A BOX OF EXS

In My Garage

Michelle Kelly

Ryegrass Publishing

CONTENTS

Title Page

Dedicated to   5

Chapter 1: Breakdown   7

Chapter 2: The Thigh Test   14

Chapter 3: The Weeds   20

Chapter 4: Moving On   25

Chapter 5: Christmas is coming   29

Chapter 6: Alice Attacks   33

Chapter 7: Gone Global   38

Chapter 8: Bloody Marvellous   47

Chapter 9: Christmas Wishes   55

Chapter 10: Fallout   63

Chapter 11: Mix up   70

Chapter 12: Alone, like Jones   77

Chapter 13: The Interrogation   85

Chapter 14: Marathon   100

Chapter 15: New Year, New Resolution   108

Chapter 16: Bye, Bye Thigh   117

Chapter 17: Volunteer Fear   124

Chapter 18: Obscene   129

Chapter 19: Falling   149

Chapter 20: Bad Loser 160

Chapter 21: Surprise Guy 166

Chapter 22: Feast or Fleeced 171

Chapter 23: Therapy Blues 179

Chapter 24: Losing The compass 186

Chapter 25: Killer Assistant 192

Chapter 26: Telling the truth 201

Chapter 27: Confessions 208

Chapter 28: The Great Knicker Caper 213

Chapter 29: Man Traps 222

Chapter 30: Step-by-Step 227

Chapter 31: Surprises 232

Chapter 32: An Ex is Back 241

Chapter 33: Run, Baby, Run 247

Chapter 34: Celebrate, Come on 251

About The Author 261

Books By This Author 263

Sally Gelee is a commitment-phobe looking for lasting love.

She works in a rest home, it's a nice, safe environment; the men there aren't fast enough to catch her and they pose no threat. Being a commitment-phobe, that suits her, but she's also a hopeless romantic searching for forever love.

Sally keeps a box of exs in the garage; a catalogue of her past dating disasters, to remind her of what she doesn't want in a relationship. She uses a thigh test to find Mr Right, if his thigh doesn't feel right then he's not the one. It can't just be a nice thigh; it has to be the right thigh.

Just when she thinks she has finally found her dream man - he plays hard to get.

Meanwhile her stalker ex, Gone Don, won't stay gone and pops up at random, freaking her out. And the new next-door neighbour is a right cretin.

Will she manage to conquer her commitment phobia and find lasting love, or will she run?

A catalogue record for this book is available at the National Library of NZ

First published 2022
Ryegrass Publishing
www.ryegrasspublishing.co.nz
19a Spencer Terrace, Takapuna, Auckland, New Zealand

ISBN: (Paperback) 978-0-473-65516-7
ISBN: (Paperback print on demand) 978-0-473-65517-4
ISBN:(PDF) 978-0-473-65520-4
ISBN: (Kindle) 978-0-473 65519-8
ISBN: (Epub) 978-0-473-65518-1

Cover design: Melody Simmons
Proof reader: Suzanne Hardy

A Box Of Exs is a combined work of fact and fiction. Some names, characters, places, events, locales, and incidents are either products of the author's imagination or used in a fictitious manner. Any resemblance to actual persons living or dead is purely coincidental, or done on purpose (mostly with consent). All joking aside this work initially began as mostly true, but as I wrote it became more of what I wished was true. Therefore, it is now almost entirely fiction, but most of the dates actually happened, and there really was a box of exs in my garage haunting me.

Dedicated To

Dedicated to the one who helped me conquer my phobia.

Acknowledgments

Special thanks to

Pamela Bestwick
Linda Gordon
Julie White
Vivienne Lingard
Suzanne Hardy

&

Special thanks to Terry for telling me,
"You know there's a happy ending."

This one is for you babe xxx

Chapter 1: Breakdown

Sal popped a chocolate in her mouth and looked at the pile of paperwork. Alice was cracking the whip. There were three new admissions, and the paperwork was piling up. This was the worst possible time for the stupid copier to break down. Sally punched in the phone number of the Fuji Xerox help desk, pressed button 2, and listened to the insipid music. She wished Alice could talk management into upping the budget so they could get a new machine. Dear God, this music was atrocious.

She glanced out the glass doors in time to see Millie wandering around the carpark – lost. How had she escaped again? The woman was a regular Houdini.

Browns Bay was a sleepy little seaside village, however, the rest home was situated on a busy corner, and she certainly didn't want a confused Millie trying to cross the road. The customer service representative answered just as Sally grabbed the arm of a passing carer. She pointed at Millie, and mouthed, "Quick, get her!"

The carer ran outdoors and began to gently coax Millie inside.

"Fuji Xerox, how can I assist," an upbeat female voice asked.

Sally thought of multiple smart-ass answers but with restraint said, "The photocopier has packed up again, and I need someone to come out to take a look at it asap!" She rattled off the details and hung up.

Smiling sweetly, Daisy, the cook, popped the food list in her in-tray. Knowing how much Sal hated doing that online order she placed a chocolate-chip cookie and a coffee on Sal's desk as a bribe, before scuttling back to the kitchen as quick as a hungry cockroach. Daisy was an excellent cook, not trained or qualified; she just knew how to make everything taste better. Her special ingredient was love.

Sal put the shopping list on top of the other urgent must do paperwork and logged into the website. But when the strapping, handsome, six-foot-something technician breezed into the office, the room temperature went up several notches. He was smoking hot. He was a George Clooney lookalike but with height and strong broad shoulders.

She honed in for the kill, fixing her hazel eyes on him. Then flashed him her award-winning smile, flicked her long blonde hair back off her face, and swept around the desk.

"Chase," he said introducing himself. "I hear you're experiencing a problem?" His blue eyes dazzled as he stretched forth his hand.

"Sally," she replied, taking his hand and holding it a second too long. She had to bite her lip to stop herself saying, I have many problems and I'd like you to solve them all. Instead offering to show him what was wrong, she sashayed across to the photocopier.

She gave him her best helpless look. "I think this is where the problem lies." Bending she wiggled the bypass tray. For a split second, Sal thought about attempting the Legally Blonde 'Bend and Snap' manoeuvre, but thought with her luck she'd probably knock him out cold.

"Don't worry, I'll have it fixed in a jiffy," he promised.

Sal sincerely hoped not. She was enjoying the distraction, but true to his word Chase had the copier fixed in a few minutes. When he came to the front desk to sign out Sal checked his ring finger – good, no ring. Not wanting him to leave so soon she flirted shamelessly, giggling like a fourteen-year-old schoolgirl. He flirted back, and there was crackling electricity in the air.

Sal drove straight home in her racy little yellow Mini singing 'I'm in love again' at the top of her lungs. She turned into the Longview Apartments; a small complex of adjoined apartments sharing a private driveway and courtyard. She shared her apartment with Kat – a gorgeous voluptuous beauty in her late twenties, with long dark tresses and legs up to her armpits. When they first met, Sal wasn't sure about Kat because she had such a flip nature, but they hit it off and had been flatting together ever since.

Sal was pleased to see she had beaten Kat home for a change. First one home got to park in the garage. Second one home parked outside in the shared drive. Kat always seemed to get home first. She worked in the city as an administrator for an advertising agency. Sal thought Kat should be modelling instead of working as a receptionist for an advertising agency. Kat had heaps of cool work stories about media stars dropping into to her workplace. Somehow Kat never had to work late to catch up on paperwork. She was either super-efficient or had nothing to do.

Sal pressed the remote, drove into the garage and parked her car. She left her bag and coat on the front seat, and jumped out of the Mini, slamming the door behind her. She needed to check her box of exs before she got in too deep. The small silver case hid on the top shelf at the rear of the garage. It was the size of a lunchbox; metal with black clasps. The box was loaded with secret memories, some things best kept in the dark. Sal found it, carefully lifted the box down, and unsnapped the clasps. She took out the first photo and stared at him. Hemi. Her first boyfriend and without a doubt her worst. He was a rebel without a cause. What she had seen in him was bad boy excitement. What a mistake he had been. Her father had been right. She shuffled the photos and stared at the next one, her first true love, David. She sighed. She had loved him, warts and all. It still made her sad that she'd had to end it but she wasn't putting up with his lying cheating ways.

"What you doing?" Kat asked, stepping into the garage, her arms laden with laundry. She had been so focused on the contents of the box that she hadn't heard Kat come home.

Sal jerked in surprise, dropping the photos. They scattered on the floor like a deck of playing cards.

She hurriedly gathered them. "I...um...am just looking through my box of exs."

Kat put the washing basket on top of the clothes drier and came closer. "Your box of what?" she asked, peering over Sal's shoulder.

Sal wanted to hide them but it was too late. "Exs. You know – ex-boyfriends."

"Really? You have that many?" Kat raised her brows. "Tell me you just have their photos and their body parts are not hanging up somewhere."

"Ha, ha, very funny," Sal said, peeved. "Not all are exs, some were just wannabes."

Kat exuded confidence. She had a warped sense of humour and always played the devil's advocate.

She swept her long dark hair back off her face as she leaned over and made a grab for the photos. "Here, give us a look."

Reluctantly, Sal handed over the bundle.

"Who's the monobrow?" Kat asked, chuckling.

"That's Hemi."

"Looks like a caveman."

"He was," Sal replied, snatching the photo.

"Why do you keep them?" Kat asked as if she thought Sal was mentally disturbed. "I mean what's the point?"

"It's to remind me of what I don't want. A kind of profiling, I guess."

"You're weird," Kat replied, with a quick shake of her head. Kat had had lots of boyfriends and there was always someone sniffing around but she was picky. "Are you going to spend all night out here, or do you want something to eat?"

"Be in soon."

Kat chucked the washing in the machine, added powder, and switched it on. "Don't be all night."

Sal flicked through the pictures, there was Tom, he was a blip. Then Marty, too intense. Phil, too controlling. Steve, good kisser but no substance and tight as a fish's bum. Kurt, nice but unreliable. Ken, too broken. Don, the stalker, who couldn't take no for an answer. Niall, who was way too young. And then, hidden underneath the black satin lining there were the dark secrets best left forgotten. She had always been unlucky in love, and always had terrible taste in men. And here she was, dreaming about a photocopier man who probably wanted nothing more than to do his job and go home.

It was time for a reality check. Chase was a tall, well-built Clooney look-alike, but he was hardly a Mills and Boons prince. He was a photocopier repairman for heaven's sakes. Hadn't she suffered enough heartbreak? She should be happy to have a boring little life with no dramas. But she liked drama and romance and hoped to one day find her forever love. Sal popped the photographs back in the case and snapped the clasps shut before heading in for dinner.

They had chicken kebabs and salad for dinner and, busy with their own thoughts, ate in silence. Sal knew it wouldn't be long before curiosity got the better of Kat and she'd ask about the box of exs.

Intrigued, Kat wanted to know more. Still, she waited until after dinner to ask. "Want to tell me in chronological order or alphabetical?

Sal poured herself a glass of wine and sighed dramatically. "It would take too long."

"I've got all night." Cat-like, Kat curled up on the couch with a glass of wine within reach and eyeballed Sal across the coffee table.

"I'm not going anywhere, and I'm all ears. Spill."

She'd noticed Hemi the moment he'd walked into the coffee shop. He wasn't handsome, but he was loud, and had a swagger about him that made you believe he was a capable, interesting dude. Turned out to be an arrogant prick, but she didn't know that then. She was young, and still at school. They'd struck up a conversation and he'd wowed her from the get go. His exploits were incredible; it didn't take too long until she realised most of them were bullshit. But being an impressionable teen, Sal was caught; hook, line and sinker.

Hemi was broke, but he had been given a car. No, it couldn't really be called a car – it was a wreck. A clothes peg held the bonnet closed.

Still, he said, when he picked her up for their first date, it had a full tank of gas.

"Let's go for a drive."

Sal was wearing a nice summer dress and strappy heels. She wrinkled her nose at the car, opened the door and climbed in.

As they drove into the country, Sal began to worry. She didn't know this guy, and they appeared to be miles from anywhere. She was freaking out when the car stopped dead.

Hemi hopped out and checked the engine, then the petrol tank. He opened the cap and stuck a long, thin, tapering stick into the tank; it came out bone dry. The gauge was faulty and they were out of gas.

"Sorry," he apologised. "Guess we are going to have to walk."

Walk! They were miles from anywhere! And because she had been trying to impress him, she had worn heels. Being five foot nothing she needed to add a little height figuring that it would make it easier for him to kiss her. She was now regretting having made that choice as they walked along the gravel road. She was beginning to think she'd have blisters the size of golf balls when Hemi suggested they pop into a farmhouse and ask if they could have some petrol. If it had been dark enough, he might have tried to pinch some, but it was a clear day with not a cloud in the sky. Footsore and grumpy, Sal agreed; asking for gas was better than walking all the way home.

Amused, the farmer watched Sal tiptoe over the cattle stop as she tried not to get her heels stuck between the gaps. She didn't want to think about what might be caking the soles of her brand-new shoes. Gunk she'd have to scrape off before getting back in the car, should they manage to get the wreck to go. A kind man, the farmer gave them a can of petrol and sent them on their way. Sal held her breath as they drove back to town. There really was something nasty caked to the bottom of her shoes. That first date was a clue that she should have run. Hemi was cheap and nasty.

After the car died, Hemi bought a motorbike, and deliberately rode through the main streets of their small home town at warp speed showing off and doing wheel stands to get attention. His bad boy image which had initially attracted her soon changed to annoyance. It was like the guy could never get enough attention, he craved it. He always wanted to be on everyone's radar and it didn't matter if it was the police radar. Hemi was all bravado and as shallow as a saucer. He was an arse. It was a blessing when it ended, and he moved away. Naturally, he didn't leave without causing drama, going quietly wasn't his style. Yeah, Hemi was her first major mistake and one of the main reasons for her commitment phobia.

Chapter 2: The Thigh Test

Most of the residents couldn't go far without their walkers. The children who visited their elderly parents were usually in their sixties, and, apart from the odd grandchild or entertainer that visited the rest home, there weren't a lot of potential singletons to choose from. That's probably why Chase looked like such a hot prospect; for a start he had all his own teeth. Damn it, she couldn't stop thinking about him. She found herself absently doodling his name on her desk pad. Why hadn't he called?

The next day the photocopier broke down – again. It was a sign! This time the hopper was jamming. Alice raised a suspicious eyebrow when Sal told her it was playing up again.

"You're doing that on purpose," Alice accused, a hand on hip. She would have made a great Sergeant Major as she barked orders and always walked like she was on parade. She had a strut like a peacock.

"It's a crap photocopier," Sal complained. "Surely we have enough money in the budget for a new one."

"Is he husband material?" tight-fisted Alice asked, giving her a meaningful look. Sal squirmed.

"Tell you what, Alice, if I marry him, you can be my bridesmaid." Sal crossed her fingers behind her back. The likelihood of her ever getting married was remote, especially since she wasn't dating anyone. Over the years Sal had forgotten how many people she had promised could be her bridesmaid – one day should the happy event ever occur; it would be a surprise to her how many people claimed the right to be her bridesmaid.

Alice shook her head. "Like that's ever going to happen. You never stay in a relationship longer than five minutes."

Sal turned her back on Alice. There was no way Alice would ever be her bridesmaid now. "Lucky for you I don't change jobs as often then, isn't it?" she muttered.

Sal picked up the phone and eagerly dialled the 0800 number to lodge a service call. A computerised voice told her she was in a priority queue, then played the same insipid music in her ear.

Suzie arrived and dropped timesheets on Sal's desk. A little pocket rocket, Suzie attacked everything with vigour. If it needed sorting, Suzie loved it. Right now, she thought Sal's love life needed sorting.

"Wish you could meet my friend Lance, he's such a honey. You'd like him. Pity he lives in Whangarei."

Sal was only half listening. "Mm?" Sal put the phone down and glanced up at Suzie. "Who? Lives where?"

Cecil appeared, interrupting their conversation. He leaned over the counter and peered down short-sightedly at Sal over his spectacles, his lined face gravely serious. Knowing what to expect, Suzie quietly slunk away. Sal glanced up at him. Cecil was a long-time resident. He'd smoked most of his life, drank like a fish, and defied the odds by living well into his nineties.

"Cecil," Sal said, patiently. "What can I do for you?"

Cecil's bushy grey eyebrows met, he cleared his throat and said, "I want to die."

Sal sighed. "Not on my watch, that's way too much paperwork. Besides, the photocopier has broken down again."

Accepting that as a reasonable excuse, Cecil shrugged. "Ok, I'll come back tomorrow." He shuffled up the hallway leaving his walker behind. Sal put the phone down. She chased him, and gave his walker back, then saw him safely to the lounge. On the way back to her desk, she bumped into Norman.

"Do you know where my room is?" Norman asked, bewildered.

"Number 53, down the end of the hall and turn left," she called back over her shoulder.

"Thank you, bless you, my dear." Norman blew kisses.

Sal sped back to her desk and dialled the Fuji Xerox 0800 number. She entered the familiar press button numbers and waited with bated breath.

Then some random Australian customer service guy answered in his thick Aussie twang, he said, "How may I help?"

Sal explained the situation, the customer rep said he'd lodged a service call. "I'll send a techie out," he promised.

Sal didn't want just any technician. She wanted Chase. "Ah, how many technicians do you have working on the Shore?" she asked.

"Fifteen. Why?"

Fifteen! It was like playing Russian roulette. She couldn't leave it to chance; she would have to ask for him by name.

Taking a breath, she brazenly said, "I'd like to request Chase, he's friendlier and much more helpful than the others." There was silence on the other end. Sal quickly added, "He really knows his stuff."

From the comfort of her air-conditioned office, Alice yelled, "'Yeah, and he's got a nice bum."

Horrors, was Alice checking him out too? Curse her!

The customer service rep laughed aloud.

Mortified, Sally squeaked, "Did you hear that?"

"Yes," the nice customer service rep happily replied tapping away at his keyboard. We love feedback. I'm just recording that for our notes. However, I'm afraid it will be whichever technician is in the area, madam."

Madam! She hated being called Madam – it made her feel a hundred years old. She hoped that Alice's remark about his cute posterior wasn't passed on to Chase. Alice was single, and even though she was older, Sal didn't need the competition.

Fuji Xerox didn't send Chase. This time they sent a young man with piercings, green hair, pimply skin, barely old enough to shave. Disappointed, Sal pointed him in the direction of the machine and got back to work.

She could hear whispering around the office. The carers popped up to reception and lingered for no apparent reason.

Vikki, the Clinical Manager, jerked her head in the direction of the boy and hissed, "Is that him?" Vikki had a Mary Poppins way about her, an air of efficiency that you knew she'd get the job done in a way that would surprise you the most. You always wondered what trick she would pull out of her bag next. She even looked like Julie Andrews.

"Don't be ridiculous," Sally snapped. "For goodness sakes, do you think I'm a cradle snatcher?"

"No, but I do think you might be a desperate thirty-something whose clock is ticking."

"For your information, I've only just turned thirty." Sal chucked a pen at Vikki. She dodged. The pen missed, hit the wall, and clattered to the floor. "It's the tall one, the one that came to fix it on Friday," Sally snapped.

"Oh," Vikki grinned, retrieving the pen and throwing it back. "The one with the nice bum."

Sally wished everyone would stop checking out Chase's bum. Ignoring Alice and Vikki who had both kept their office doors open in the hope of more entertainment, Sal immersed herself in her work, and the young one kept his distance.

Later, in the relative calm of the lunchroom, Sally slowly sipped her coffee while she plotted how to catch her man. The box of exs haunted her thoughts day and night, and made her depressed. She knew what she didn't want. Those men were rejects, and she mustn't make the same mistake again.

That night, Sal curled up on the couch, a melting bowl of hokey pokey ice cream in her lap and wine glass strategically placed on the coffee table within reach, and contemplated how she had come to this.

Kat was eagerly waiting for the next instalment. "So, about the exs," she paused, toying with her wine glass. "Do tell."

Sal cast her mind back. "Well, let's see, there was Curtis. Curtis. Nice guy, built like a giant teddy bear, but you know…" Sal shrugged, trying to find the right words.

"No spark?" Kat guessed.

Sal pointed the spoon at Kat. "Zip. Nada. Nothing."

"So, what happened?"

Sal shamefacedly admitted, "He got me at a weak moment, I should have said no when he asked me out on a date, but somehow I said yes."

Kat narrowed her gaze. "How old were you?"

"Still at school. I panicked when he said he wanted to take me out on the weekend. Figuring I needed a human shield I insisted my friend Jenna came along too, and because he had a kind heart, he agreed. He picked us up in a taxi, took us out for lunch, and paid for Jenna too. Every time he went for my hand it was Jenna's job to get in the way. She was a fantastic third wheel, she even sat between us at the movies. Poor Curtis, he did so much to impress. When he finally managed to shake Jenna off and got me alone, he went in for a kiss."

"Yeah, and...?" encouraged Kat.

Sal screwed up her face. "He kissed like a lip-sucking octopus."

"Hmm," Kat looked thoughtful as she sliced a thin piece of cheese and delicately placed it on a cracker. "I've never kissed a giant octopus but I like the analogy and it gives me a pretty graphic picture."

Sal still felt guilty as she remembered the massive bouquet that arrived at her parents' house the next day. She could see things were going to quickly spiral out of control.

"Poor guy, there was no way to gently tell him that I didn't want to go out with him. I had to be brutal before the gifts became even more elaborate."

"What did you do?"

"I told him I was in love with someone else."

Kat rolled her eyes and snorted. "At fifteen, you'd be more likely to be infatuated. Who were you 'in love' with?"

"No-one, but it was easier than telling him I wasn't into him."

"You are such a people pleaser, Sally Gelee. Poor guy, he put a lot of effort in for nothing."

"Yeah, I felt bad but when the spark's not there, well it's just wasted time, isn't it?"

"So, he wasn't a drop kick, he just wasn't..."

"Right." Sal finished for her. "He wasn't right."

"How does the runaway bride know when it's right?" Kat

asked, interested.

"Well, it has a lot to do with the thigh test."

"The thigh test?" Kat arched an eyebrow. She leaned in. "What do you mean?"

"It's kind of hard to explain but it's when you touch the thigh and it kind of feels right, strong, dependable." Sal gave the cushion beside her a little squeeze.

Kat laughed. "Sally Gelee, you're a weirdo." Kat picked up a photo and held it up so Sal could see. "Who's this one?" The photos were still out of order. Should she put them in alphabetical or chronological order? No, random probably suited best.

"Phil." Phil, like his name, was a fill-in. He was the one after the significant one and was as bland as milky coffee without sugar, but it was comfortable. Nothing happened; they dated for a while until it kind of fizzled out.

"And this one?"

"Toby." Toby was a blind date. He was good-looking, had a sort of menswear charm as he worked in the clothing industry but the brain cells of an amoeba.

Kat was enjoying herself. "Did you tell him you were in love with someone else?"

Sal nodded.

"I might be shallow but you are predictable." Kat laughed.

Kat had to go to some flash work function so she popped the lid back on the box, and told Sal she was looking forward to tomorrow and the next instalment of Sal's dating disasters.

Chapter 3: The Weeds

Andie was Sal's favourite care worker. He was flamboyant, and excessive in every way. Nothing about Andie was boring. He was overtly interesting and oozed exuberance. Sal admired three things: wit, exuberance and height.

"Oh, darling," Andie gushed. "I love that colour green on you. It matches your beautiful eyes. I'm warning you, if you leave that jacket somewhere I'll steal it, I absolutely adore it!"

Sal didn't want to damage his ego by telling him it would be much too small for him so she played along.

"Honey, if I find another like it in the shops, I'll buy you one. Now finish filling in the uniform request for me, I want to get that order in by tonight."

"Oh, you are such a bossy bunny. You are a treat-them-mean to keep-them-keen kind of girl, aren't you? Here you go," Andie said, handing over the completed form. He cast a glance at the front door, his mouth popping open in an exaggerated O. "Uh-oh, don't look now but Gone Don is coming."

Andie stepped aside so Sal could see, but it was too late to escape. There was nowhere to hide. Don had to be the only man who never believed her when she told him it was over.

Pretending to straighten the information packs, Andie hovered in reception to eavesdrop. For one mad moment Sal thought about introducing Andie as her boyfriend but no one was ever going to buy that, and especially not Don.

Don said he popped into the office in the hope of finding a rest-home apartment for his elderly parents. Sally knew it was just a ruse to see her. Besides, this care home wasn't a fancy new one with apartments or units which was more suited to Don's tastes. It was an old-style rest home that housed one person per room, and if you were lucky, you got a bathroom that you might only have to share with one other resident.

"There's nothing available," she said, dismissing him. Tapping the keyboard, she said, "Now if you'll excuse me, I've got work to do." She wanted to scream, 'Get lost and leave me alone' but her mother had taught her to be polite so she tried to ignore him instead. She was good at channelling her inner ostrich.

Nose like a ferret, Alice sniffed a sale and hurried out of her office. "Is it for you or your parents?" she enquired in her perfect sales voice, handing Don an application pack.

Don scowled at Alice as he accepted the pack, mouth twitching in distaste. "For my parents, of course," he replied snippily. Then giving Sally an exaggerated wink, and a pistol grip finger, he said, "Be seeing you, darling."

As the glass doors closed after him, Sal resisted the urge to head-butt her desk.

Andie tossed his long dark ponytail, "Goodness darling, what were you thinking? He's so terribly beige."

"I don't know. I can't have been in my right mind at the time," muttered Sal.

What was wrong with her? She was such a failure when it came to relationships. Sal was still feeling down when she got home. And to make matters worse, Kat had beaten her home and had snaffled the garage.

After dinner, Kat switched off the telly and picked up the box of exs.

It was an out-of-focus back profile.

"Stuart," answered Sal. "My accidental date."

Kat coughed in surprise. "An accidental date? How does one have an accidental date."

Stuart was a building inspector from Liverpool, and seemed like a nice guy. One day when he was inspecting the rest home, she asked him how his day was. He said he was happy enough, but all he needed to make his life complete was a deaf, blind nymphomaniac whose father owned a brewery.

Sal had replied, "My father doesn't own a brewery."

After a moment's stunned silence, he asked her if she'd like to join him at the local. After all, it was 5 p.m. on a Friday. She thought he would be perfect for her friend Lyn. After all, they were both from the UK. And the British pub, Speakers Corner would be an ideal place for them to meet.

When he went to the bar to order the drinks, she phoned Lyn. Unfortunately, Lyn was busy, but told Sal to get as much info as possible and to take a sneaky pic of him to send to her so she could vet him. Sal only managed to get a fuzzy back profile to send. She quizzed him asking questions that she thought Lyn might want to know. He was flattered and asked her to go out with him on the weekend. Embarrassed, she had to tell him no as she was already seeing someone, and being the jealous kind, he'd not take well to her dating another man. Stuart was disappointed and worse still, Lyn wasn't the slightest bit interested.

Kat laughed. "Can't believe you said that. No wonder he was keen – what man doesn't want a nympho." She returned Stuart to the box and picked up another. "Ok, who is this guy wearing the groovy 70's shades?"

Kurt. They had been out on a couple of coffee dates when Kurt suggested he take her to visit his favourite wild west coast beach. When she'd mentioned going to Karekare beach to her friends, they looked horrified, telling her she was naïve. Karekare was remote. Like what did she know about this guy? Didn't she watch those CSI murder programmes where the girl ends up buried near some isolated beach?

"Look out for ropes and a shovel when you get in his car," warned her sister, Paula. Vikki advised her to make sure she was within cell phone range and to call them to let them know she was ok.

By the time Kurt picked her up in his beat-up old builder's wagon she was seriously freaking out but couldn't figure out how to get out of the date. They chatted while he drove. Sal glanced nervously at the big meaty hands on the steering wheel and pictured them tightening on her neck. Her friends were right, what did she know about him; he could be a serial killer.

They were in the country when she glanced over the back and noticed a sack, ropes, and a shovel! Then she really started to freak out. She grew really quiet and pressed herself up against the door wondering how much damage she would do if she had to bail out of the car at speed.

The car slowed as the road got rougher and Sal moved further away from him until she almost meshed into the door. Her imagination running wild, Sal couldn't think of a single sensible thing to say. Certain that whatever came out of her mouth would be complete gibberish, she kept quiet. Kurt noticed and asked her if she was tired. She shook her head, assured him she was wide awake, and kept her eyes on the road, still checking the speedo.

He pulled into a car park, turned to her, grinning wickedly he said, "I've got something special planned for you."

Every crime documentary and movie she had ever watched flashed before her eyes. Oh God, I'm going to die! He got out of the car and retrieved the picnic basket from the back of the van.

He opened her door. "Come on, the beach is just through here," he said, reaching for her hand.

Sal wondered if she should try and steal the van, or make a mad dash through the dunes. Heart beating rapidly, she walked wobbly-legged across the sand. A handful of people were scattered along the shoreline so it wasn't entirely deserted, but the beach was wild, and an ominous shark fin like rock stuck out of the sea reminding her of the movie 'Jaws'. A chill ran down her spine and she shuddered. Kurt asked, if she was cold, and did she want him to put a blanket around her shoulders? Alarmed, she shook her head. Kurt spread a picnic blanket near a weather-eroded log and took out champagne and oysters.

"This is the perfect place to watch the sunset," Kurt said popping the champagne cork and pouring her a glass. The rest of the evening had been beautifully romantic. He really was a sweetie.

Sal smiled sheepishly as she told Kat the only danger she was in, was getting a little too tipsy.

"How much did you have to drink?" questioned Kat.

Sal pinched her fingers together. "Two teeny tiny little," she paused, before adding, "bottles."

Kat raised her eyebrows. "Bottles! Sally Gelee, you lush!"

Reminiscing, Sal smiled her secret little Mona Lisa smile. For a burly builder, Kurt had a strong romantic streak, but he didn't pass the thigh test.

Kat's ears pricked up. "The thigh test again? What was wrong with his thigh?"

"Too arthritic." Sal yawned. "I'm off to bed."

Chapter 4: Moving On

Kat was gawking out the window, watching the moving truck reverse into the neighbours driveway. The adjoining apartment had been empty for less than a week when the Sold sign went up. Mrs Robinson had been widowed for many years and the place was getting too much for her. She hadn't told them who the new owners were; she was just happy to get the price she wanted so she could move into the retirement village of her choice.

Mrs Robinson huffed when Sal suggested she might like Serenity Shores Rest Home. Saying she wasn't that incapacitated yet; no siree, she wanted some place with pizazz and get up and go. She wanted a retirement village lifestyle like Kensington Park advertised for her twilight years, thank you very much.

Sal felt defensive. She liked her sleepy little rest home. Sure, it didn't have the glamour of the big retirement villages with individual units and independent living but everyone was like family and it was a lovely caring place. There had been rumours that the new owners of Serenity Shores were going to tear down the old home at some stage and build a three-storey complex on the site. Sal hoped it didn't happen for a while, she liked things how they were. All she really wanted was a new photocopier, and Chase.

Kat was dying to see what their new neighbours were like. All she had seen so far was the moving van and a couple of guys emptying the back of the truck. They would miss Mrs Robinson's home baking that she would bring over once in a while. Still, it was nice to think there would be others nearer their age living in the complex. There were the wrinklies, an elderly couple living in the end apartment, next to them lived old Mrs Mac and her two small dogs who Kat affectionately dubbed the Maccas. Then in the middle lived the Dinklahs (double income no kids left at home). They seldom saw the Dinklahs; if they weren't working, they were holidaying abroad. Next to them lived the Saffers. The Saffers were South African skilled migrants in their forties, only recently arrived and with such broad accents that it was difficult to understand them. And now, these blokes next door who looked relatively normal and somewhere in their late twenties or early thirties.

"Come away from there," hissed Sal. "They'll see you."

"I hope so. They're young blood. Couple of blokes. Maybe they are a couple, it's hard to tell," Kat told her, still leering out the window. "Makes a change from the middle-aged wrinkly brigade. Helps bring down the average age in the block."

Sal came up behind Kat and peered out the window. "I wish we didn't have to share the driveway with everyone. Have you seen the way the Dinklahs drive, it's like they are always running late, I'm worried they might run over the Maccas if they get out."

"It's not the dogs I'm worried about," Kat answered. "I'm worried about the wrinklies reversing out the drive. They almost side-swiped my mirror the other day." Kat let the curtain fall.

The rest of Saturday was spent on the usual housekeeping, shopping routine, and Saturday night was a big night in.

"Oi! I was watching that," protested Sal when Kat turned the telly off.

"No, you weren't. You were dreaming about the photocopier man."

"No, I wasn't," Sal argued – but she was.

"Yes, you were. You've got that goofy look on your face."

"I just can't understand it," Sal pouted, wrapping her arms about herself indignantly. "I wear a name badge, for goodness's sake. He knows where I work. It is easy to track me down on social media. How many others have a name like mine? There's none that I know of, no one else's mother was so cruel to give them a rhyming name." Sally's mother was proud of her husband's French heritage. It hadn't crossed Joyce's mind that Sally would rhyme with Gelee (the French word for Jelly) and kids at school would tease her, calling her Smelly Sally Jelly.

Sal frowned as a terrible thought occurred to her. "Perhaps I've lost my pulling power."

"Perhaps he's gay." Kat helpfully suggested.

Sal hugged the fluffy cushion. "Didn't seem gay when he flirted with me."

Kat screwed a brightly polished finger in her temple. "Well then, perhaps he's retarded." Kat had her *now you listen to me* look on. "He'd have to be stupid not to go after you."

"Thanks," Sal mumbled, not believing it.

"Now for heaven's sake, forget about him, and move on."

Sal sulked like a five-year-old. Realising they weren't done yet, Kat made herself a coffee and one for Sal. She plonked the cup down in front of Sal and opened the box of exs.

Kat picked up another photo, brows knitting, she asked, "Who's Lawrence of Arabia?"

Different cultures, different religions and Niall was six years her junior. She felt like such a cradle-snatcher. He cried when she told him he needed to find the right girl for him, and she wasn't the one. When he didn't believe her and tried to convince her that they were made for each other she told him that she was in love with someone else.

"This one?"

"Scott. Rebound. Lasted a weekend."

"And this one?"

"Mike. Funny, separated, not ready for divorce. Blip." She'd met his ex-wife, Sharon, once. She was wearing a t-shirt that said *my next husband will be normal.*

Kat laughed. "Who's the short old grey guy?

"Marty."

"Shame on you, old enough to be your dad." Kat picked up another. "And this one?"

"You're enjoying this," Sal accused.

"You bet." Kat laughed. She waved the photo under Kat's nose. "Come on, spill."

"Grant the plumber."

"How the hell did he get in tight places? No, on second

thoughts I don't want to know." She put the photo back.

"He didn't get in my tight spaces."

"Didn't do your plumbing." Kat grinned suggestively.

Sal rolled her eyes. Grant was a big guy, big and of above average height, and nice, but nice in a boring, predictable kind of way nice. He asked her out for dinner but she brushed him off saying she already had a date. The poor man was still hopeful but eventually gave up and disappeared.

"Now who's this?" she asked, picking out a photo that had been taken at a bar. "He looks like a dwarf."

The Hobbit, as she nicknamed him, was short. Shorter than she was, and that didn't happen often. He came up to her boobs and spoke mostly to them. What he lacked in height he made up for in self-confidence. He was bombastic, and had a belly laugh like Father Christmas and eyes that twinkled like he was up to no good. There was no point doing a thigh test on him, he definitely wasn't for her. And to have a quiet drink without being perved at, she opted to change her Friday night hangout.

Kat tried another tactic. "Do you think that maybe you're a major commitment-phobe?"

"No, of course not." Sal retorted. "Who made you an expert at relationships?"

Kat shrugged. "Well, I've been in a few."

"Do I need to point out you're not even in one at present?" Sal reminded her.

"Point taken. I'm just saying, it seems to me if they are easy to catch and into you, you become bored, but if they play hard to get you are interested." Kat switched the telly back on signalling the counselling session was over.

Needled by Kat's brutal honesty, Sal stretched and faked a yawn. "I've got to get some sleep, big day tomorrow."

Tomorrow she was going to get the Big Guy on the job.

Chapter 5: Christmas Is Coming

Sal was enjoying the lead-up to Christmas at church when out of the corner of her eye she spied Gone Don directly behind her. Overnight Don had become a believer! Now, not even church guaranteed sanctuary. And gross, he was giving her the eye – in church! Sally squeezed her eyes shut and prayed he'd disappear. Could life get any crazier? She couldn't catch one man and couldn't get rid of another.

Don had wooed her from the start, taking her to fine dining restaurants, shows, and away for long weekends. He had expensive tastes and always wore designer clothes, but his salary didn't match his lifestyle and Sal was mortified when she learned the truth. He was a pretender. He'd been nice to her, attentive and all that but there was no depth to his character, and his lack of friends should have given her a clue that he wouldn't fit into her hyper- social lifestyle.

As soon as the service ended, she rushed for the nearest exit. But Don was waiting in the foyer. Fortunately, he didn't see her. Sal spun around and ran back through the church, and out the side entrance. Ignoring greetings, Sal tugged her collar up around her ears, and weaved between the parked cars towards her little yellow Mini. She slid behind the wheel and started the engine. She reversed out of the car park and slammed the car into drive. Sally braked hard as Don stepped in front of the Mini.

Don flashed his trademark cheesy grin and waved. By reflex Sally limply raised her arm and waved back. Angry with herself for not giving him the finger she drove home promising herself next time she saw Don, she'd floor it and run the annoying little weasel over. Surely, God must make allowances when you are pushed too far.

Sally was still fuming when she got home. She vented her frustration to Kat, who rolled her eyes like she had heard it all before. "Why don't you just tell him to get lost," she advised.

"I did," Sal protested, indignant.

Kat crossed her arms. "Are you sure? Did you say those exact words?"

Sal's face told Kat what she already knew.

"You are too nice; he doesn't take you seriously. You seem to have a problem with saying no. Guys don't know that you have friend-zoned them because you are too nice to tell them."

Kat made them coffee and telling Sal to put her feet up, joined her on the couch. Kat positioned the box of exs on the coffee table and snapped open the lid.

Kat shuffled the photos like they were a deck of cards. She plucked another from the pile. "This guy looks interesting." Kat dangled a photo before Sal's eyes. She winced at the memory. She'd loved Ken.

Ken, gardener, come landscaper, come handyman, was bandy, and rolled rather than walked; it was almost as if he'd been pile-driven into the earth. She met him online on Findsomeone. He was witty and confident online but in reality, he was shy. They had spoken online, and on the phone, and she enjoyed the easy-going banter but when she'd finally agreed to meet him, she immediately regretted it.

His nose was too long, and a bit crooked from a break not set right. Dark-haired, he had warm brown eyes and was intelligent, but he'd been knocked around by life. Their coffee meeting had been a disaster. If he'd tried to sell himself, he went the wrong way about it. Everything he said, just made her want to turn and run.

She had arranged a friend to text while she was at coffee and they had organised a ruse should she need to flee. Even though she was freaked out by everything that was wrong with the guy she knew he'd not harm her in any way. He had a kind heart and others had taken advantage of his generous nature. When Sal received the text which was her out, she assured her alibi that everything was fine. Still, she left the building feeling incredibly disillusioned with the whole online dating thing and vowed she'd never do that again.

But Ken was persistent. He called her and offered a no-strings-attached cruise on the Auckland harbour. Having been duped before, she asked him to send a pic of the boat expecting it to be dingy. She wasn't expecting the 70ft luxury liner that looked like the *Love Boat*. It wasn't his of course, but a friend's. They had danced, singing along to Bruno Mars, *I think I want to marry you*, it was fun and he was fun. Whenever they went out, they were invariably approached by someone who would stop for a moment, stare, snap their fingers and say to Ken, "You look just like that movie star, what's his name?"

"Richard Gere," Ken would confidently reply.

"No, no, the guy with the big nose, you know the funny guy... lots of movies..." they would flounder before declaring, "I know – Robin Williams."

Kind and funny, Ken grew on her, but he still was broken by life, and the cracks showed. Sal tried to ignore the obvious signs. Her nature made her want to fix people and things but, in the end, she had to admit she wasn't up to the challenge. Ken needed professional help and was suffering from depression. At times she saw the black dog sitting heavily on his shoulders and he seemed genuinely incapable of shaking it off. Winter affected him badly, he wanted to hibernate when the long shadows of winter altered his moods and everything looked bleak and uninviting.

Sal was unsure how to handle this kind of behaviour. Being a people person, she flitted between events and outings and loved the stimulus of being around others. People gave her energy and made her feel alive. The relationship teetered between ups and downs and near the end there were more downs than ups.

He was always broke. Not that her finances were much better. One morning when they went out for breakfast, she insisted they go Dutch. As she was paying the bill the sexy-looking Latino guy behind the counter suggested that if she was free, she should come along to Salsa class on Wednesday. Sal thanked the waiter, and told him it sounded like a bit of fun. Ken was as chilly as Antarctica on the way home and she guessed the reason why.

Thinking it best to clear the air, Sal brought it up. "I think Marko thought I was single because we paid separately."

"Marko Sharko." Ken snorted. "Wait a minute, how do you know his name? he demanded.

"He was wearing a name badge," she replied.

Ken grunted as if he didn't believe her story.

Sal's mobile rang.

"Oh, let me guess," he said starchily. "I suppose that's him now. You probably slipped him your number when I wasn't looking."

"Don't be silly," Sal replied, trying to appease him while absently checking her phone. It was the beginning of the end.

Feeling insecure, Ken had been pushing for a relationship; he wanted to be called her boyfriend. Wary by then, she awarded Ken one letter at a time, he was given boy first before he got boyf, boyfr, i-e-n but he never got his last letter. He never became her actual boyfriend. The word used to stick in her throat and make her feel sick. She did have feelings for him. They were going nowhere. It was a nice thigh but not the right thigh.

It was disturbing to think that perhaps Kat might be right. When anything started looking too committed, she got scared, and ran.

Perhaps some of these photos and memories were best kept buried in the box and left there. "Think I will head to bed," Sal said, faking a yawn.

"Night, chick, sleep well," Kat told her.

Somehow Sal doubted she would.

Chapter 6: Alice Attacks

From Fiji, Pearl loved flowers and colour. There was tinsel and poinsettia everywhere. Each day Pearl added more décor to the reception area until Sal felt like her desk and surrounding area resembled something like the inside of Santa's grotto.

As if by a miracle, the photocopier broke down – again. Sal happily lodged a service call and, two hours later, Chase breezed into the office.

"Hello! Long time, no see," he said, leaning across her counter to grab a pen to write in the register.

Her prayers had been answered.

Sally explained the latest problem. "I think it's time for a new one," she said loud enough for Alice to hear.

Alice yelled, "What? Another man? Not again, Sally Gelee!"

Sal grimaced and ignored Alice. She hovered by Chase's elbow. He had such a warm smile and nice blue eyes. She had to crane her neck to look at him. It would do wonders for getting rid of that double chin that was starting to form.

She wanted to scream, *Take me now!*

"I have you trapped behind the photocopier," he said with a wicked grin.

Her face flamed red. Could he read her mind? The phone rang, she went to answer it and left Chase to fix the copier. Her imagination running wild, Sally found herself impossibly distracted. Then, she spotted Millie in the carpark. That little Houdini was out again.

She hurried outside. "Where are you going, dear?" she asked Millie, taking her frail arm.

Bewildered, Millie stared at Sal. "Have you seen Mum and Dad? Are they coming to pick me up soon?"

Sal didn't wish to upset Millie by telling her she very much doubted they were still alive; it would be too much of a shock.

Gently guiding Millie back indoors, she said, "No, honey, I haven't but I expect they won't be too long." Finding the nearest carer she handed Millie over and asked her to see Millie safely back inside the secure wing.

Sally hurried back to the office. She couldn't leave her post for too long, Alice was on the hunt.

Chase packed away his tools. "There, all done," he said wiping his hands on a damp rag. He came up to the front desk to sign himself out. Sal wanted to say can you write your mobile number and relationship status down as well, but resisted.

"Christmas tree looks nice," he commented.

Pearl was walking past at the time. Overhearing, she beamed her big beautiful smile, happy that someone appreciated her flair for colour and design.

"Pearl hasn't finished putting up the decorations yet," Sal told him, wishing for a strategically placed piece of mistletoe.

Chase put the pen down. "You going away for the holidays?" he asked.

"No." She held her breath. This was his chance.

"No rest for the wicked, hey." He handed her the pen. "Well, that old beast shouldn't give you any more trouble."

Did he mean Alice or the photocopier?

Then to Sal's horror, Alice marched up and stabbing her finger at him asked, "Are you married?"

The phone rang. Sally glared at it willing it to stop. She wanted to know the answer too.

"No," he replied, his mouth popping open like a goldfish. He took a step back.

Brrpp, brrpp. Damned phone!

Alice moved in for the kill. "Are you seeing anyone?"

Brrrppp! BBBRRRPPPP! Sally picked up the phone. "Good afternoon, Serenity Shores Rest Home," she said distractedly.

He inched his way to the glass doors. "No."

Alice barred his escape, "Are you gay?"

"No."

Not gay. Good. Someone was talking in her ear but she

couldn't concentrate on what they were saying.

"Good," Alice said prodding him with her jewel-encrusted finger, "Because Sally is breaking our photocopier on purpose just so you'll visit."

Mortified, pretending to have dropped her pen, Sal ducked beneath her desk. The person on the other end of the phone hung up. She prayed Chase would be gone by the time she emerged but there's only so long one can stay under a desk without reason – perhaps a nice earthquake would happen now. She surfaced to find Chase looking as if he half expected her to wrestle him to the ground and force a wedding ring on his finger.

Old steam roller Alice, was on a roll. "You should take Sally out for coffee," she suggested with all the subtly of a charging rhino. Around the office, there were murmurings of ascent.

Vikki opened her big mouth, and said, "Yeah, Sally needs a good man, she's had a series of failures."

Chase looked at Sally like he thought she was a man-eating piranha. "Ah, got to go," he said, and almost ran into the automatic doors in his hurry to leave. He threw his tools on the front seat of his vehicle, climbed in the other side, and high-tailed it out of the carpark.

Certain Alice had scared Chase off for good, Sal wanted to strangle her. But before she could give Alice a good piece of her mind, Alice was conveniently called to an emergency in the dementia ward.

Feeling depressed, Sal called into the supermarket on the way home to get supplies. She entered the store and had just grabbed a shopping basket when she spied Gone Don in the meat department. Rats! Sal hid behind a rack of specials and waited for Don to move on, then she tiptoed towards the deli freezer.

Being picky, Don dallied in the meat department until he had selected the perfect cut. When he turned down the confectionery aisle, she headed to the wine section. Sal watched him go through the checkout. She waited until he had walked out into the carpark before breathing a sigh of relief.

Why had she ever gone out with him? And, how was she ever

going to get rid of him? She couldn't keep hiding forever. This situation called for comfort food. She stood at the checkout with a bottle of wine and a tub of gold standard chocolate ice cream.

"Bad day?" The pimply young checkout boy dinged the bell and waited for his supervisor to come.

Sal let out a huge sigh. "The worst."

Young eyes dancing with mischief, he said, "Can I see your ID for that bottle of wine?"

Sally chuckled. "Keep that up and you'll get all the girls."

"Made your day better, didn't I?" he asked hopefully.

"You certainly did," she said with a grin. "I'll tell management they need to give you a pay increase for excellent customer service."

She was relieved to be home. She pulled into the driveway and parked outside the garage. With a heavy heart, she opened the picket gate with a kick and walked up to the front door.

"This is dinner tonight," she told Kat plonking the ice cream on the kitchen bench. "And no, I don't want to talk about it."

Kat popped her head up. "Somebody die?"

"No, I just want to. Is it possible to die of embarrassment?"

Sal spilled the beans.

It didn't help that Kat was amused, and told Sal she needed to deal with it.

Once they were settled in for the night, Kat pointed to the silver box resting on the coffee table, "Ok then, tell me who was the next ex?"

"I can't remember."

Sal sighed. Clearly, her dating disasters were going to be Kat's new source of entertainment.

"Oh, who's this then?" She held up a photo.

"Steve." Short, tanned, reasonable looking with good taste in clothes and furnishings. An international traveller, Steve was a good kisser but he was tighter than a fish's bum. He squeaked when he walked. He had money to burn because he spent none. He had a nice car and house and travelled, but he made Sal feel like she owed him.

The crunch came when she drove him home from Deep Creek Brewery which was within walking distance from his house albeit uphill so he didn't have to pay for gas. She dropped him off at the door and thinking she better get the thigh test in before things went any further, she leaned across pretending to get an invisible something and touched his thigh. Nothing. It was a nice thigh, nothing wrong with it, but it just didn't feel right. After that, Sal stopped taking his calls and went for long walks to avoid him. He disappeared off the grid and she was happy with that. He might be a rich man but a life with him would be a miserable one.

Sal finished the whole tub of ice-cream in one sitting. Comfort eating was becoming her new thing. She licked the spoon then popped it in the dishwasher. She washed out the cardboard tub and went outside to drop it in the recycling bin. Talking about these old ex's was getting her down. Why did she have great taste in ice-cream and terrible taste in men? Sal went back inside, closed and locked the door. She felt a growing sense of unease as she climbed the stairs for bed knowing she would probably dream about one of her many ex's tonight. Some things were better left alone she thought, as she wearily climbed into bed and closed her tired eyes. It took a while but finally she drifted off to sleep but it wasn't men she dreamed about – it was the nasty sugar plum fairy. She was trapped in Willie Wonka's Chocolate Factory and had turned into a puffed-up chocolate Oompa Loompa.

Chapter 7: Gone Global

Sal was tapping away on her keyboard while Suzie was hovering. Tenacious to the core, Suzie was still hell-bent on match-making Sal with a friend of hers. Some guy from Whangarei. Sal reminded her that a long-distance relationship wasn't ideal, and she had no intentions of moving out of Auckland.

"Suzie," Sal said, "If by some incredible miracle I ever get married you can be my bridesmaid," she promised.

Suzie used her best whiny voice. "You have to meet him. He's so worth it," she persisted. "Just one date, Sal, go on."

They were interrupted by a commotion in the reception area. Amos had lost his wallet – again, and was in a panic.

Suzie sighed. "Are you sure it's not in your jacket pocket?"

"No, it's not!" Amos snapped.

"I'll leave you to help Amos, but remember Lance is a super nice guy and you should meet him, ok?" Suzie shot her a warning look that said, I'm not giving up.

"Ok," Sal wearily agreed.

Sal got up from her desk and went to check Amos' pockets. A technician wearing Fuji Xerox shirt and nice black trousers entered the building. His grooming was impeccable. His shoes were so highly polished they gleamed like a mirror. He looked startled to find the receptionist frisking an elderly gentleman at the counter.

"Here's your wallet Amos," Sal said triumphantly, fishing the wallet from his trouser pocket.

"Bless you, my angel," Amos praised her, kissing first his wallet, then both her cheeks. Sal missed the discreet wink Amos gave the technician as she resumed her post behind her desk.

"Amos, why don't you go to the lounge for a nice cup of tea and a biscuit?" suggested Sal. "Daisy has made lovely Anzac biscuits today."

Amos shuffled down the hall while Sal turned her attention back to the smartly dressed gentleman.

"How can I help you?" she asked, confused.

"Am I also to be patted down?" he asked with a sleazy grin.

"That won't be necessary," Sal answered snippily. "Why are you here?" She frowned up at him.

The man scribbled his name in the register. He gave her a smarmy smile showing perfect teeth. "Pierre. I'm here to take a look at the photocopier."

"But I didn't lodge a call. The machine has just been fixed."

"Routine service," he replied smoothly. Pierre was a good-looking guy, with a sexy French accent, but Chase was the one she was attracted to – dammit.

Sal pointed him in the direction of the photocopier, and Pierre set to work. Now and then, Sally felt his leery eyes watching her. Suspicious that Chase might have vomited all the gory details about a desperate thirty-something receptionist who would attack anything in trousers, she thought it best to clear the air.

"Did Chase tell you what happened the other day?" Sally asked, trying hard not to blush.

He grinned, blinding her with his dazzling white teeth, "He certainly did," he said in his sexy French accent. "Thought I'd come and check things out. Ah, I mean the photocopier," he corrected himself.

Sally felt humiliated. Fuji Xerox worldwide had probably been told she'd practically tied Chase to the photocopier and tried to have her wicked way with him. Not that she didn't want to, but she didn't want anyone else knowing that.

Glowing beet-red and wishing for the ground to swallow her whole, she mumbled, "Please tell him I'm sorry." Why was she apologising? Alice should apologise. Bloody Alice.

They were interrupted by the phone ringing. Sally answered it while Pierre signed himself out. "Bonjour, ma chérie," smoozed Pierre, giving her a small bow before he disappeared out the main door, and into the carpark. She didn't know if he'd even serviced the machine. She hadn't bothered to ask.

Vikki popped out of her office to check the register. "Pierre?" She grinned at Sal. "Shall we call the first one, Nice Bum, the second, Pimply Boy and the third, Pierre Cardin." Laughing at her own joke she wandered up the hall chuckling to herself.

A week passed – still nothing. Depressed, Sally had eaten the entire stash of chocolates in the top drawer of her desk and the photocopier was working fine. Everyone in the office was giving her heaps about Chase, and still no phone call. Bloody Alice.

What was it about Chase that she found so magnetic? Perhaps it was his height and his kind blue eyes, perhaps it was the way he was good with his tools, or his cute bum, but whatever it was, Sally kept obsessing about him.

***

After her morning shower, Sal stepped on her bathroom scales naked, and was horrified when the dial went up 2 kilos. Alarmed, she jumped off, then stepped on again, convinced they must be wrong. The dial went up 3 kilos. She hopped off again. 1 whole kilo in a milli-second! Taking a deep breath then exhaling, she timidly got on again with her eyes closed, then slowly opened them, and glanced down at the dial. 3.2 kilos up! Appalled, she cursed Daisy's delicious cooking!

Outraged, she slipped her slippers on, wrapped herself in her bathrobe, picked up the offending scales, and wresting the gate open she marched up the driveway to where the rubbish bin was waiting to be emptied. Sal opened the lid and threw the scales into the bin. With a satisfied smack of her hands, she told the perfectly portioned jogger running past. "That lying bastard had to go!"

The pretty jogger tittered and continued on her way, her blonde ponytail bouncing. She had hardly broken into a sweat, her hot pink spandex gear fit her toned body like a glove.

Sal was still grumpy when she arrived at work. Stupid, bloody scales! If she kept eating at the rate she was going she would need industrial scales.

Sal pulled her smock tight across her tummy. "Do I look fat to you?" she asked Andie.

"You're looking healthy, darling," Andie said diplomatically.

"Go on, say it – I'm looking fat. It's all these chocolates the resident's families keep giving me. That and Daisy's fine cooking."

"Oh, baby," Andie flapped a hand, "so what if you are a bit cuddly, you are still gorgeous. There's just more of you to love. Besides, you have lush hair."

Before Sal could say anything, Andie grabbed a trolley of towels, and whisked it up the hallway, hand covering the side of his mouth, he whispered a warning to others along the way to keep away from reception today, Sal had PMS or something.

At morning tea time Daisy deposited a gingerbread biscuit shaped like a Christmas tree in front of Sal. She politely refused, telling Daisy she was trying to lose weight.

Daisy snorted in disgust. "Stupid time to diet right on Christmas," she said taking the plate away, and still muttering under her breath, she stalked up the hallway in a huff, tea towel draped over her shoulder.

When lunchtime arrived, Sal looked despairingly at her salad and piece of fruit but reminded herself that she had to be good. By the end of the day, she was hungry and couldn't wait to get home to eat.

"I'm starving," she told Kat as she dumped her handbag on the dining chair. "What's for tea?"

"Mac and cheese."

"No, no, that won't do. Will have to be a lettuce leaf and a can of tuna," sighed Sal.

"Suit yourself." Kat shrugged. "Your loss."

Kat ate her mac and cheese while Sal stuck to her salad, all the while looking longingly at Kat's plate.

After they'd cleaned up, Kat said, "Now come on, tell me about another ex."

They sat outside on the upstairs balcony off Kat's bedroom enjoying the last shreds of sunshine; Kat with a glass of wine and Sal a glass of water. Like a centrepiece, the box of exs sat on the outdoor table. Sal squirmed as Kat clicked open the silver box and began to riffle through the photos.

She found one tinged yellow with age. She gasped and flung a photo in Sal's face taunting her with it.

"Paedophile," Kat accused. "This is a primary school class photo!"

"First crush, Kenny Rogers."

"Really? For real? Did his mother name him after the country star, Kenny Rogers?"

Sal gave her a half-smile. "I reckon she did," she drawled in her best country accent.

"How old were you?"

"Five. "

Kenny Rogers played hard to get, and at five he was more interested in her mother's chocolate chip cookies than Sal. Perhaps that was where the challenge lay, the thrill of the kill. Trying to catch Chase was similar. It was like trying to catch Kenny Rogers all over again.

Kat was busy randomly picking out photos. She held up another. It was a primary school reunion photo.

"Warren."

At their primary school reunion, Warren asked her to dance. They boogied, then he plucked up the courage and invited her out for a coffee date. Flattered by the admission he'd had a crush on her at school, Sal accepted the invite. But there was no spark, nothing, she didn't need to implement the thigh test. There was simply no attraction. She let him down gently by telling him she was seeing someone, which wasn't strictly true then but it was only a matter of time.

Kat picked up another photo. Sal flapped a disinterested hand. "Boring."

"And this one," Kat asked, picking up another.

"Suffocating."

Kat put the photo back in the box and picked up another. She waved it at Sal.

Sal yawned. "Suffocatingly boring."

Kat picked out another.

"Too young."

Kat put that reject to the back of the pile and held up a photo of a guy who looked in his forties.

"Too old."

Kat discarded the rejected forty-something year old. "You sound like Goldilocks."

"Goldilocks?"

"Too hot, too cold, too young, too old, I hope one of these days you will find one that will be just right." Kat held up a new photo.

"And this one?"

"Didn't pass the thigh test."

Kat studied her thoughtfully. "Were there any who got away?"

"A couple," Sal admitted and drained her glass of water. Longing for a proper drink she frowned at the empty glass. Water just wasn't doing it for her.

"So," Kat drawled. "Tell me about the ones who didn't get in the box, the ones that got away."

"Matteau. I was ten."

"What happened?"

"He moved to the other side of town and went to a new school."

Kat shook her head. "I'm not talking about infants. Were there any grownups that got away?"

Sal remembered him fondly. Her sister Paula was working at a business advisor's office in Browns Bay, and Sal was meeting Paula for lunch. The business premises were upstairs situated between shops. Sal had just taken a couple of steps up the narrow flight of stairs when a dashing young man came flying down the stairs two at a time; he collided with her almost knocking her over.

Apologising profusely, he held her steady saying, "Sorry, I

didn't mean to bowl you over. Are you alright?"

The attraction was instant. Sal thought he was hot. "I'm Sal. I'm here to see my sister, Paula," she told him.

"Cool. She's upstairs. Sorry, I'd love to stay and chat but I'm late for an appointment. Must dash, name is Dave. See ya." And then he was gone.

Was Paula holding out on her? Probably didn't want to risk Sal going out with one of her workmates and then have her dump them for no good reason as far as she was concerned. Stuff her, the sisterhood pact needed to be tested. Sal interrogated Paula over lunch. According to Paula, Dave was Canadian, single, and a super nice guy. Sal had lunch with Paula every day for the next fortnight hoping to catch sight of Dave, and every time she saw him, he was just dashing off. Sal kind of wanted him to pull a hamstring or break a leg, anything to slow him down a bit so she could get to know him. If she didn't know better, she'd think he was avoiding her on purpose, but Paula told her that he'd mentioned in passing that your sister is pretty cute, isn't she?

And then the worst happened. Everyone in their office, except for Paula and the manager, were made redundant. Devastated, Dave moved back to Canada. When Sal bemoaned the fact that she would never see Dashing Dave again, Paula remarked that Sal wasn't actually in a relationship with the guy. Paula knew how to burst Sal's dream bubble saying, everyone can be idolised until you get to know them properly.

Sal had finally stopped fantasying about a dream life in Canada with Dave when Paula casually mentioned Dashing Dave was holidaying from Canada and would be joining her and her husband Alistair for dinner at their house, and did she want to come? Hell, yeah!

Dave was just as handsome as ever, but he brought his boring anaemic Canadian wife with him. They'd been married less than a month. All Sal's hopes were dashed. She ate a double helping of dessert that night.

Kat tapped Sally on the leg bringing her back to the present. "Sally Gelee, you are a major commitment-phobe."

"No, I'm not!" Sal declared. "I want love and marriage."

Kat gave her that look. "You say that but the moment anything looks serious you turn tail and run." She held up her hand to prevent Sal from arguing.

Sal narrowed her eyes. What made Kat think she knew all there was to know about relationships? Why did she assume she knew everything about her life – she didn't know squat.

"You need to get away and forget about what's-his-face," she said. "The guy with the nice bum?"

Sally looked over the rim of her glass. "Chase," she said bleakly.

"Yeah, him," Kat said, shaking her head. "Chick, he's not worth the space he's occupying in your head."

"But I like him," Sal said, knowing she sounded childish.

"You don't even know him," Kat reminded her. "He's only perfect in your imagination. He's a fantasy, just like dashing Dave, perfect from afar."

Was Kat, right? Did she have to be so in control that she had to be the one in pursuit, not the one being pursued? Nah, that was bulldust.

Kat pushed again. "You need to get out there, babe, and date a real man, not a figment of your imagination."

Sal could feel her bottom lip droop. "How? What do you suggest?"

"Online," Kat said emphatically.

"Too risky," Sally replied, hugging her empty glass to her chest.

"No riskier than meeting someone in a pub," argued Kat.

"Yes, but, but..." Sal floundered.

"I'll build you a profile," Kat offered reaching for her tablet.

"No, not yet," Sally said resolutely. "That's how I met Kurt, and Ken."

That night she dreamed about two perfect men that got away. She woke up feeling tired and out of sorts. She told Kat over a light breakfast about her dream.

Distracted, Kat ah-hummed. She was nosing out the window

trying to catch a glimpse of the new neighbours. "You met the guys next door yet?" she asked. "They look a bit of alright."

"No, I haven't. Guess it's only a matter of time. But that fire service ute takes up a fair chunk of the driveway. Did you want to bake cookies for them or something to welcome them to the neighbourhood? Then you could tell him to park properly."

Kat was not known for her cooking skills. She faked a laugh. "You're so funny." She moved away from the window. "You, Little Miss Bossy, can tell them to park better."

"What's your nickname for them?" Sal inquired. "New kids on the block?"

"Nice, I like it but I think we'll just call them The Guys." Kat refocused her attention. "Right, back to the ones that got away."

Sal couldn't recall any others.

"You have a pretty good hit rate."

"So, why won't Chase call?" whined Sal.

Kat cried, "Stop moping! And for heaven's sake eat something other than lettuce. This stupid diet is making you unbearable."

Mm, perhaps she should go online to find a new flatmate. She wondered if there was any room in the flat next door?

Chapter 8: Bloody Marvellous

Work was so busy the week went by in a blur. Poor Nancy who always wore purple, had a fall, and the ambulance had to take her to hospital. Then, there was an infectious gastro outbreak, and some residents had to be isolated. Sal prayed she didn't get it.

Howard, the caretaker, was changing the lightbulbs, and testing and tagging equipment in the reception area. He had a grumbling morose way about him that made everything sound like a problem. Sal couldn't help being reminded of Eeyore from Winnie the Pooh. Alice was busy instructing Howard on which bulbs needed changing, Vikki was busy with residents' medical problems, both real, and imagined, and Pat, the cleaner was trying to vacuum under Sal's desk and muttering about staples sticking in the carpet.

Andie arrived amid this chaos, puffing, "Honey, have you seen Amos?" Howard was particularly wary of Andie, he always seemed uncomfortable around him. He packed up his ladder and disappeared.

Sally tried to remember the last time she'd seen Amos. "Not since morning tea, he was in the dining room then," she told Andie.

Carla came running into reception, "It's ok, he was over at the police station reporting his wallet as being stolen."

"For heaven's sake, it will be in his pocket," Alice said, stalking down the corridor, arms swinging, presumably on her way to find Amos. Sal sighed. Roll on Christmas – she sure needed a break.

"Are you alright, dear?" Ethel called from the other side of the reception counter. Sal loved her job; she loved the staff and the residents but she hated Sid Snot. Sid Snot was her nickname for the rest home safe. Sid opened at will but not at Sal's will.

She'd punch in the numbers on the keypad and the stupid thing wouldn't budge. Cursing under her breath, Sal had another go. You got three shots at getting the sequence and timing right before it locked you out for half an hour.

Ethel was growing impatient. "You haven't lost my money, have you, dear?"

Sal clenched her jaw and tugged. "No Ethel, it's perfectly safe. Even those with the combination can't touch it," Sal replied wrenching the handle, then by a stroke of sheer good luck Sid opened. Sal let out a sigh of relief. Ethel smiled as Sal dished out forty dollars in cash and marked it off her comfort account. Ethel tucked the money into the bra that held her matronly bosom, and toddled up the hallway as happy as a wee clam. Sal knew Ethel's first stop would be the fish and chip shop for a good feed of grease, then she'd be off to the stationery shops to buy a couple of magazines before returning home again. In a place where life was unpredictable, some things were wonderfully predictable.

Later in the day the hairdresser came in, and competing for the best lavender wash and set the ladies eagerly lined up. Sal felt fat and dowdy, if she couldn't lose weight then she could at least get a new hairstyle. Kat kept reminding her that just because she worked in a rest home, she needn't let herself go. Her hair was growing at an alarming rate, and her fringe was covering her eyes. She felt like a shaggy old English sheepdog. Not wanting her hair dyed lilac or shaped into a soft boofy perm, Sal decided that she would indulge in a little pampering, and booked a hair appointment for herself at the new salon that had just opened up the road from work.

Gino introduced himself, led her to the chair, and asked her to sit down. Mediterranean, Gino knew how to flatter a woman.

"Beautiful," he murmured running his fingers softly through her long fair hair and drawing it gently away from her face, he asked, in a soothing chocolatey voice, "What would you like, my darling?"

"Roots," Sally replied. Then feeling like she had suggested

something terribly rude, hurriedly added, "and some foils."

"Yes, yes, my darling," he enthusiastically agreed and set to work. Hours passed. Gino was very attentive. He massaged her scalp, he had lovely hands and she relaxed under his care.

He stopped working, comb poised in mid-air, and asked, "Are you single, darling?"

"Yes," Sal answered, surprised he'd asked.

"I can tell you are beautiful inside and out, I would like to marry you."

How did this stuff happen to her? Gino might be exotic and a fantastic hairdresser, and although it would be nice to have her hair professionally done for free, he was probably only looking for citizenship. Other than the initial attraction there was nothing right about Gino, she didn't even have to attempt the thigh test to know that.

"I'm flattered but...but...I'm in love with someone else."

"Oh," he said crestfallen. "Lucky man."

***

Pearl was finishing putting up the last Christmas decorations.

"I've got the residents making cards and more decorations for the hallway."

"Don't forget the mistletoe, Pearl, darling," chirped Andie. He blew air kisses at Howard who shuffled off grumbling something about sexual harassment in the workplace, Christmas humbug and all sorts of carry on.

"You must stop teasing him," Sal chastised Andie.

Andie pooh-poohed her. "Oh, darling, he's just so much fun to tease."

Sal could think of a lot of words to describe Howard but fun wasn't one of them.

Vikki suddenly appeared behind Sal, startling her. She stilled her beating heart. "If you are looking for Scrooge," she pointed at the shambling figure of Howard who had just made it to the first set of double doors, "he went that way."

Even Alice was getting into the Christmas spirit. "Daisy has made a fabulous Christmas dinner menu. I won't have to cook on Christmas day because I'm going to have lunch here. I couldn't be happier," Alice enthused. "What are you doing for Christmas, Sal?"

Christmas alone, Sal thought bleakly. Sal's mother was down South and would be having Christmas with her new love. How come her Mum could find a decent normal guy while she seemed to attract all the weirdos on the planet? Maybe there was a better breed of men down South. Her sister and brother-in-law were going away, and her brother and his wife and kids were going camping. Kat was an orphan since both her parents had passed but she was probably having Christmas with her old aunt.

"I'll tell Daisy to count me in for Christmas lunch too," Sal said. She might as well eat as the diet didn't seem to be working and, her clothes still felt tight.

Vikki was waiting for the doctor to arrive; hands clasped behind her back and rocking impatiently on her heels. He came every Monday to do his weekly rounds; nice guy, a streak of a man with wispy blonde hair and spectacles.

"Heard from the photocopier man yet, Sal?" Vikki asked.

"Alice scared him off," Sal muttered darkly. Bloody Alice!

Pearl knotted the last wreath in place. "You better not hear from that other stalker of yours or I'll tear him limb from limb," she growled. "I'd like to stuff him down a chimney and light him on fire."

"Now, now, darling," Andie tutted, "that's hardly the Christmas spirit, however, if you need help..." Andie grinned.

Pearl told them that the last time she'd taken the mini-van out she'd seen Gone Don in his black Holden. She pulled up beside him at the traffic lights, and winding the window down, yelled out, "Oi you, get a life and stop annoying Sally, or I'll set this lot onto you." She thrust her thumb at those sitting in the back.

Taking their cue the residents shouted abuse, banging

the windows with their canes and growling like they were possessed.

Norman, who couldn't remember his name, gave Don the fingers and yelled out that in a past life he'd been a champion boxer, adding, at least I think so, as an afterthought. "At any rate, I can still take that little weed on," he muttered to Pearl.

"You should have seen Gone Don's face, he almost pee-ed his pants," Pearl said, with a naughty little giggle.

"You did a good job of scaring him Pearl, haven't heard a peep from him since." She had to admit she almost missed the attention. What was wrong with her? Was she crazy?

Sal went to the staff room to have lunch and overhead some carers swearing.

"Hey, hey, language," she remonstrated, frowning at Clara. "You lot will be donating to the swear jar, and the rest of us will be enjoying dinner out on you guys."

"We aren't swearing, darling," explained Andie. "We are talking about Bloody Marvellous."

Sal's eyebrows shot up.

"Who's 'bloody marvellous'?" she asked, picturing a retired circus performer, maybe he'd once been shot out of a canyon.

"Marvin. He's Australian, he's the new admission. He says everything is bloody marvellous, all the time. And insists we call him Bloody Marvellous. He reckons all his mates call him that. Bet he was like Crocodile Dundee in his day."

Sal racked her brain. "Really? I don't remember him. He sounds like a character I wouldn't forget."

Later that same afternoon, Sal was running around distributing the mail to the residents when she heard a man with a booming voice say, "Well, that's bloody marvellous, that is."

She stopped and went over to the man in a wheelchair. He wore a big sloppy blue cardigan over a red checked shirt, beige trousers, and corduroy slippers. Not a bit like Mick Dundee.

Sal crouched down so they were face-to-face. Like Santa, his face was whiskery, he had nose hairs like grey spider legs and big bushy eyebrows. "You must be Bloody Marvellous," she said with a smile.

He ginned widely, a spark in his milky blue eyes, "And you must be Bloody Beautiful."

She laughed. "You old flirt. I bet you say that to all the girls. Keep that up and I'll send you outside to do three laps around the courtyard in your chair."

"Anything for you, darling."

***

Sal was still chuckling when she got home. She kicked off her shoes at the front door.

"Heard anything?" began Kat.

Sal drew a blank. "From?"

Kat gave her *that* look. "You know who."

Sal sighed. "No. Nothing."

Apologetic, Kat said, "I don't know why you go for losers. Look at you, apart from your lousy taste in men you are smart, funny, and good company. However, your dress sense could do with improving"

"What's wrong with it?" Sal said, instantly defensive. "I had my hair done."

"Your hair looks good, but look at yourself, chick." Kat waved a manicured hand. "The rest of you needs a makeover. You may work in a rest home, but you don't have to dress like you belong there. You look positively dowdy."

Sally looked down at her baggy sweater and lose-fitting pants feeling as flat as a squished dead hedgehog. "I'll have you know I was hit on today by Bloody Marvellous."

"Let me guess, he was eighty. You need to mix with people your own age."

"Why don't you fix me up with one of your superstar clients then?" Sal huffed.

"Because they are already taken," Kat retorted. "They are either married, or in a relationship because they have a life."

Sal crunched miserably on a carrot stick. Even the residents were having more fun than she was. Why only yesterday Walt was found in Ethel's room, and there had been some very eyebrow raising suggestive bantering in the reception area beforehand.

Sal sat on the couch, a water bottle in one hand, twirling a stick of celery in the other, staring blanky into space.

Kat was unloading the dishwasher. "You're doing it again."

Startled, Sally asked, "What?"

Kat sighed. "Dreaming about Mr Photocopier guy."

Tucking her legs under her she sat on the couch, flicked the telly on, trying to block out Kat.

Kat wasn't going to be ignored and joined her on the couch. "Come on," she said like she was coaching a puppy out of hiding, "Forget him, he's not that into you or he would have called."

Sal dug into her pocket, took the folded paper out and passed the invitation to Kat. She didn't need to read it, she'd designed it.

"Since I'm single do you want to be my date for Saturday night? It's my work's Christmas Party. The theme is to Give a Little Love this Christmas. It's not just our rest home, it's for the staff of the five Oceancare rest homes and other community volunteers. Instead of buying each other presents, we are to donate a present for a deserving person in our community, and then the rest home managers give them out a few days before Christmas so there's something under the tree for them. If you are stuck for ideas there are a few hints on what to buy on the other side of the invitation."

Kat brightened. "Oh, what a lovely idea. I'd love to go." She sucked in a breath. "Oh no, it's a dress-up." Not a fan of dress-ups, Kat suddenly seemed in two minds about going.

"You don't have to dress up if you don't want to," Sal said glumly.

"Because it's for charity I'll make an exception," Kat conceded.

She jogged Sal's arm. "It'll be fun. Bit of music and dancing is just what you need to cheer you up. It will help you get over your infatuation, and who knows, you might meet someone who isn't geriatric."

Sal pulled a face. "Ha, ha."

Kat snorted, "You probably can't fit another photo in the box of dating disasters, but you look like you need a good bonk."

Sal lifted her chin. "I want more than a one-night stand, thank you very much," she replied tartly.

"Oh yeah, that's right, you are looking for Mr Right, aren't you?" Kat said cynically. "Well, good luck with that."

Sal's bottom lip protruded. She was going off Kat, pity she didn't have an off button.

Kat sighed. "Come on, chick, you've got to get over yourself. Sitting here moping isn't going to change your life. And think about it, if Don…"

"Don?" Sal looked up sharply. "What's he got to do with it?"

"Right now, he thinks he's still got a chance because you are still single. He stalks you so he knows you aren't seeing anyone but if he sees you with someone else, then he'll leave you alone, right."

Sal thought it sounded feasible, and as it was a community event. Maybe Chase might be there too. "Yeah, you're right. Let's do it."

Chapter 9: Christmas Wishes

Friday night, Sal was still deciding what to wear, when, ready and rearing to go, Kat pounded on her bedroom door. Sal opened the door to find Kat standing there in a parcel hat and sparkly red Christmas stocking dress with a furry white collar, her black boots peeking beneath the drawstring bottom. She looked great. Kat could look good in a paper bag.

Staring, Kat squeaked in disbelief, "Are you going like that?"

"Don't be silly," Sally flipped a hand. "I'm still in my dressing gown. Give me five."

Sally dug in the bottom of the wardrobe and found a battered Christmas hat and stuck it on. She appeared downstairs, wearing minimal makeup, her long blonde straight hair pulled back into a ponytail, and dressed in a navy-blue jacket and shirt with shiny black heels.

Eyebrow's meeting, Kat frowned. "And you are?"

"Santa's event manager," she said tapping her clipboard.

Kat rolled her eyes and flapped a sparkly red manicured hand. "Oh, now it's obvious," she said in a voice thick with sarcasm.

They popped their presents on the back seat of Kat's car, and for once Sally was allowed to drive. Only because Kat's costume was too gathered at the bottom for her to manipulate the pedals. It was just going on dark, and a few splatters of rain hit the windshield.

Kat shook her head. "Anyone would think you were a real estate agent going to some corporate event. You should have worn your dressing gown at least then you'd look like 'the night before Christmas'."

Sally wished she'd made a better attempt to get in the spirit of Christmas. Usually, she'd be all in for a dress up, but she was down and couldn't get in the mood. Still, she reasoned, there were probably going to be a hundred little Santa's there, so if nothing else she should stand out.

Sal turned on the GPS and after a slight detour, thanks to Google, she found the place and took the first available carpark.

"You could have parked a bit closer," moaned Kat.

"The walk will do you good," Sal replied.

Sal couldn't suppress a giggle as she watched Kat mince geisha style up the path towards the front door, balancing her present in one hand and hitching the side of her stocking up with the other.

The hall was dripping with tinsel. Much to her shame, Sally felt seriously under-dressed. Everyone had gone all out. There were Christmas trees, reindeers, elves, angels, snowmen, and heaps of Santa's. She almost bumped into Jesus who walked past her wearing a sign saying, 'I'm the reason for the season.'

Pearl was dressed as Mrs Claus; she took their presents for the needy and placed them under the huge Christmas tree in the foyer.

The fairy lights, draped end-to-end across the ceiling, made the hall pretty and inviting. People were really getting into the swing of things and enjoying themselves. Collection booths were set up and a video screen flashed up showing Christmas stories of previous years' deserving families blessed with gifts they otherwise wouldn't have had. Sal scouted the room, maybe if she was lucky Santa would bring her the Christmas gift she wanted – Chase.

The music was blaring, the band was good, and a few bodies were strutting their stuff on the dance floor. Kat started to hand jive as they walked to their table. They strategically chose a table near the dance floor, yet conveniently close to the bar. Nope, no sign of Chase. Maybe a Christmas miracle would happen, and he would suddenly appear, and she'd fall into his arms and..., damn, she was daydreaming again.

Alice, dressed in angel garb, was working the room. Unable to see properly in the dark, Sal bumped into Alice skewing one of Alice's wings. She hurriedly introduced Kat as her flatmate, and told Kat, Alice was her boss.

"Pleasure," Alice smiled approvingly at Kat, then turning on Sal, Alice said, "You might have made more of an effort, Sal." Then whisking herself away she went to hobnob with the managers from the other care facilities.

"See what you mean, she's all heart that one," commented Kat.

Explaining that her costume was too restrictive, Kat gave Sally the job of getting the drinks.

"Didn't you get the memo that it was fancy dress?" asked a sympathetic snowman as Sal made her way to the bar. Sally sighed. It was going to be a long night.

Stuff having a lowly glass of water – after all it was Christmas. "Two glasses of bubbles, please," Sally said to the reindeer behind the bar.

"Coming right up, little lady," he replied, his nose blinking like a lighthouse beacon.

Careful not to spill a drop, Sal held the drinks aloft and negotiated her way through swarms of people.

"Here," she handed Kat a glass. "Bottoms up."

"We should be so lucky," Kat joked, chugging it back.

"Take it easy, girlfriend. A couple more of these and you'll be on your ear," warned Sal.

"Unlike you, I can handle more than a couple."

Andie came over to say 'hi.' Flamboyant as ever, he was dressed as a Christmas Fairy and enjoying every moment. Long black hair was piled up in a bun, with a halo of tinsel circling it. He wore silver eye shadow and lipstick to match. "Darling," Andie air-kissed Sal's cheeks. "Did you forget it was a dress-up, babe?"

A grinch waved at Andie from across the room and before Sal could answer, Andie was gone with a wave of red and green painted fingertips. "Tootles, honey, have fun."

"What a sweetie," Kat said, watching Andie weave his way across the room.

"Yeah, told you that you would love him. Andie's a honey," Sal agreed. "He's awesome with the residents and so caring.

Everyone loves Andie. Everyone except Howard. Howard's dead scared of him."

"Oh, why?" Kat wanted to know.

"Phobic."

"Shame."

The bubbles were tickling her nose. The laser lights flashed; the noise was deafening. They sat in companionable silence watching the uninhibited and the more inebriated boogie on the dance floor and commenting on their different costumes. One guy had come dressed as the Simpson's dog, Santa's Little Helper.

A guy Sal knew from one of the other rest homes, dressed as a Christmas bauble, walked past them, and shouted over the noise, "Didn't you know it was fancy dress, Sal?"

"What are you?" Sal asked a support worker clad in a red, green, and white bed sheet with eye and mouth holes cut out.

"Why I'm the spirit of Christmas," he proudly told her. Puzzled, he asked, "And you are?"

"Myself,' muttered Sal.

Kat jostled Sal's arm. "Cheer up, your gloomy face is scaring off the talent."

"What talent?" Sally squinted in the darkness. "I know most of these guys and I can't see any talent."

"Put your glasses on, nana," Kat said jerking her head at the group of guys at the next table.

"I'm telling you I can't see anything decent." One of the guys did look alright.

Kat snorted. "That's rich coming from you, girlfriend. Weren't you the one that went out with Soggy?"

"Short old gray guy? He wasn't so bad. Just, well…a little - old."

"He was like the walking dead," joked Kat. "Now, if you are going to keep scowling, chicky, you can go sit somewhere else. You are ruining the power of attraction."

Sal faked a smile that looked more like a grimace.

Kat nudged her. "No seriously, do you know the hot present at the next table?"

Sal glanced over. Sal had to admit he was pretty cute. Even under his red and white striped boxed costume, you could still see he was tanned, and heavily tattooed.

"Nope, he must work one of the other homes, or is a guest of someone who does, or maybe he's one of the first responders."

"Wonder if he's single? Kat smiled and batted her long lashes at the dude.

Sal squinted. "Can't see a ring. Can't see much at all in this light."

The Christmas box swaggered towards them. "Hi, I'm Rob. Would you like to dance?" he asked Kat.

Kat glanced uneasily at Sally. "Will you be ok, chick?"

A bit miffed that Rob hadn't asked her to dance, Sal replied, "Of course, go on, go."

Kat slipped off the stool, "Love to, but I'm having a little trouble with my bottom half."

Rob laughed. Kat was mortified when she realised what she'd said.

"Mine wasn't the most practical costume either," he said, attempting to make her feel better. "You'd think an architect would choose a better design. Loosen your drawstrings or you may face- plant."

At the word architect Kat's eyes lit up. "Let's go," Kat said taking his arm. They made their way to the dance floor.

Sally sank another glass of champagne and giggled while she watched Kat and Rob dance as best as they could in their outfits.

"Great party, Sal." Suzie slid past in a slinky little Santa suit giving her the thumbs up. "Can't wait to introduce you to my friend Lance, he's coming to Auckland soon."

Sal fixed a grin and gave her the thumbs up.

Someone tapped her on the shoulder and a husky voice asked. "Wanna dance?"

Sally turned slowly. From what she could see in the semi-darkness the guy was about 6 feet, dark-haired, and average. He towered over her but then when you are five foot three at a push everyone towered above you. He was dressed as Santa but didn't have the stomach; he was the more modern healthy version.

She shrugged. "Sure." Anything was better than sitting around looking at everyone else having a good time. Sal put down her glass, squeezed past people, and followed him onto the crowded dance floor.

Perhaps she'd had too much champagne. Her legs felt kind of wobbly. Maybe she was dancing sexy, then again – probably not.

"What's your name?" he bellowed over the music.

"Sally. Yours?"

"Hector."

Hector? That was a name she associated with dolphins or Silence of the Lambs.

"Do you work for Oceancare?"

"No, I came with a mate of mine who does."

"What do you do for a job, Hector?" Sally shouted. The band was winding down to take a break and the music ended abruptly.

Hector yelled, "I work at the prison. I'm a sexual psychologist for serious sex offenders."

Everyone stared at them like they were some kind of freak show. Sally wanted to die of embarrassment. She was dancing with some kind of Hannibal Lector wannabe. Hannibal Hector worked at the prison. No wonder he liked her outfit. Uniforms were probably his thing.

"Shame the band is taking a break," Hector said, escorting Sally back to her table. "When they start up again, I'll come to get you for another dance, hey?"

"Yeah, great," she murmured, her eyes searching for the nearest exit. Oh no! Was that Gone Don over there in the shadows? Please God, no!

Back at the table, she found Kat cuddling up to the present called Rob. He told her he was designing a new Oceancare facility in the city. Meanwhile Kat was impressing his friends with her work stories about the celebs she knew, and was in no hurry to leave.

"I think I'll call it a night, I'm not really in the mood. I'll call an uber," Sally told her, handing Kat the car keys.

"Lighten up, the night is just getting interesting." Kat said, "That guy who asked you to dance, he's a bit of alright, isn't he?"

Sally rolled her eyes. "He's a shrink for serious sex offenders at the prison."

"Really?" Kat was fascinated. "Bet he knows some kinky shit. Hey," Kat said brightening, "you should ask him how to handle stalkers so you can get rid of Not Gone Don, better still, perhaps he can lock him up."

Sal swallowed. "Yeah, well, I think Gone Don is lurking over there in the shadows."

"Where?" Kat strained her eyes. "No, you're seeing things girlfriend, that's not him, just a look-alike."

Sal was freaking out. "I don't want to encourage another stalker now, do I?"

Kat sighed. "Go if you must, I'll either get a ride home or a taxi. Here," Kat reached into her handbag and took out a small slip of paper, "I've got a couple of free taxi vouchers, if there's a taxi outside use that and you'll get a free ride."

"No jokes," Sal warned. "Ok, you stay here with the present and I'll head off. You're sure you'll be, ok?"

"I'm fine. Don't worry, I won't drink and drive. I'll leave the car here tonight and catch a ride home with Rob," Kat winked, "Don't wait up, I have a feeling things will go well without the handbrake around."

"Handbrake." Sal snorted indignantly.

Desperate to flee before Hector came back and wondering if there was some sort of invisible tattoo on her forehead that said if you're a super weirdo loser, pick me. Sal swiftly made her way to the exit.

She noticed a white car waiting out front. Assuming it was a taxi, Sal opened the door and bumped her head as she eagerly climbed in the back.

"Oww," she cried rubbing the bump and passed the voucher to the driver.

He twisted around and said, "Hi, I'm Trent, and you are?" He wore a Santa hat and beard. Everyone was in the spirit of

Christmas. She felt like such a grinch. She should have worn a grinch outfit; it would have matched her mood.

"Sally. 4/12 Shelly Way." She glanced back over her shoulder. "Ah, can you step on it, I'm kind of in a hurry."

"Your wish is my command, my lady." He nodded and pulled away from the kerb.

"Did you have a nice evening?" he asked, checking her reaction in his rear vision window.

"It was ok, but I have a headache, so I thought I'd call it a night."

"I'm not surprised, banging your head like that."

She didn't need to be reminded how much of a klutz she was. She slunk down in the back seat and checked her phone. He took the hint and didn't pester her further.

"Just drop me here, please," she told him as they pulled into the street. "That'll be fine, thank you."

"You're welcome," Trent replied, his voice muffled by his fake beard.

"Is that voucher enough or do I owe you some?" She asked as she opened her phone to retrieve her card.

"No, nothing, keep it. Merry Christmas – tonight is on the house. It's Christmas and I believe in paying it forward."

She tentatively opened the car door. "Really? That's very nice of you. Are you sure?"

"Yeah, it's all good," he assured her. "I'll swap my Santa hat for angel wings later."

Sal shut the door and watched the car pull away. She staggered inside, switching on the light and kicking off her shoes. Damn, she needed a coffee.

At three a.m., sitting bolt upright in bed, blinking like a startled owl, she wished she hadn't had that damn coffee. On the up side, she heard Kat come home. There was the squeak of the door, a bit of staggering down the hall, shoes dropping as she went, the creak of a stair. Sal listened but could only hear one set of footsteps not two. Then Kat's bedroom door closed and there was silence.

Chapter 10: Fallout

Kat had bulldog eyes in the morning. Sal teased Kat, threatening to take photos and post them on social media so Rob could see what she really looked like in the morning.

"Oh, get lost – you don't look much better," griped Kat, reaching for the painkillers. Sal watched as Kat greedily wolfed down a greasy feed of bacon and eggs for breakfast to help soak up the alcohol. After they had picked up the car, Kat put herself back to bed to sleep off her hangover.

It was late in the afternoon when Sal knocked on Kat's bedroom door to check if she was still alive.

"Yeah," came the feeble answer.

Sal handed Kat a coffee and then plopped herself down on the bed. "So, did you have a good night?"

"I did." Kat nudged Sal with her foot. "Despite you being a total killjoy."

"Sorry," mumbled Sal. "But at least you weren't hampered by the handbrake."

"True that," Kat grinned. "Rob's really nice. We are meeting up tonight. He's an architect and a volunteer firefighter. He'd look great on the Firefighters calendar, don't you think?"

With his buzz cut and heavily tattooed arms, Sal thought he looked like he belonged in the services or prison. She hadn't picked him for an architect or a firefighter.

Sal listened while Kat droned on about Rob until she'd heard enough. "Ok, I give up, build me a profile."

"If I do this for you, promise to leave me alone, I need to get some beauty sleep."

"Pinkie promise."

Kat dusted off her tablet and clicked onto the online dating site. Full of nervous anticipation Sally filled in the details only lying about her height, weight, and age.

"I've always been bad at right and left, what if I swipe right when I mean to swipe left, or is it the other way round?" Sal fretted.

"You'll figure it out. Now let me sleep," Kat pleaded as she crashed back on the pillow and closed her eyes.

***

It's just coffee, Sally told herself as she walked into Starbucks. Carl was waiting for her. Tick. At least he was early. Tick. He had showed up. Carl was good-looking and not unlike his profile photo. He was wearing faded blue jeans and a plain black t-shirt, and appeared normal. So far so good. He stood when she entered. He must have recognised her from her profile. Tick. He had manners. He offered to buy the coffee so she let him. Tick. Generous.

They sat in the comfy chairs near the front window, close to the door. Easier for escape Sally reasoned.

Carl began by asking questions. "So, do you live around here?"

Sally felt her pulse quicken. Kat had told her, don't let him know where you live. Don't tell him anything personal. You don't need another stalker.

"Not far away." Vague but true. "I'm an administrator for a rest home," she volunteered. "I love it." That much was true. She tried to sound chill as she asked, "And you? What do you do?"

He put down his coffee and leaned in. "I'm a solo dad. I'm currently unemployed, but you know, I'm hopeful."

Strike one. Unemployed. Strike two, solo father.

"Dylan's thirteen."

Eek! She had no intention of going through the teen thing with anyone. She wanted a family but not a ready-made one. Sally slowly took a sip of coffee and waited for some inspiration. "So, tell me a little about yourself?"

"Well, I've spent many years in and out of institutions, up until recently I've lived in a commune."

Strike three. Warning lights flashed before Sal's eyes. Terminate! Abort! Abandon!

"Really?" Not knowing what to reply to that she drank her coffee and listened.

"I've been in recovery now for two years and the Doc says I'm doing really well." He jiggled his leg incessantly, and not meeting her eye, he picked at a loose thread on the arm of the chair.

Someone once told her that men at her age were like car parks, all the good ones were gone and only the disabled ones were left.

"Ah…is that the time?" Sally glanced at her watch. Horrors, it had only been fifteen minutes since they sat down yet it felt like an eternity.

She bit her lip. "Yeah, well, um it's been interesting," she said in a breathy rush. "Um sorry, but I have to be somewhere, so I have to go."

"Can I see you again?" Carl ventured, seemingly undeterred by her reaction. Was the entire male population mad?

"Um, no, I think not." Sally hurried outside. In case Carl followed her car, she thought she'd give him the slip so she drove to the mall. After all, Sal needed to cheer herself up and needed to get her Mum a Christmas present. She ducked into the Music shop. Her life was so not going to plan. Her mother, who was in her sixties, bless her, had a 69-year-old boyfriend who was the love of her life. Sal's dad had passed away ten years before. When Joyce met Bernard, she fell in love all over again. Her mother lit up like a Christmas tree whenever Bernard's name was mentioned and giggled away like a gooey-eyed teenager. It was endearing and nauseating at the same time. How come her Mum could find lasting love, not once but twice, and she couldn't?

Sal flicked through the sales racks searching for a particular DVD that would make a nice present for her Mum for Christmas and found the perfect gift; a doco-film named 'Young at Heart.'

"I hear this is sad," the guy behind the counter commented, as he processed the transaction.

Sally glanced at his name badge. Bill was the new store manager and was kind of cute, in a British sort of way. Short, with a wiry build, black hair and scruffy five o'clock shadow, Bill had a cheeky sense of humour.

"I've already seen it, it's a bit of everything," Sal told him. "Funny and sad, but inspiring. It's for my Mum, she's 64 and got a 69-year-old boyfriend."

"That's great," Bill said, bagging the gift and handing it to her.

"They are living life to the max." Sal could hear herself babbling but couldn't stop. "That's why I think my mother will like it. She's living life to the max."

Bill raised his eyebrows. "Really?"

Sal quipped, "Yeah, it's tragic when your mother's sex life is better than your own."

Bill paused for a split second, glanced at his watch then looked her dead in the eye. "I'm free at four o'clock."

God's truth, she was tempted. English blokes weren't usually her type, but Bill was cute and an opportunist, and had a quick wit to boot. And, by the look of the ring on his finger had a wife. She wasn't going there. Unable to think of a suitable reply, Sally laughed nervously and glowed pink. She went home with nothing but the DVD for company. At this rate, she was going to be single forever.

Sal parked and unlatched the picket gate; the gate was sticking so she gave it a shove. Once inside the flat she was surprised to find a guy who looked vaguely familiar sitting with Kat at their kitchen table drinking coffee. Dark-haired, he had striking blue eyes, a sharpish nose, and a moustache. He was chatting to Kat like they were old friends. Then, she clicked.

Sal rubbed her chin and frowned. "Hello? Aren't you…?"

"Santa?" He laughed, chuckling at his own joke.

Sal rolled her eyes; so the guy thought he was a comedian. Wait?! Was the slimy so-and-so stalking her because he knew where she lived?

"Trent Powell," he offered, nodding at her. "Your local taxi driver."

"What are you doing here? Did you change your mind and come to collect?" Sal asked, searching in her handbag for her card. She tried to keep calm but her heart was starting to race.

"No," he assured her. "Relax, I live in the townhouse next door. My mate, Anton, and I moved in last Saturday. I bought the place and he's flatting with me to help me pay the mortgage."

"What?" Sal asked, puzzled. She didn't like being on the back foot. "Why didn't you tell me?" she demanded.

"You didn't give me a chance. You jumped in the back of my car and barked an order so I thought I better do as I was told."

Sal flushed with embarrassment. "What were you doing outside the hall?"

"I was dropping off some of my mates and was about to look for a carpark when a pretty girl jumped in the back and told me to drive her to the house next to mine." He put down his cup. "You seemed a little upset and a bit tipsy so I drove you home." He shrugged. "It was no skin off my nose. Actually, I was driving Anton's car, mine's the fire service Ute parked in the driveway."

The one hogging the driveway, Sal wanted to say. Instead, she mumbled an embarrassed thanks.

"Tea? Coffee?" Kat got up and put the jug on.

She pulled a face. "I've just had one, remember – the coffee date."

Kat dismissed that as of no consequence. "Oh yeah, but you could have another. Guess what?" Without waiting for Sal to guess, Kat continued, "Our worlds are colliding. Trent, Anton, and Rob, all know each other."

"Really?" Sal eyed Trent with suspicion.

"They are volunteer firefighters but Trent is a paid firefighter as well." Kat explained, clearly impressed.

"Please don't start with the pole jokes," Trent warned. "I've heard them all."

"Coffee, please," Sal said, changing her mind. "Small world," she agreed, taking a seat.

"It is around here," Trent smiled. "Everybody knows everybody."

She wondered if he'd heard the rumours about her disastrous love life, or if he knew Gone Don as well. Trent and Kat chatted about the dance and what a good night it had been. She wished she hadn't had to bail early but she seriously didn't want to have to fend off the sexual psychologist for the rest of the evening.

"So? How did *IT* go?" Kat emphasised it so Sal would know what she was referring to.

Sal played dumb. "How did what go?"

"Your date?" Kat jogged Sal's arm almost spilling her coffee.

Sal still felt nauseous and didn't want to revisit it. "It was a complete mare."

Her usual flippant self, Kat replied, "Oh well, never mind there's plenty more profiles to choose from."

Then Kat felt obliged to fill Trent in. "Sal's a serial dater, you know, she's terribly bad at commitment," Kat informed him. "I'm going to get her new running shoes for Christmas."

Sal glared daggers at Kat willing her to shut up.

"Why don't you tell him about some of the famous people you know. Some of your work stories," Sal hinted. Ignoring her, Kat continued giving Trent an insight into Sal's disastrous love life.

Enjoying the stories, Trent wasn't in any hurry to leave. Sal wished he would. She didn't like the smug look on his face and thought she'd suffered enough humiliation for one day. Her abysmal love life was not something she wanted to discuss with the new neighbour.

He eventually picked up on it. "Think I better get going, I've still got lots of unpacking to do," Trent said, excusing himself. "Thanks for the coffee, Kat." He hesitated, then said, "By the way, if you girls are interested in joining the Fire Service, we are looking for recruits."

"Really? Join the brigade?" Kat's eyes lit up. "We'll think about it, won't we, Sal."

Sal choked on her coffee, and spluttered a goodbye.

Kat saw him to the door. "See ya."

"Laters," he grinned.

As soon as he was gone, Kat pressed herself against the door and said, "Fire Service could be a bit of fun. What do you think?"

"Maybe after Christmas," Sal said fobbing it off as another one of Kat's good ideas that wouldn't last long. Hopefully Kat would soon forget all about it.

Undeterred, Kat replied, "Ok, we'll talk about it in the New Year."

Kat returned to the dining table, reached over and patted Sal's hand. "Never mind, it was just one bad experience, don't give up."

Sal changed the subject. "How well do you know this Trent guy?"

"Why? You interested in him now?" Kat joked. "Don't blame you, he's easy on the eye."

Sal rolled her eyes. But his looks hadn't escaped her. When Trent stood up, she noticed he towered over her and that his uniform fitted his expansive shoulders and tapered nicely down to his belt. The trousers were fitted but she didn't check out his backside. It would be rude to be checking out the new neighbour's bum on their first meeting. She heard a small inner voice say, didn't stop you checking out the photocopier guy though, did it.

Kat was burbling on. "Haven't met him until today. Nice enough guy though, isn't he, giving you a lift home, and all that." Kat collected the cups. "Can't believe that he knows Rob, nice coincidence, hey."

"Nice," Sal begrudgingly admitted.

"My head hurts," Kat grumbled, rubbing her temples. "Bloody hangover but got to pull myself together. I'm meeting Rob soon."

Rob must have been absolutely smitten because Kat's mobile was vibrating with multiple messages.

"Might even start my own box of exs," she ribbed Sal. Unfortunately, Rob was to become a regular visitor.

Chapter 11: Mix Up

As Christmas got nearer, Alice was ramping up the entertainment. Today, the rest home had a petting zoo visit. The animals were dressed in little Christmas outfits. There were bunnies, dogs, cats, and even a baby goat wearing nappies that jumped all over the place, up on the chairs, and cavorted around the lounge. Once all the animals were rounded up, and back in their cages, things settled down. The residents loved it. Everyone was in a good mood after the petting zoo's visit.

That wily little minx, Suzie, sidled up to the front desk.

"Sally," she smiled sweetly, and stroked the counter with her freshly polished fingertips, "I was wondering..." she wheedled in a cutesy voice that meant she wanted something.

Distracted, Sal frowned at her sent emails trying to locate the urgent order she thought she'd sent yesterday. "Yes?"

"Well, my friend Laurie would like to take you out to lunch. He wants to talk to you about house-sitting."

Rats! Why couldn't she find that damn email? She lifted files and moved them from one stack to the other, perhaps the printout was somewhere on her desk.

Undeterred, Suzie continued, "You used to house sit, didn't you?"

"Huh?" Sal glanced up at her. "Oh yeah, lots, before I moved in with Kat."

"Laurie is dying to meet you. I've told him all about you. And, you'd be doing me a huge favour. Don't worry he'll spring for lunch."

"I'm a little busy." Sal could feel herself caving. Why did she find it so hard to say no? Nothing was worse than a blind date. House-sitting. Yeah right! She gave Suzie ten out of ten for originality.

"I told him you would." Suzie hastily added, "Don't hurry,

take your time, I'll mind the front desk for you," she offered.

Sal sighed, resigned to the power of Suzie's persuasion. "Oh, I give up." Sal threw her hands in the air. She would have to rewrite the email and send it again after lunch. Sal reached for her handbag.

"Thanks, Sal, you're a honey," Suzie said, shooing Sal away. "He's waiting for you in the carpark."

Laurie wasn't anything like she had imagined. He wasn't the muscular bronze hunk she had envisaged. He was short, thin, balding, and wore glasses. "You must be the lovely Sally," he beamed hurrying towards her, his arms outstretched.

Sal didn't need the thigh test to tell her Laurie wasn't her type.

They went into The Beach café. After checking out the food cabinet, Sal decided in case the scales were right, and the spare tyre around her tummy was not just bloating, she'd have a salad with a glass of water. Laurie said he wasn't overly hungry, and coffee and a muffin would do him. Laurie paid, and they sat outside enjoying the sunshine and watched as people strolled past on the boardwalk walking their dogs. Sally kept her shades on in an effort to be incognito. He was chatty enough, and reasonable company, but it was like she was on a job interview. He seemed genuinely interested in house-sitting and asked Sally all kinds of questions like how one went about getting jobs, and what house-minding entailed.

"So, you are from Whangarei," she commented when there was a lull in the conversation.

"No," Laurie answered taken aback. "Whangamata."

"Whangamata?" Sal repeated. Strange, she could have sworn Suzie said Whangarei.

"So, how's the landscaping business going?" she asked, finishing her glass of water.

He laughed. "I'm quite fond of pot plants if you get my drift but I'm no gardener."

"Oh, right," Sal gave an awkward laugh. Suzie told her he was a landscaper. Was Suzie losing it? Sal was waiting for him to ask for her number, or if they could meet up again, and had rehearsed in her head what she would say, but the moment didn't come.

She glanced at her watch. "Ah, I must get back we are super busy at work."

He escorted Sal back to the office where he thanked her and kissed her lightly on the cheek. It was on the tip of her tongue to tell him that although he was a nice guy, she wasn't ready for a relationship, but he merely grinned, waved, and then he was gone.

Perplexed, Sal walked through the sliding glass doors into the foyer.

Suzie vacated Sal's chair. "So, how was lunch?"

"Yeah, ok," Sally replied, surprised that she had enjoyed Laurie's company. "He seems really interested in house-sitting."

"Yeah, Laurie and his wife, Jade, are thinking about setting up a professional house-sitting business. Didn't he tell you?"

What? Wait? He's married? "No."

Suzie continued, "Oh yeah, now, about Lance, the dark and handsome landscaper I've been harping on about you meeting. He's coming down from Whangarei this weekend and would like to take you out for dinner. What do you say?"

Lance! Laurie! Laurie wasn't the guy Suzie had been trying to set her up with?! Laurie was a short, pasty white guy from Whangamata who just wanted to pick her brains about house-sitting. "Um, ah, I don't think long-distance relationships work," muttered Sal. Sal felt sick. Oh God, that could have gone terribly wrong. Laurie was married. How embarrassing! She could have easily said something stupid and Laurie would have thought she had lost her mind.

Suzie misread the look on Sal's face. "You are not still hankering after the photocopier guy, are you?"

Ignoring her, Sal slid behind her desk and checked her to-do list.

"You do look a bit peaky," Suzie said, with a worried frown, touching a hand to Sal's damp forehead. "You, ok?"

Sal swallowed. "Yeah, fine," she replied. Can one die of embarrassment? Well, it could certainly make you feel sick.

That afternoon, lovely Rose passed away. It was a gentle passing. That was Rose, she never wanted to be a bother. She just went to sleep in the lounge watching telly and didn't wake up. The staff mourned the loss of Rose, at eighty-six she had been a long-term favourite with everyone. They were going to miss her. Sal was not the only one who shed a few tears. Sadness covered the rest home like a heavy blanket.

Kat could tell something had happened the moment Sal stepped through the door. Hers was not a poker face.

"You ok, honey?" Kat asked. Dropping everything she went to Sal.

"Rose died today," Sal told her, eyes misting with tears.

Kat's own eyes grew moist and she wrapped her arms around Sal and hugged her tight.

"Oh, babe, I'm sorry." Kat empathised. She knew Sal cared about the oldies. Kat almost felt she knew them as well, as Sal spoke of them so often.

Affected by Rose's death, Sal was quiet. After dinner, Sal suddenly said, "Do you ever worry about what someone might say at your funeral?"

"Nope, not really." Kat shrugged. "Why do you ask? Do you?"

"Yeah, I worry that they might say that Sal was a cheeky little ratbag."

"Oh, they won't say that," Kat reassured her, adding, "They'll say, you had terrible taste in men."

Sal threw a fluffy cushion at Kat, who dodged in time and the cushion hit the wall.

***

Sal had only seen Anton and Trent once since they moved in. Trent introduced her to Anton, yelling across the box hedge that separated their two properties as she was going out and they were coming in, "This is Anton. Anton, meet Sally."

There was a quick exchange of pleasantries but nothing more. Sal had no idea what Anton did for a job, but she knew they were volunteer firefighters, and unfortunately, Kat had not given up on the idea of joining the brigade.

Rose's death prompted Sal that she needed to put things in order. It was time to get her insurance updated – just in case. She made an appointment with Sovereign Assurance at the bank.

She made it on time with a couple of minutes to spare. After announcing her arrival to one of the tellers she patiently sat on the couch and waited for the broker to call her name.

"Sally?" inquired a thin blonde man, in a nice grey suit with a white shirt and blue-striped tie. Very business-like; Sally approved. And he was handsome too with intense blue eyes. Sal smiled, "Yes, that's me."

"Andrew," he beamed, shaking her hand. "Come in, come in." He ushered her into his office. "Take a seat," he insisted, pulling out a chair for her to sit on. Feeling an instant attraction, Sal sat down her eyes fixed on him.

"There are a few questions we have to go through but I promise it's all relatively painless."

Andrew told her if they entered all the details directly into the computer system, it could generate a quote immediately.

"Great," Sal nodded, eager to begin.

"We'll get started then," Andrew smiled and loaded the questionnaire.

"Marital status?" Andrew asked, his mouse hovering over the choices.

"Single."

"Surprising," he commented clicking the appropriate response.

After name and address, came the date of birth.

Sal hesitated.

"It's alright I promise not to disclose to another party outside the company," he said, crossing his heart.

Laughing, she told him her age. "I'm the big three zero."

"You must be kidding I was sure you were in your early

twenties."

Flattered, she smiled.

He became business-like again. "Height?"

"Short."

He laughed. "Can you be a bit more specific?"

"I think I'm 5' 3 but everyone thinks I'm only 5 feet." Why couldn't she be a 6 foot supermodel?

"Weight?"

Ouch. "Heavy." She'd rather cut out her tongue than tell him her current weight, for despite walking, and trying to eat lettuce, she'd gained another couple of pounds.

He gave her a sly knowing grin. "Now it's important we fill in the online form accurately."

Reluctantly, she gave him her weight. She got the feeling he was enjoying watching her squirm.

"You told me this was going to be painless," she complained.

"Relatively, but not entirely," he consoled her.

Why couldn't this insurance broker be a crusty old man that she didn't feel attracted to?

His fingers busily tapping on the keyboard, they bumbled through the computerised questionnaire with Andrew finding out she was blind as a bat without her contacts, deaf as a doorknob in her right ear, hopeless with money, and on a tragically low income. Sal dutifully answered questions on her financial status and her family history. As they proceeded through the questionnaire the questions got increasingly personal.

"Any sexual diseases? HIV? "

"No," Sal replied, her face going pink.

When he finished entering all the information, he pushed the magic button that gave her the premium she'd have to pay.

"Wow, that's great!" she enthused, surprised at how low the premiums were.

"Ah," Andrew scratched his beard, "something's wrong, it should be more than that." He flicked back through tabs and checked the data he'd entered. "Oh," he said, realising his mistake. "I'm afraid we are going to have to do that all over again, I've put you in as a male."

Sal was offended. "Do I look like a bloke?"

"No, quite the contrary, you're very feminine."

Complimented, Sally smiled, her cheeks growing hot. Suddenly indignant at the discrimination, Sally frowned, "How come blokes pay less?"

"Statistically we're healthier because we rarely go to the doctors," Andrew told her, "And we drop dead earlier, because we rarely go to the doctors, so we cost the Insurers less."

"Oh, I guess that's good news then," Sal replied mollified.

"Besides," he shrugged, "It's your fault I stuffed up – you distracted me."

When they reached the bottom of the long questionnaire for the second time Sally sighed with relief, "Man, they should use this questionnaire on online dating sites. It would save a lot of time and trouble."

"Yeah, and for the record, I'm 38, divorced, single, and got a ten-year-old son, and you know what I do for a job. Oh yes, and I have no sexual diseases."

Sally couldn't believe Andrew was blatantly coming on to her. What a way to sell himself.

"Well, I'll put a package together that will cover life, income protection, redundancy, and health and give you a call," he said with an award-winning marketing smile.

He saw her to the door and shook her hand. "Might be after Christmas now since there are not many business days left, but I'll be in touch." His eyes met hers and held them a little longer than necessary.

Sal left the mall feeling flattered, flirted with, and a tad depressed, her insurance premiums were higher than she expected but, on the upside, Andrew was interesting and available. Chase still hadn't called. Perhaps everyone was right. Perhaps she should start looking elsewhere.

Chapter 12: Alone, Like Jones

On Christmas Eve, Sal sat on the couch alone watching a marathon of Bridget Jones movies with 'All by myself' playing loudly in the background. It felt like her theme song. Being loved up, Kat had stopped asking about the box of exs and spent most of her time canoodling with her tattooed buzz cut, architect Rob. Although Kat teased Sal about her commitment phobia, Sal hadn't told her the whole story. She hadn't shared the goodbye letters with Kat that were hidden at the bottom of the box; they were too personal. They were the real reason she was commitment-phobic.

Sal picked up one yellowed piece of paper. On the outside of the tattered paper was written – The Deserter. She held the unfolded letter to her chest, but unable to open it, she put it away again. Sal saw the other two letters there, but she couldn't bear to read them either. She couldn't change the past or hide the scars but she could bury them. She tucked them underneath the lining, just like she buried the hurt in her broken heart.

Sal bit her lip. All she'd ever wanted was to find lasting love, but experience had disappointed her so much that she feared committing again, although she couldn't explain it to anyone. These guys were the reason she kept bailing. She bailed before she got hurt. They were her true heartbreaks. Kat was right, she was crazy. She was damaged, here's hoping she wasn't beyond repair, and one day she'd stop running and find love that lasted just like her mothers had, not just once but twice.

Kat was staying the night at Rob's so she could wake up and have Christmas morning with him. Anton and Trent had invited her over to their flat for late-night Christmas drinks, but she wasn't in the mood for company. She thought Anton was nice, he was a bit of a shy guy who worked in management for an electrical company in the city. She was impressed that Trent was not only a volunteer firefighter but a paid firefighter as well, however she was still miffed at him for deceiving her with that stupid taxi driver stunt. He seemed to get a kick out of making fun of her.

Sal had decided that she would have Christmas lunch with the residents at the home and would join the neighbours for the communal BBQ after that. She stumbled off to bed, feeling woefully sorry for herself. Surely if Bridget Jones could get her man, so could she.

She woke up early Christmas morning to her phone ringing.

"Hello, Mum," she answered groggily. Only her mother would call her at sparrow's fart on Christmas morning.

"Merry Christmas, dear!" Joyce was brimming with excitement. "Have you opened your present yet?"

"Not yet, Mum. Hang on, I'll get it." She fumbled, rolled out of bed, and picked up the small parcel resting on the dresser.

"I've opened mine, thank you, darling," Joyce said gleefully. I've watched the DVD already, and I loved it so much I'm thinking of joining a choir."

"You'll be great." Rustling the paper Sal ripped opened her present. It was a lovely pair of silver hoop earrings. "Thank you, Mum, they are lovely. I'll wear them today."

Sal listened as her Mum told her that Bernard was coming over for Christmas lunch and what else she had planned for the day. She was happy that her Mum was happy but wished she didn't feel so miserable. It sucked being single on Christmas Day. She hung up and padded out to the kitchen. She phoned her brother and sister and wished them Merry Christmas but they had both gone away for Christmas with their families, and the calls went to voicemail. She was the tragic family singleton.

She poured herself a big bowl of rice bubbles and added milk. "Merry Christmas Sal, happy singledom," she said aloud.

Kat had left a present for her on the kitchen table along with a note, saying, *Merry Christmas, chick, see you at 4pm for the neighbourhood BBQ.* Sal opened the present; it was a book called *Moving on and Getting on With Your Life.* Thanks, Kat!

Stuff it, she wasn't going to mope all day. She'd go celebrate with her other family. She needed them as much as they needed her. Sal borrowed Kat's Christmas sack outfit from her wardrobe, and put her much loved Christmas hat on, and drove to work.

Christmas day at the home was lovely, the staff were amazing, everyone was dressed in costume for the occasion. It was difficult to tell who was who – everyone looked so festive.

First, Sal went to the Christmas service held in the rest home chapel. She sang the Christmas carols, joining in harmony with the choir, with Natalie playing the piano. During the service there were some murmured amens and a few hearty outbursts of 'bloody marvellous' after the prayers were said.

Alice wore her angel outfit. Andie, glamorously dressed as a Christmas fairy, waltzed around with tinsel decorating any resident who looked underdone. Howard was typically a grinch and didn't need to wear a costume to prove it. Andie dusted Howard off with his wand and wrapped some tinsel around the old man's neck and shoulders. Blowing air kisses, he waltzed away and grabbed Phyllis twirling her on the spot. Dizzy, Phyllis sat down giggling with delight.

Sal had a present for each of the residents. She minced along the hall behind the trolley laden with gifts, handing out soaps, gingerbread men, and cards. She was delighted by the rest home staff and their generous Christmas spirit, some staff even choosing to come in when they weren't even rostered on. Daisy had outdone herself with the menu: ham, turkey, new potatoes, salads and so many desserts with lashings of cream. Everyone who was allowed to drink had a glass of champagne, while those whose medication wouldn't allow alcohol, had to make do with grape juice or lemonade.

Old cheapskate Alice had organised Santa, who had a strong Australian accent and repeated everything, and everyone was bloody marvellous, and entertainment for the day was anyone who had a talent, or some musical gift, getting up and performing.

Sal smiled wistfully, she may be single, but love was all

around her. This was what Christmas was all about. Spending time with the people you love.

Even Alice was merry, and it wasn't just the bubbles. Then when everyone was full to bursting, and heads drooping with sleep, Sal hugged everyone goodbye, and set off home with a warm fuzzy Christmassy feeling in her belly, proud and happy that she worked in such a loving caring rest home.

Turning sharply into the apartments shared driveway she almost ran Anton over. Wearing a Santa hat, and a Santa BBQ apron over his bare chest and skimpy bike shorts, Anton was cooking sausages on the barbie, a bottle of beer in his hand. Trent was wearing his traditional blue t-shirt and shorts. It appeared every item of clothing he owned was blue.

The boys had set up tables and deck chairs, while the neighbours had gathered and set up their BBQs, sun umbrellas, chilly bins, and beers. The wrinklies and Saffers came, and old Mrs Mac was there with her two dogs, Penny and Bonny. It was a charming festive New Zealand Christmas scene and it warmed Sal's heart. She may be single on Christmas day but life wasn't really so bad. Sal parked the Mini, and went to join in.

"Merry Christmas, chick!" Kat cried, handing Sal a glass of bubbles. Kat looked lovely and fresh in her white summer frock and gold sandals.

"Merry Christmas!" shouted Rob raising his beer.

Trent popped another bottle of champagne. "And here's to a fantastic New Year."

"Best Christmas ever. I can't wait for New Years'," Kat cried. They clinked glasses and drank many toasts. They toasted everything. The Saffers kept muttering that it was nothing like a *braai* and next Christmas they would treat the rest of them to a proper Southern African *braai*. Anton got a little snotty and said, he was happy to pass the apron on next year.

Mrs Mac fell asleep in her deck chair, head nodding to one side, mouth open, dribbling, and snoring lightly. The wrinklies patted their full tummies and said they were off home for a nap. Mrs Saffer complimented the chef telling Anton he did a good job with the sausages but wait until he had tasted *boerewors*, now that was something else. She promised to buy and cook him some as a special treat. In the interest of diplomacy, Mr Saffer took her arm and led her home.

Rob said there was a group of them going camping down at Tarawera for New Year and it was going to be great fun. He suggested that the girls join them.

Mrs Mac woke up. Alarmed, she scolded him, saying she couldn't possibly go, she had the dogs to think of. Then she packed up her deck chair and waddled home, her dicky hips clicking as she walked. Kat and Sal glanced at each other and burst out laughing.

"You keen?" Kat asked Sal, her voice slurry with champagne.

"You girls wouldn't be interested," Trent insisted. "You might break a nail or something."

"I'd miss my squeeze too much. I can't leave you behind can I, babe," Rob nuzzled Kat's neck.

"I don't think Trent likes me," Sal whispered to Kat. "He doesn't seem overly keen on the idea of me tagging along."

"Nonsense, what's not to like," countered Kat.

They sat around in a semi-circle of deck chairs in the shared drive talking long into the night, and by the end of it, both girls had agreed to go camping.

When Sal staggered out of bed on boxing day, she vaguely remembered agreeing to go camping, but not the details.

Kat was ecstatic. "Come on, it will be a blast, I promise."

"Pinkie promise."

"Pinkie promise," Kat smiled beguilingly.

Well, anything had to be better than moping around the house alone on New Year's Eve, didn't it? Could she have been more wrong?

***

The trip to Tawarewa was a long one. Leaving at five in the morning they drove down in convoy stopping for breakfast along the way. Kat and Rob in his car, the guys in theirs, and Rob's friends Ethan and Jayne behind them, while Sal doggedly followed up the rear alone in her little Mini packed to the gunnels with camping gear. They were to meet the Parkers, friends of Rob's, at the camp.

Sal's first impression of Ethan was that he was a hunter-gatherer kind of dude. He was smooth, a capable guy that made you relax and think he must have been a good boy scout. His wife Jayne seemed equally qualified as a camper, being familiar with the camping lifestyle and practical as she had packed everything they could possibly need. They looked like they should be the perfect fit. Unfortunately, their relationship was on the rocks.

When the convoy stopped at McDonalds in Rotorua, Ethan and Jayne had an argument over who was paying for breakfast. They argued throughout breakfast until exasperated, Jayne stood up and said, "You've paid for it – you can have it," and she poured the remainder of her coke over Ethan's head. Stalking out, she got in the car slamming the door behind her. Sal half expected Jayne to drive off but she didn't.

It was super awkward. No one spoke. Everyone wondered what Ethan would do. Without a word he calmly walked outside opened the car boot and got his wash bag and a clean t-shirt then he used the café's toilet to change.

Sal anticipated that Ethan would ask her if he or Jayne could travel the remainder of the way in her car but neither did. Sally thought, seriously, who goes away for a holiday with someone they are breaking up with? That's like guaranteed misery.

Once Ethan was cleaned up, they hit the road again. The others leading the way into the forest and Sal bringing up the rear. The drive down was long, the gravel road through the forest longer still. She was hot, tired, and dusty by the time they arrived but so was everyone else. Rob's friends, the Parkers, Pete and Mindy were already there.

Peter Parker was nothing like Spiderman. He was a businessman wearing label clothes, with short grey hair and a bit paunchy round the middle. Like a good trophy wife, Mindy was a good-looking tanned girl with sparkling blue eyes, long straight blonde hair and a peaches and cream complexion, and she knew how to work it. Her nails were manicured to perfection and she was wearing full makeup on a camping trip! She had a body to be proud of, and had all the guys running around after her. Mindy insisted on having the best campsite and supervised the parking of the campervan and the placement of all the camp tables and chairs without lifting a finger to help. Everyone wanted to strangle her and it was only the first day.

"No one said anything about a long drop." Sally looked accusingly at Kat.

Kat raised a perfectly plucked sardonic eyebrow. "Would her ladyship prefer the bush?"

"Mmmph!" Sal snorted.

Sal dragged her tent from the car and threw it on the grass. A family-sized tent for one, how ridiculous! Bone-shaken, she was in no mood for pitching a tent but unless she wanted to sleep under the stars, she had no choice.

Sally started feeling guilty about her stink attitude. Once her tent was up and supplies safely stored, she went to see if anyone else needed a hand, but she discovered the others were pretty much under control.

Trent had a pop-up tent, Rob and Kat were sharing a two-man tent, and Ethan and Jayne had a small family tent (and needed a much larger one so they could have their own corners), while Peter and Mindy's campervan was like a three-room palace. Everyone was organised – everyone except Anton.

No one offered to help him put up his tent because no one knew how, or where to begin. Sally was challenged by jigsaw puzzles at the best of times and Anton's tent was a scientific architectural challenge that would probably test Stephen Hawkings' capabilities. It was silver and like a tubular Rubik cube mixed with a game of pickup sticks.

Fascinated, Sal sat on the grass enjoying a cool drink while Anton tried to erect his tent. He spent ages pegging it out while the rest of the campsite drank beer and offered advice. Anton crawled about sticking one pole into another, the igloo ensemble transformed many times before it finally resembled something he could doss down in for the night. Trent finally offered to help.

"We'll crack out the cards when the entertainment is over."

Rob laughed, amused as he watched his mates wrestle with the tent.

"You are the architect, why don't you help?" Sal asked Rob.

"What and miss out on all the fun?" he replied.

Anton grinned broadly when the last pole was finally in place. Trent stood up, dusted himself off, put the mallet down, and reached for a can of beer. There was a loud snap, crackle, and pop as the tent twitched and creaked before ripping itself out of the ground like a giant bouncing plastic pretzel.

Rob shook with laughter. "Cards might have to wait till tomorrow night, mate." Sally felt sorry for Anton, but she was starving, and food was beckoning so she wandered off with the group to the communal BBQ table where pre-dinner nibbles and drinks were waiting. Finally, at dusk, looking exhausted, Anton arrived, a can of beer in his hand.

"New, got it for Christmas," he said by way of explanation. He suffered more good-natured ribbing but took it on the chin. When Mindy wasn't telling her husband what to do, she was telling everyone else what to do. At first, Sal thought Pete was quiet, but it turned out he was as opinionated as she was, he just needed her to be quiet long enough for him to get a word in edgeways. The Parkers had the best of everything, the very latest and greatest thing in camping gear, and they kept going on about how you really should get one of these, they're the absolute best. It wasn't only the Parkers and the mosquitoes irritating her – Kat had deserted her. She and Rob were inseparable, all over each other like bad rashes. Ethan and Jayne fought through putting up their tent, and then fought through dinner, and now weren't speaking to each other. Yep, should be a tip-top holiday. Should've stayed at home, she thought.

Chapter 13: The Interrogation

Sally's internal alarm clock hadn't gone on holiday and she woke up at daybreak. "Where's the showers?" she asked.

"Didn't you bring a solar shower?" Mindy asked, looking at her like she had three heads. Mindy didn't offer her the use of their campervan shower.

"No one told me I needed to." Sal glowered at Kat wondering if Kat could see the steam coming out of her ears.

"There's the river," Rob said, pointing her in the right direction. "Did you remember to bring a towel?"

Stuff the lot of them, Sal thought angrily as she grabbed her towel and searched for a discreet spot on the river to bathe. She kept her togs on in case she should be seen by anyone on the prowl. Dipping one toe in the water, she discovered what she had already guessed, the water was bone-chillingly, spine-tinglingly cold. Her river bath was super quick, a real quick dip.

Now what? The whole day loomed ahead with nothing to do but enjoy the serenity. Five minutes later serenity was *boring.* Kat and Rob's gooey eyes and constant cuddling made her want to throw-up, and the others were driving her mad as they seemed interested in doing nothing but lounging around reading the latest bestselling action-packed novel. It must be good as everyone had their noses stuck in it and only surfaced to fish and eat. Sal decided it was time to find some new friends, or at least to find someone whose nose wasn't stuck in a book. The only book Sally had taken on holiday was the one Kat had given her for Christmas, written by some stupid clinical psychologist about *Moving on and Getting on With Your Life*. She didn't want another cheater, heartbreaker, or stalker in her life and would do anything to avoid it, so she better read it. She opened it – Chapter One was entitled, The Death of a Relationship. Cheery start.

"I'm going for a walk. Do you want to join me?" Anton asked.

Anton was always up-to-date on the latest theories on health and now that he'd come out of his shell, he was happy to share them with her.

"Sure," Sally shrugged. Well, anything was better than struggling to read that awful book. Sally's idea of a scenic walk was a nice meander through the bush at a leisurely pace. Anton, on the other hand, was part mountain goat. Into cycling, and taking care of his body, he walked briskly, taking long-legged strides. He never once tripped over a tree root, or faltered, but moved through the bush at an incredible speed and it was everything Sally could do to keep pace with him. Stubborn to the bone she was never going to admit she was tired or ask him to slow down.

The sky was hidden by the treetops. It had to have been thirty degrees in the shade. The track snaked around the river; parts of it were easy-going, parts of it dry and dusty, and other areas covered in lush ferns which they had to duck under, and tree roots to step over. They walked for hours. Anton was a bit of a theorist and gave her a taste of some of his ideology while they walked. Sally slipped under a tangled supplejack vine which whacked her on the back. Her legs were feeling mutinous. He held a fern frond back as she ducked beneath.

"Done a bit of hiking then, have you?" she puffed.

"Hunting, actually," he answered as he stepped over a fallen branch.

"Hunting?"

"Yeah, I used to," Anton told her a couple of hunting stories as they progressed along the track. He finished with, "Now I mostly take photos, but you can't beat a good venison steak and they make great salami."

He didn't look like a Bambi killer.

"Talking about hunting, Trent's told me about your box of *exs*," he began. "What's the story? No-one good enough, or what?"

"Did he?" she broke off with a snort. How dare Trent discuss her love life! What did it have to do with him?

"I get it – the dating world can be a scary place, it's full of nutters."

Like you.

"But you shouldn't keep focusing on the past. You need to think about the future, after all you are not getting any younger and the old egg clock will be ticking."

What the hell?! I'm not getting any younger, fumed Sal. What did he think he was? God's gift to women and available to keep the human race populated? He wasn't that young! His tadpoles were probably past their use-by date anyway.

He stopped suddenly and put a finger to his lips. "Shhh!"

"What? What is it?"

Using hand signals, he beckoned her to hunker down and keep quiet. A large fern twitched. Frightened it might be a wild pig, Sally hid behind him.

"A wallaby," he whispered hoarsely.

Sal snorted. "Yeah, yeah, fair dinkum. Pull the other one, mate, we live in New Zealand, not Australia."

"No honestly, there are wallabies in this bush." He remained very still his eyes riveted to the spot.

"Oh, whatever!" Sally shook her head.

But whatever it was – it was gone.

She'd gone quiet and if he knew her, he'd know that she was sulking, but she was determined not to let it show. She wasn't happy about everyone giving her a hard time about her love life, or her age. Where did they get off? Apart from Kat and Rob, everyone else's relationships didn't look good, and the rest of them were single and her age.

When they reached the clearing they came across a rock pool, it was picture-postcard magical.

"Oh, it's lovely," Sally breathed softly with awed reverence.

Anton agreed and started to peel off his t-shirt. "I'm going in." Sal sat on the rocks, baking in the hot sun with her feet in the water watching as Anton enjoyed swimming around as playful as a seal in the cool water. Kids leapt from a large rock into the gorgeous turquoise water, tremendous whoops and hollers filled the air as they laughed, teased, and splashed their friends. She was that peeved, she would have walked back alone if she was sure of the way, but because she didn't want to get lost, she waited for him.

He came out of the water and dried out sunbathing on some large flat stones. When he was dry, he put his shirt back on. Finally, he was ready. He walked ahead leading the way. Sal didn't speak a word. She was eager to get back to the camp and away from him. What made him think he was qualified and could dish out advice? She hoped the giant igloo thing broke apart during the night and trapped him like a Venus flytrap, it would serve him right for being so rude.

They made it back to the campsite to find the others had already cracked open the beers and were having pre-dinner drinks. Their fellow campers greeted them with knowing smiles as if they'd been up to no good. Good grief, did everyone think she'd attack anything in trousers?

Sally's legs were killing her. She wanted nothing more than to collapse onto her air bed and sleep. Instead, she fell into a waiting deck chair and raised her glass for filling, figuring her legs were already unsteady so a couple of wines couldn't possibly make them any worse; in fact, it was probably medicinal. She was mad at everyone. They all made her feel like a serial dater and a complete failure and now, she was worried about the state of her eggs. Bugger the lot of them, she was fine on her own. She didn't need anyone – not even Chase. Well, maybe Chase, but definitely not anyone else.

"Sorry chick," Kat apologised, pulling up a camp chair. "I know you are not having any fun, but please stop sulking."

"I'm not the one spending all day in a tent," she pointed out.

"Jealously is not an attractive quality either, Sally Gelee," Kat reminded her.

***

The campground was still sleeping soundly when Sally

unzipped the fly of her family-sized tent. She made herself a coffee and munched on some brekkie, and sat in the deck chair staring across the campground, thinking. Much to her annoyance Anton's geometric igloo thingy had survived the night and was still standing. She had willed it to snap apart while he was asleep and change into a giant robot that would stalk the land. She was surprised that anyone had managed to sleep last night. Anton's snores could be heard as far away as the upper campground. If anyone had managed to get a whole night's shut-eye they must have been in an alcoholic coma.

The whole day loomed with nothing to do! She was bored witless. Picking up *Moving on and Getting on with Your Life*, Sally meandered down to the lake's edge. Finding a large log down by the water's edge, she sat down, opened the book, and read the heading again. Chapter One – The Death of a Relationship. Sigh. She flicked through the other chapter headings, How to spot a Narcissist, Classic Gaslighting Behaviours. She knew what they looked like, she knew how to avoid them, what she really needed was a book on how to combat commitment phobia.

Sandflies nipped at her ankles, she took off her jandal and slapped at one, splattering blood. She itched the irritated spot.

"Hi," a deep male voice resonated from behind her.

She turned to see a lofty, tanned, athletic man with a buzz-cut hairstyle astride a mountain bike wearing nothing but a scanty pair of shorts, and a dazzling white smile. He was showing off the most impressive six-pack she had ever seen. His washboard stomach was incredible. Sally swallowed. She hadn't had sex in so long even the vegetables were starting to look good, and here he was with the body of a Greek god, oozing sex appeal. She almost dribbled when she looked at him. Then, she noticed the kids on their bikes. There must have been eight of them. All boys around eight- to ten-year-olds.

"Early riser too, huh?" she grinned.

"Yeah," he chuckled. "That's why I got the job of looking after the kids so their parents can have a lie-in."

"Not all yours then?"

"Nah, none of them are. I'm their uncle."

Thank goodness they weren't all his!

"You here by yourself?" he asked wheeling closer. Sally studied his tanned toned muscular thighs, then her eyes travelled upwards to his handsome chiselled face.

"No, I'm here with friends," she explained. "But they are dead boring. If they aren't fishing or sleeping, they're reading. They're all reading the same action-packed thriller, and can't seem to put it down. I didn't come on holiday to read."

He cocked an eyebrow. "Yet you are – reading."

"Oh yeah," she thrust the book behind her back.

"The book you're reading looks pretty heavy duty," he commented.

Rats, he must have already seen the title.

Oh yeah, duh. "I'm studying. Psychology," she lied.

"Gus," he said. He had cute dimples.

"Sally," she said, feeling stupid.

"Very pleased to meet you, Sally." His eyes flickered with interest.

It was early in the morning but the temperature just went up a few degrees! This was as good a distraction from Chase as she could hope to get. Had her Christmas wish been granted?

"Sally," he smiled invitingly. "Why don't you come up to our campsite and meet Sarah, she's the only girl with us at present and I'm sure she'd love some female company."

Rats! Sarah was probably his girlfriend. "Why not," Sal replied lifting her shoulder in a nonchalant shrug. "It's nice to meet other early risers. Is it far? Do I need a bike to get there?"

"Nah," he laughed. "We are just at the top of the rise, mustard brown and red tent. Look for my bike. I'll see you up there." He seemed fairly confident that she would follow.

Why not? She needed some new friends, and as Kat and Rob had so kindly pointed out, she needed to get out more. Sally went back to her tent and ditched the book. After quickly applying a thick layer of cherry lip-gloss she went in search of Gus. When she came over the brow of the hill, she saw him sitting on the grass talking to a woman she presumed to be Sarah.

Grinning widely, Gus stood up and greeted her. "Sarah, this is Sally." He turned to Sarah, "See, I told you I'd find you some girly company."

Rats, Sarah was his girlfriend. Darn!

"How thoughtful of you," Sarah said drolly as if she expected as much.

Gus grinned. "And she's sexy too, huh."

Mm, not something you'd say to a girlfriend – or a wife.

Sarah agreed, nodding her approval.

Sally blushed. "Hi, Sarah."

"Pull up a blade of grass," Sarah said, patting the spot beside her. "My man's out fishing, but you'll get to meet him later."

Gus was available! This could be a good camping trip after all.

Dark-haired, tanned, and with a face full of freckles, Sarah was lovely. Laid back, she was the kind of person that made you comfortable in her presence. Mother of two of the eight kids, hers were twins, the others were cousins and friends. Sarah explained that although their family originally came from the Deep South they now lived in Tauranga.

"Really?! I come from the Deep South," Sal said, rapt to discover a fellow Southerner. "Where are you from?"

"A little tinpot town called Hokonui. You probably haven't heard of it," Sarah said with a forgiving smile.

Sally stared at Sarah in wide-eyed disbelief. "Really? I have an aunt who lives there."

Sarah's eyes widened. "What's your aunt's name?"

"Vera Henderson."

"No way!" Sarah cried, shocked. "She's my aunt too. Good Lord, we are related!" Delighted, Sarah hugged her. "Hello cuz!" She let go. "My sister, Wendy is arriving at four. You can meet her, and then we'll have a drink to celebrate being long-lost cousins," promised Sarah.

After a crash course on the family tree, Sally decided she liked her new cousin. Sarah was chatty, energetic, and funny, and then when Wendy turned up with her brood, Sally liked her even more. Two years younger than Sarah, Wendy's hair was bleached blonde, she was curvier and taller. She had a face full of sun kisses and a good sense of humour. These guys were looking more interesting than the friends she came with. And Gus was way more interesting – what a hot body!

Gus suggested they all take a walk to the rock pool. Still sore from yesterday's excursion, Sally stiffened, but the thought of spending a bit more time perving at that fantastic six-pack and checking out those small tight buns in his skimpy shorts was appealing, so she agreed.

Everyone came to the rock pool. There was Gus, Sarah, Wendy, and their respective husbands, Hamish and Josh, and all the kids. Gnarly tree roots sprouted from the uneven ground. Sally tripped a couple of times. Her heart skipped a beat when Gus put out his arm to save her and his hand lingered a little longer than necessary. His biceps were as hard as steel. Sally hadn't thought about Chase all day. Kat was right. This was proving to be a great holiday.

Gus said he was into all kinds of sports, but triathlons were his passion, and he told her he'd just won an Ironman challenge. She believed it. He was a 100 percent athlete. And, although he didn't have any children of his own, he seemed to be everyone's favourite uncle.

"The twins can be a bit of a handful," he told Sal. "So, I help Sarah and Hamish out now and then. Gives them a bit of a break, hey," he said cheerfully.

When they reached the rock pool, the kids whooped and hollered and dove in, they climbed up the rock ledges and dive bombed into the emerald-green water below making tremendous splashes.

"Want to go for a swim?" Gus asked slipping off his runners.

It seemed like a rhetorical question. How opportune, she had her bikini on under her clothes. "Yeah sure."

The water was cold but after the long walk, a swim was wonderfully refreshing as she gingerly lowered herself into its icy cool, green depths. Gus dove straight in, showing off with the kids. His perfect bronzed physique glistened in the sun. She had visions of him wrestling alligators with his bare hands and tearing them apart like Tarzan. Down girl, get a grip!

On the return journey to base camp, Sarah and the others went ahead, while they lagged behind. He seemed in no apparent hurry and walked alongside her, chatting. It thrilled her that he would deliberately slow down his ironman stride just to walk with her.

"You should have left your clothes off," he said, bemused.

"I didn't want people to think I was walking around in my undies," she explained, tugging the bum of her shorts away from her bottom. He was right of course, she should have left them off, but with no towel to dry herself, or to hide behind so she could whip her bikini bottoms off and go commando, she had pulled her pants back on and trudging along behind him with a big wet patch on her bum, which looked like she'd wet her pants. Hardly a sexy look, but it was too late, not much she could do about it now.

They parted company when they reached the lake with Gus promising to take her water-skiing tomorrow. Water-skiing! Now there was a challenge. She could barely stand on her own two feet on land let alone on skis. She reminded herself that she'd promised herself this was a year for saying yes to everything. And with such a good-looking incentive dangling in front of her eyeballs, why wouldn't she?

Nestled under the trees, cap resting low over his eyes, Trent was lounging in a deck chair, the squeezed tube of sunblock was lying beside him. His legs stuck out at right angles; the book propped open on his lap. He was wearing his regular blue t-shirt and shorts. God, he was predictably boring!

Sally faked a yawn. "Still reading?"

He pushed his cap back. "Almost finished." He held it up so she could see how far he'd read. "How are you getting along with your book?"

She hadn't got past Page One. "I've got better things to do at the moment," she replied tartly.

"So, I see," Trent commented, his eyes drifting to the retreating figure of Gus. There was an unnatural pause. "He must work out heaps."

"I reckon." Sally fanned her face. "Wouldn't Gus look awesome on the Firefighters calendar. He's so hot!"

Trent snorted. "So are you."

Sal raised her eyebrows. "Was that a compliment?"

"You're sunburnt," he clarified, turning the page. "You should have put sunblock on, it's a bit late now but you can help yourself to mine." He kicked the tube of sunblock towards her.

Kat arrived. Lifting her sunglasses, she blinked at Sal. "Was the Ironman just here?"

Trent rolled his eyes. "Yeah, bet you're sorry you missed him," he replied.

"Aww, stink," Kat said disappointed. "I hear he's got an incredible physique."

"Who told you that?" Sal asked.

"Trent."

What? Was Trent gay? Was he checking Gus out? He was her eye candy and they needed to back off.

Sal nodded. "Hot enough to melt the eyes."

Kat grinned, "I bet that's a good distraction from what's-his - face."

"Who?" Trent piped up. "Which one of the many *exs*?"

Sal scowled at him. "Oh, shut up and go back to your book."

Shaking his head, Trent picked up his book and turned the page.

Sal was utterly exhausted; she had never walked so much in her life. In desperate need of a lie-down, she crawled into her tent and was asleep in minutes.

"Where have you been hiding?" Ethan asked when Sally finally joined the others at the dinner table.

"I've been hanging out with people who aren't spending their entire holidays snogging, fighting, or reading," Sally retorted.

"It's a great book,'" Ethan said. "Looks better than the rubbish you are reading."

"I'll have you know that book was a present from a friend."

"Do they hate you?" Ethan asked.

Finger to her lips, and mouthing, shush, Sal jerked her head in Kat's direction. Too late, Kat had heard.

"Careful, or I will buy you a present," she warned Ethan.

Mindy wasn't happy that there wasn't any internet but was consoling herself by reading the latest gossip magazines, sunbathing and drinking cocktails.

"Right now, I've got more exciting things to do than reading," Sal proudly told them. "I'm going water-skiing tomorrow."

"Cool," Ethan said clearly impressed. "Who with?"

"The Greek god," Kat answered for her.

Sal nodded, pleased that Kat thought Gus was a bit of alright.

The guys had managed to put their bestselling novel down long enough to take the dingy out and had caught a couple of fish for tea. They were super proud of their catch.

Mindy balked when she was offered fresh fish burgers for dinner. "I'm allergic," she told them.

The little princess was adamant if she ate fish she'd swell up like a giant balloon and be covered in large red welts. Sally thought it would be interesting to watch but resisted the temptation to sneak a little bit of fish onto Mindy's plate. Mindy piled high her plate with salad but kept going on and on about a diet lacking in protein was bad for you until finally, Pete cooked a steak to shut her up.

Jayne and Ethan were giving each other the silent treatment. Rob and Kat were making everyone sick with their over-the-top affection. Pete was doing whatever Mindy told him. Anton had gone for a bike ride while Trent still had his nose buried in his book. He was so utterly boring he could put one into a coma.

Jayne decided to turn in early but the rest of them stayed up playing cards. "Come on, Sally, join us," Ethan implored.

"Nah, I'll give it a miss," she told him, when it came to games, she was super competitive. Not wishing to damage her 'nice girl image' she flatly refused.

"Come on, Sal, let's see what you are made of," Trent

cajoled. Man, he knew how to push all her buttons.

"She's mean when she wins, and even worse when she loses," Kat said, putting her two cents in.

Sal still refused to play and just watched the first couple of games. When Trent had to duck off to the toilet while a hand was being dealt. Ethan loaded Trent's hand with all the best playing cards. Trent couldn't believe his luck when he returned, saying, "You won't believe the hand I've got."

They all knew the hand he had. Sal managed to keep a straight face as Trent played the best cards one by one, and still lost. Trent scowled at them and accused them of cheating.

"What shall we play next?" Anton asked, shuffling the deck.

Ethan suggested, "We could alphabetize Sal's exs for fun." He winked. "Looks like she's planning on adding another to the box."

Kat laughed. "Pretty sure, there's a couple of Gs in there already."

Sal's lip curled. They were all jerks.

A torch flickered in the darkness, the light growing stronger as Gus appeared out of the gloom.

He was wearing stone wash worn jeans and a mustard hoodie. The other girls stared, transfixed.

"Anyone fancy a walk?" Gus asked.

Trent snorted, "No thanks mate, we're playing cards."

"Some of us are playing quite badly," Anton said, nudging Trent.

Sal heard herself say, "Don't mind if I do." Her legs protested as she stood.

"Have fun, kids." Kat shooed them away. Sal knew they'd be talking behind her back the moment they left. Well let them talk. This guy was hot and there was no denying it.

With all the walking she'd been doing Sal was convinced she'd be able to enter triathlons soon. They walked down to the bridge. Gus shone his torch on the water where little black water crayfish called koura wriggled and dug into the sand trying to hide from the light.

"Come on," Gus said, pushing back a large fern frond and leading the way into the bush.

They moved through the bush as softly as shadows. Sal held her breath when twigs snapped underfoot. She started to feel uneasy. Could she trust him? Too late, she couldn't back out now.

They hadn't gone far when he stopped dead. "Shh!" Gus whispered, touching a finger to his lips and crouching down.

Sal's heart thumped. She remained frozen to the spot thinking she was going to be pounced on by a rabid possum, or a wild pig.

"There!" Gus breathed, pointing.

Sal couldn't believe her eyes. It was a wallaby! Anton was telling the truth!

"Wow!" she said in disbelief.

The wallaby hopped away disappearing into the scrub.

Standing, Gus brushed the dirt from his jeans. "They may look harmless and cute but they are destroying the native bush, they are pests like rabbits."

"You want to head back, unless of course, you would like to," he paused, "stay a little longer?" he said suggestively.

She glanced around. What if he was a weirdo? "Ah, no, let's head back."

It didn't take long to make it back to camp. When they strolled past Anton's tent, they heard him snoring like a souped-up leaf blower. Noises were coming from Kat and Rob's tent making Sal want to stuff her ears with cottonwool. They must be at it again! They'd puncture their air bed if they weren't careful. Pete and Mindy had gone to bed. Ethan and Jayne were sitting at opposite ends of the table, not speaking to each other. Trent was still up, sitting in his camp chair nursing a bottle of beer. He looked up as they approached.

Gus said goodnight, giving her a quick peck on the cheek, then he disappeared into the gloom, the torch bobbing and weaving as he went back to his campsite.

"Nice moon." She sat down in the chair beside Trent. "You star gazing?" she asked.

"Yeah, it's a beautiful night and I'm feeling a little philosophical," he replied turning to face her. "It might be the beer talking but I've been wondering about why you have a box of exs? I mean that's not normal, is it?"

"That's personal," Sal said, miffed that he'd brought it up yet again.

He shrugged. "Just curious. I mean you seem kind of normal, a little quirky, a bit ditzy at times, but relatively normal, but everyone tells me you're a commitment-phobe whose main talent is running."

"Gee, thanks for the compliment. Nice to know I'm good at something," she snapped.

"What's with keeping their photos," he asked. "That's a bit sick, isn't it?"

How rude! "It's to remind me what I don't want," snapped Sal. I don't want to be with another arse like you!

He raised his eyebrows. "You haven't been out with every letter of the alphabet, surely?"

"No, I don't believe I have." Her voice was icy cold. She wasn't going to stay another minute. He'd only tell her what was wrong with her and why she couldn't maintain a relationship longer than a couple of minutes. She went to get up but her legs had seized.

Trent hadn't finished. "I couldn't help seeing the title of the book you're reading. Moving on, seems to be the one thing you are good at, don't you think?"

"You know what? When I met you, I was prepared to give you the benefit of the doubt but now I know you are a total arse! Good night!" Sal pushed herself out of her chair and marched off, arms swinging.

Alone in her family-sized tent, she changed into her summer PJs and flopped on her bed. The air bed had developed a slow leak and she hoped it would stay up all night. Sal shut her tired eyes but she was too angry to sleep. She had been hoping that the box of exs wasn't going to haunt her while on holiday but everyone kept throwing her serial dating in her face. She was over people giving her heaps about her past. It was nothing to do with them. She was a runner because she'd been hurt – it was that simple.

The truth was she had only ever been in love twice, and both times she'd been badly hurt. Crushed really. She fell for David because of his wicked good looks and witty charm. And why did she loathe him? Because he was a lying, cheating, betraying bastard. She had loved Ken but he was too broken, too damaged by life and she couldn't fix him. And she thought she loved Gone Don because he pretended to be everything she had ever wanted, but that was just an illusion, and when they split up, she never cried – not once. She realised then she didn't love him at all, she only thought she did. These men were the reason she couldn't trust anyone. She'd been so disappointed, she doubted she would ever trust her heart to love again. She would have to read more of *Moving on and Getting on With Your Life*, clearly, she wasn't over it, and she was still holding onto the past.

Still, tomorrow was looking promising, water-ski-ing with the gorgeous Gus as her instructor. Things were looking up!

Chapter 14: Marathon

Sal decided against wearing a bikini, with her luck she'd probably lose the bottoms. Wearing a hot new pink swimsuit, she put her sunnies on and slung a beach towel over her shoulder.

Wearing his traditional blue t-shirt and shorts, Trent was entrenched in his comfy outdoor chair. She hoped to get past him without having to speak.

He glanced up as Sally passed. "Where are you off to?"

"Water-skiing," she said, unable to hide the excited squeak in her voice.

"Another one down, and another one down, another one for the box," he sang taunting her.

"Oh, shut up!" she growled and stalked off, head held high.

He went back to his reading. She flipped him the bird when she thought he wasn't looking. How dare he! He didn't sound anything like Freddie Mercury either. He might be good-looking but he was an absolute tosser.

Water-skiing was way harder than it looked. Gus was patient and explained the best way to position herself, how to hold the bar and how to keep the skis apart. He started the boat slowly, and she rose but then face-planted – again and again. Coughing and spluttering with her lungs full of water, she waited for him to come back and throw the rope to her one more time. Sally's cousins hollered encouragement from the shore while they downed beer after beer. She didn't manage to succeed in getting up and by the end of the afternoon, she felt as if her arms had been ripped clean out of their sockets. Sal was convinced she looked like a cartoon character with excessively long spaghetti arms.

Exhausted, Sally trudged wearily back to her tent wanting nothing more than to collapse and die. The sunblock she had hurriedly slapped on earlier had worn off and even without the benefit of a full-length mirror she knew she was the same colour as her hot pink togs. The heat in the tent was unbearable. Too knackered to take off her togs she crashed out on the half-deflated air bed and quickly fell asleep.

Someone was calling her name. Startled, she woke up on her tummy, dribble running from the corner of her mouth.

"Huh?" Sally said, wiping the dribble away from her chin.

Trent poked his head inside. "Would you like a cuppa? I'm boiling the billy."

"Go away I'm not talking to you," Sal groaned.

"I'm apologising for being an arse. Now, would you like a cuppa?" he repeated.

It was decent of him to offer. Still, he needed to redeem himself. "Yes, please. Tea please – white and one."

Sal heard the chilli-bin lid open and close. Attempting to get up she rolled off the airbed and tried to push herself up, but her arms were numb.

She lay groaning on the floor.

Trent brought the cup to her. Shocked at the sight of her lying like a giant sunburnt slug on the plastic floor, he put her cup of tea on top of her book. Crouching beside her, he asked "You ok?"

Sal whimpered. "No, I'm never going water-skiing again!"

"Here, give me your hand." Trent helped her sit up. She winced as he touched her burned shoulders. She was burnt to a crisp, felt as if she had been tortured on the rack, her legs were like jelly and every muscle in her sunburned body, ached. Ironic – that her name was Sally Gelee and her legs were as wobbly as jelly.

"What time is it?" Sal asked, confused.

"Six,' he told her. "I got worried, thought you might be in a coma and thought I better come check on you."

"I wish I was dead," she groaned.

He tutted. "I've got some aloe vera you can put on that sunburn."

"Thanks," she muttered, feeling like a naughty child. She

stared at the cup of tea, willing it to come to her by magic.

"Here's the aloe vera." He popped the tube down beside her. She must have looked pathetic because he thought better of it, and kneeling down applied a good squirt of the soothing gel to her back, gently massaging it in, then he handed her the tube. Startled by his gentle touch, she couldn't speak.

"You'll be able to reach the rest of it. It won't be long till grubs up," Trent told her and disappeared again, closing the tent flap behind him. She used a good dollop of aloe vera gel and smothered the rest of her sunburn. That was nice of him, she thought, puzzled. But then again, he was a first responder and probably thought it his duty to care for the injured.

Still feeling waterlogged, Sal managed to slowly swallow sips of tea, until she had drunk enough. Somehow, she made it to the camp BBQ table alive. She put her forehead on the BBQ table, and let out a low moan. Every bit of her body hurt.

Shirtless, displaying his tatts, and an ear-to-ear grin, Rob slapped her on her sunburnt shoulder. "You alright, love?"

Sal flinched. "Ouch, careful," she said through gritted teeth. She might be slathered head to toe with aloe vera but it wasn't by any means a miracle cure.

Unperturbed, Rob continued, "Where have you been hiding?"

That's rich coming from you, you rabbit. "I've been hanging with more interesting people, and it's killing me."

"SOOO?" he asked, one eyebrow raised in anticipation as if he was waiting for the goss.

Knowing what he was hinting at, Sal played dumb. "So what?"

"I hear you got another bloke keen on you."

Sal didn't reply. It wasn't any of his business. Why didn't she just tell him to keep his nose out of it?

"Something to drink?" interrupted Trent, handing Rob a can.

"Thanks mate." Rob patted his tanned belly. "I'm seriously hungry mate. What's there to eat?"

Trent shrugged. "Anton's king of the BBQ, ask him."

"Feel free to help yourself to whatever is in my chilli-bin," Sal told him. "Just don't ask me to get it for you."

Rob rummaged around in Sal's chilli-bin and found buns, burgers, and salad greens. "This will do for now."

"Please make something for me too, I can barely move," Sal called.

Rob grinned and replied, "That good a day, was it?"

"No problem," Anton said striding to the barbie like a man on a mission. "By the look of you, Sal, you need a ripper-sized burger."

"I don't think I've got the energy to eat," she said pathetically.

Kat landed in the deck chair next to her, hair awry, and her top on inside out. "So, how's the Greek god?" Kat asked Sal, giving her a playful nudge.

"Great. Gus is great. I'm wrecked."

Kat sniggered. "Go, girl."

"It's not what you think," she told Kat. She must stop giving them ammunition to tease her with.

"Sure, it's not," grinned Kat.

Sal didn't have the energy to argue. Anton was dishing up the burgers.

"Here," Trent said handing Sal a burger. "Anton said there's plenty more so tuck in."

"Thanks, Anton, thanks, Trent." Sal gratefully took a bite. "Mm that's good."

"Sal doesn't look like she'll last the night," Rob said. "Reckon you'll be hitting the hay early."

Yeah, not only do my arms not work but I am covered in mosquito bites the size of small planets. I haven't had a hot shower in days. I am constipated because the long drop terrifies me. I'm sunburnt to blazes and every muscle in my body is cramping. I'm grumpy as hell because everyone is giving me heaps about being a serial dater. And to top it all off, I'm eating my dinner off a plastic plate, and we are running low on wine. Bring on tomorrow.

Sal endured a challenging night of very little sleep due to Anton's ear-splitting snores which reverberated like a freight train in her head. She would have to either move her tent further away or drown him. After a bit of tricky wrangling trying not to hurt her sunburned body she managed to dress. She was grateful Trent had left her the aloe vera cooling gel, and this time smothered herself head to foot in sunblock.

Anton was cooking breakfast. "Sleep well?" he asked cheerfully.

Sal shook her head. She was going to have to drown him. Trent was waving his mobile in the air trying to get signal.

"You need to stand outside the long drop, and lean to the left, about ten degrees, then you'll get coverage." She told him.

"Oh, yeah, thanks. I forgot." Trent walked up the rise towards the outdoor loo and met Gus coming from the opposite direction. They acknowledged each other with a cursory nod.

Wearing nothing but his skimpy shorts, a cap, and his trainers, Gus called out, "Hey, gorgeous," to Sally.

"Hey," she smiled back, her heart racing.

"What are you up to?" he asked, a slow grin spreading across his handsome chiselled face.

Dying, she thought. Every muscle in my body is in agony and my arms are as long as an orangutans. "Nothing."

"Want to come for a walk?"

"Sure," she answered. Her body protested – what the hell? Her mind argued back. Put one foot in front of the other and you'll be fine, you can numb the pain with wine later. It was not easy for her to keep up with Gus's long-legged strides, but he noticed she was struggling and slowed his pace.

Tiredness made her clumsy and she managed to find more tree roots to trip over today than she had yesterday. She stumbled.

Gus caught her by the hand and pulled her to him. "You, ok?" he asked.

"Um, yeah, a little dizzy, low blood pressure," she lied.

"I like dizzy blondes – like you," he added, his eyes meeting hers in a head-on collision. She blushed. He held her for a few moments longer before letting go.

They continued walking. "Sarah likes you too. I can't believe you are cousins." Gus shook his head. "You girls are nothing alike."

"Yeah, it's crazy, hey," Sal agreed, weaving her way between ferns. "Hokonui is such a small place, most people haven't heard of it."

"Oh, I've heard about those small places, I hear everyone's related." He teased, crossing his eyes.

Having heard that lame joke many times before Sal didn't rise to the bait.

They came to a broader place in the track where they could walk side-by-side. When they reached the waterfall, Gus suggested they take a few minutes to enjoy the scenery.

Glad for a break, Sal sat down on the nearest rock and Gus sat beside her. She moved over a bit to give him room, but he shuffled closer.

"It's lovely," Sal said taking in the majesty of the waterfall.

"Truly beautiful," Gus said, looking at her.

Self-conscious, Sal picked up a fallen leaf and dipped it in the water. "You are pretty good at water-skiing."

"We were brought up on the water." He chuckled. "I learned to do a lot of things young." The innuendo was unmistakable. He was radiating heat. Maybe Kat was right. She did like to be in control, she did like to do the chasing, and not be the chasee.

"So, moving on?'

"Huh?" she said, distractedly.

"The book you're reading?"

Oh, right, the book. "I have a mental disorder," she said flippantly. "I'm forgetful."

"Seriously?" Gus's eyebrows met and he looked as if he believed her.

"Yes, memory loss," she quipped.

"You been studying psychology long?"

"No, not long." About five minutes. She was such a liar. "We should head back."

Gus reluctantly agreed.

As they walked back, he told her a little more about himself, while she was deliberately evasive about her past, believing no one wanted to know there was a box of exs that was almost full, an ex-boyfriend stalking her, and likely to pop up at the most unexpected times, or the fact that up until very recently she had been considering the possibility of a liaison with a very elusive photocopier repairman.

For her New Year's resolution, she intended to lose three kilos and get fit, surely all this walking would help achieve that goal, but what she wanted now was a cup of tea, a chocolate biscuit, and a lie-down. Finally, the bridge was in sight. Gus suggested Sally join them for a barbeque dinner.

"Join us, we are having fish burgers," he said proudly.

Sal was torn. As much as she wanted to be with Gus, she felt bad for deserting her friends. "I think I better chill with my mates tonight."

"Later then," he winked, an unmistakable look in his eye. She didn't have the energy to entertain even the suggestion of a twinkle and felt quite faint at the thought.

Without bothering to kick off her jandals, Sally unzipped her tent, staggered a few paces, and fell on the semi-deflated air bed.

There was a polite tap on the tent pole. "You, ok?" Trent called.

She groaned. "Yeah, just stuffed,"

"Want anything?"

A new pair of legs would be good. Instead, she replied, "Nah, all good."

Trent persisted, "Tea, coffee, water?"

"Wine? I need to be anesthetised," she answered, sounding truly pathetic.

"Can you make it to the table?"

"I couldn't possibly take another step. Could you be a dear and deliver?" She couldn't believe she was asking him a favour – she must be desperate.

"As you wish, your ladyship," he mocked.

She had never felt less ladylike in her life. She felt like an absolute train wreck. Like she'd been on a three-month safari across Africa. She hadn't shaved her legs for a week and was sure she'd grown a forest of underarm hair.

Trent returned. She felt his shadow and opened one eye. With a wry smile, he handed her a plastic goblet filled to the brim.

"Thanks," Sal said, meaning it. Trying not to spill a drop, she struggled to sit up. She took a grateful sip.

"And will your ladyship be joining us for dinner tonight?"

"Depends, I'm more tired than hungry."

"Anton, Ethan, and I went fishing, there's fish for tea."

"OMG! I am going to grow gills!" Sal cried.

"Well, you do drink like a fish. Don't worry, there are sausages as well because as you know, Mindy is allergic to fish."

Sal toasted Mindy. She finally had a reason to be thankful for Mindy's presence.

She gave Trent a querulous look. "Have you finished reading that damn book yet?"

"Yep, finished it," Trent replied. "Fancy a walk later?"

She choked on her wine and in a coughing fit managed to splutter, "No, no, I don't."

Chapter 15: New Year, New Resolution

The night was balmy and the sky ablaze with stars as they sat around the communal BBQ table chatting. The lantern sitting on the table lit their faces making them look ghostly, and drew the bugs. Sal had smothered herself head to toe in insect repellent before leaving her tent, but it was too late. They'd already had a good feed and some angry red welts were appearing and making her itch like crazy. There were some animated discussions around religion and politics. As the drink flowed everyone got louder, more animated, and more opinionated.

Mindy, dressed in the finest designer gear and wearing baby doll pink lip-gloss, was whining like an annoying mosquito. Sal wanted to strangle her. Anton was quiet, he'd been for a massive mountain bike ride and was still recovering. The other guys had been for a body roll down the river in their wetsuits, and although covered in bruises they were pumped with adrenalin and still relishing re-telling the event.

Trent seemed to have stopped picking on her. And anyone who brought her a cup of tea or a glass of wine when she could barely move, couldn't be all bad. Ethan played it cool making a few wisecracks here and there. Thin, blue-eyed, Jayne looked brittle – like she might break. The poor thing – the last thing Jayne needed was to be around Kat and Rob acting like a couple of loved-up teenagers when she was in the throes of separation.

Sal whispered, "Are you ok?" as she gently patted Jayne's arm.

"Yeah, I'm alright," Jayne replied, her face telling a different story. "It is just hard knowing this is the last time we will be camping together, knowing that it's over. It feels, you know," she searched for the words, "final."

"Do you want it to work?"

Jayne sadly shook her head. "Too late, there's too much water under the bridge. I guess I'm scared of what happens next."

"I understand," Sal said, squeezing her hand. *Moving on and Getting on With Your Life* sprung to mind, but how could she recommend the book to Jayne when she had barely made it past the contents page.

It was well after ten when Sally announced, "I've been invited up to my cousins for a drink to celebrate New Year. Anyone else want to come?" Well, it was only decent to ask.

"Nah, you go right ahead," Kat told her, giving her a knowing smile. "We wouldn't want to cramp your style."

"No, you wouldn't want to be known as the handbrake now, would you," Sal pointedly reminded Kat.

"Touché!" Kat raised her glass in mock toast. "Goodbye, Mr photocopier guy."

Sal felt like maybe, for once in her life, she would throw caution to the wind and be entirely irresponsible. What did one wear as seduction garb when one was camping? In the finish, she pulled on her skin-tight jeans and yanked a flowery feminine pink blouse over her head. She tucked a sweatshirt under her arm for later, when it got cooler. Her sunburn was slowly being replaced by a tan. She touched up her lip gloss, then picking up a magnum of champagne, Sally set off to celebrate. As she passed by the long drop, her phone beeped. It was Don. *Thinking of you. Miss you, babe. Love you xxx.*

Would he ever give up? She'd been given a new knife set for Christmas, God help him, she might just use it. She deleted his message.

She arrived at the campsite to find the party in full swing. She had wanted to have been celebrating the New Year with Chase but no such luck. Maybe Kat was right, she was dreaming about the impossible and maybe it was time for her to live a little and misbehave.

Gus wore a tight black muscle tee which showed off his bulging biceps, and his tight blue jeans hugged all the right places. Those buns were buns of steel. Mouth suddenly dry, Sal swallowed. Oh God, it had been so long.

"Hello gorgeous," he said, pecking her cheek.

Tongue-tied, she went the same shade of pink as her blouse. This was probably only going to be a summer fling. He lived in Tauranga, and she was in Auckland so it couldn't go anywhere – could it?

He led her into the inner circle of the group and they stood next to Wendy's, husband, Josh. A down-to-earth, Southern guy, every word Josh uttered sounded like a slow rumble. His southern burr was strong as he rolled every "r" in words that didn't even contain an r.

Wow, could Wendy and Sarah drink! In typical generous Southern style, the girls kept topping up Sal's glass until she had no idea what stage she was at, and before she knew it, she had gone from bubbles to brandy. Gus remained attentively glued to her side. She could feel him undressing her with his eyes. Nervous, she struggled to find anything intelligent to say.

"Another?" he whispered in her ear as he picked up the brandy bottle.

She yawned and waved it away. "No, no, better pace myself, or I'll never see midnight."

"Can't have you passing out before I get my New Year's kiss," he said, handing the bottle back to Josh.

Gus asked, "So, what do you do for exercise, Sal?'

I chase a few old men around the rest home. No, no, not the right answer. "Um, nothing really," Sal admitted. "I like to dance."

"Then let's dance." Gus disappeared into his tent and returned with an old battery-operated CD player and stuck in ABBA's Greatest Hits. The strains of Dancing Queen belted out.

"Come on, my dancing queen, let's dance," Gus yelled, his arms outstretched. Don loved ABBA. Agrh, now was not the time to be thinking of Don. Even Chase disappeared from her mind when Gus pulled her close. Trouble was, she was as coordinated as a new born foal. How was she going to dance when she could barely feel her legs? Gus held her tight against his solid muscular frame. Oh God, was he gyrating?"

"I love dirty dancing, don't you?" She gasped when his hands slipped lower and he squeezed her butt cheeks. Obviously, Gus was expecting way more than just a kiss. Sal began to flounder. As much as she wanted to be a wanton woman of the world, she felt completely out of her depth.

With a voice as loud as a megaphone, Wendy shouted, "It's almost midnight!" She started pouring glasses of champagne, ready for the countdown,

"I can't wait," Gus said, smiling down at Sal.

Sarah handed Sally a plastic goblet. Five, four, three, two, one.... Everyone shouted. HAPPY NEW YEAR!

Gus kissed her so passionately that all thought of resistance melted. Then, everyone hugged and air-kissed, shouting, "Happy New Year!" to each other.

"You, come with me," Sarah said, taking Sal firmly by the arm. Flanking her, Wendy took hold of Sal's other arm.

"Where are we going?" Sal innocently asked as they tripped across the lumpy ground dodging tent pegs and guide ropes.

"To the latrine," Sarah told her.

"But I don't need to go."

"There's safety in numbers," Wendy added, "We're all going in case we meet a possum, or a Gruffalo, or something."

Sal was baffled. "A what?"

"Gus has set his sights set on you," Wendy told her.

Well, hello – was that supposed to be news?

"He's the danger," Sarah said keeping her voice low. "And although we love him dearly, he's a bit of a player. You're our cousin and we don't want you to end up just being another notch on his bedpost."

"Yeah, you're family, and no one messes with our family," Wendy said firmly.

What? Did she belong to the mafia? Typical, just when she had resolved to play up, others decided to protect her chastity.

Sarah waved the torch about so much that the three of them had trouble seeing where they were going.

"I can take care of myself," Sal replied, tripping.

Wendy jerked Sal upright. "We don't want him to take

advantage of you."

"Yeah," agreed Sarah. "We don't want you to do something you may regret later."

Sal doubted she'd regret it. Instead, she suspected she'd rather enjoy it.

Sal's phone went mental when they arrived at the long drop as Happy New Year's messages poured in. With no time to check them and unable to focus properly, she ignored them. Wendy went to the loo first, then Sarah, both girls stood like bouncers outside while Sally went. Then, after a quick wash of their hands with hand sanitiser they set off again.

"But won't Gus wonder what happened to me?" Sal asked, worried he would feel abandoned.

"We'll tell him you were tired and went to bed," Sarah replied. "Believe me, you'll thank us tomorrow."

Then three torches approached. It was Ethan, Anton and Trent, looking for her.

In a disproving voice, Trent told her cousins, "We could hear Sal giggling all over the campground and thought they better come rescue her."

Hugging Sal goodnight, the cousins willingly handed her over. Much to her disappointment, the boys saw Sal safely back to her tent. She appreciated their concern, but it was New Year and she wanted to live a little dangerously. Wouldn't a summer fling be the perfect thing to take her mind off a crappy year and the fact Chase hadn't called?

Anton gave Sal a little shove towards her tent. "Night."

She stumbled inside and sat heavily on the saggy airbed.

Ethan zipped the door closed. "Night."

"Sleep tight," called Trent.

Sally lay on her deflated bed feeling like an absolute failure, she couldn't even muster the art of seduction properly with a man who clearly wanted her. She lifted the window flap and watched the lights weave across the campground until they went out.

It was a new year, a fresh year, a year full of endless

possibilities and she had been very close to being intimate with an Ironman. Now she knew she'd never have the guts to go back to Gus's campsite, not that she could find it in the dark anyway. Definitely not without breaking her neck.

She closed her eyes and tried to sleep, but sleep eluded her. She started to feel guilty about ditching her friends and realised she hadn't wished any of them a Happy New Year. It was pointless messaging any of them now – they'd all be asleep. She'd see who was still awake in the group and say Happy New Year in person. Rolling off the saggy mattress she landed on her hands and knees, and she waited a full minute for the spinning sensation to subside, then, when the nausea passed, she crawled to the opening and had a lengthy wrestle with the zip before fighting her way free.

Everyone else must have gone to sleep already, the party poopers. Other than the snores coming from Anton's tent, all was quiet. Trent's tent was the only tent still lit. His lantern was shining golden through the thin silver walls. Sal decided to go wish Trent Happy New Year and apologise for her anti-social behaviour. After all, anyone who could make a decent cup of tea, brought aloe vera, sunblock, and wine to her when she needed it, deserved thanks. He was quite sweet in an annoying arsehole kind of way. She found his tent flap was unzipped and crawled through the gap on her hands and knees.

Trent sat bolt upright.

"Happy New Year!" She cried falling face-first on the floor.

"You're drunk," he accused, clutching his sleeping bag to his bare chest.

"I'm a tad tipsy," she admitted. Getting up and crawling towards him, she said, "I felt bad because I haven't wished you Happy New Year and I wanted to tell you I'm sorry for thinking you were such a self-righteous arsehole. You're not that bad really. You have some good points, like you make a good cup of tea."

He checked his watch. "It's past one."

She began to hiccup. "Is it?"

"You think I'm an arsehole. Do you know how annoying you are?"

"I was trying to be nice and apologise but it seems like I was right, you are an arsehole. I didn't mean to piss you off, sorry."

He shook his head at her like she was a naughty child. "We were worried about you," he remonstrated. "We could hear you giggling all over the campground. I mean, come on, what do you know about this guy? He could be a predator."

"Hic! Sorry for enjoying myself, and God forbid, for drinking on New Year's with family and a freakishly handsome hunk."

"Go to bed," he told her sternly.

"Oh, sorry, Dad. Hic, you're right, I am a little tired." She lay down and closed her eyes.

"I meant your own bed – in your own tent."

Suddenly the tent's framework moved in and out like it was a living, breathing animal. Everything was moving, heaving and spinning, faster and faster like a merry-go-round gone rogue, and it wouldn't stop.

"Oh God," she cried. "I think I'm going to be sick." Scrambling, she made a mad dash to the entrance and squeezing through the flaps, made it to the bushes, and puked.

"Are you ok?" a deep voice behind her asked.

From her position on all fours, all Sal could see was a pair of hairy legs.

"I'm trying to find my tent," she answered.

"What's it look like?" the stranger asked.

"It's red and brown and realllllllyyyyy BIG." Climbing up his legs, Sally squinted up at him, his face was separating, and he looked as if he had four to eight eyes. Was he a spider? "I think it may be over there." She pointed with her chin, knowing she should let go of him but the ground was kind of wavy, so she held on tightly. She'd never been afraid of spiders.

Like a zombie, Trent loomed out of the darkness. He'd put a t-shirt on and was wearing shorts and was holding his torch like a police batten.

"Hammered, I'm afraid," Trent said as he prised Sal's fingers off the guy's legs.

"This your missus, mate?" The guy asked as if he pitied him.

"Nope, but seems like she's my responsibility," Trent begrudgingly replied. "Come on," he said, hoisting Sal over his shoulder in a fireman's lift and walking like he was a slaughterman carrying a sheep carcass. "It's this way, and don't you dare puke down my back."

When they made it back to Sally's tent, he carefully lowered her to the floor, then she collapsed back onto her flat air bed and squeezed her eyes shut.

She groaned. "Please make the spinning stop."

He shook his head reproachfully. "Serves you right," was all the sympathy she got.

Trent helped her remove her shoes, and threw them in the corner. Then taking hold of her arms, he tugged her into a sitting position.

He handed her a large glass of water, and ordered, "Drink this – all of it."

"Tastes funny," she complained, wrinkling her nose.

"That's because it's non-alcoholic," he said disapprovingly. "Drink all of it."

He stood over her while she drank it down. Then she let go of the glass and fell back in a swoon like a dying swan.

Squinting up at him she commented, "You should wear different colours. You always wear blue. You remind me of an overgrown smurf; you could do with some serious styling."

"Nice to know." Trent plonked a bucket on the groundsheet near her head. "Here's the dishwashing bucket; throw up in there if you need to."

"You're not leaving me?" she asked, alarmed. "What if I asphyxiate?"

"You'll be fine," he insisted.

"I don't think I will be," she moaned.

"How melodramatic can you get? Get some sleep, little princess, you're bound to have a killer of a headache tomorrow, but you'll live."

She covered her head with her hands and cried, "Men! They are never there for me when I need them."

"I'm not far away. Now go to sleep," he said firmly. She heard the zip close; then, everything went black.

Chapter 16: Bye, Bye Thigh

The urgency of her bladder woke her. Firstly, Sal wondered where she was? Secondly, why her eyebrows hurt? Then, she couldn't figure out why she was fully dressed lying spread-eagled on top of her sleeping bag. But then, she saw the dishwashing bucket beside her, and last night came back like a flood to haunt her. Good Lord! She had thwarted Gus's hopes and thrown up outside Trent's tent and climbed up some random stranger's legs.

She clutched her aching head. Dear God, she wished she was dead. She had probably confirmed Trent's suspicions that she was a raging alcoholic, and after anything in shorts! She cringed. It must have been the combination of the brandy and the champagne. She'd never drunk that much in her life. People said it wasn't wise to mix your drinks, now she knew why. She felt terrible. Her tongue felt furry, like she had licked the cat. Her new New Year's resolution was to never drink again.

Grunting, Sal rolled off the bed and lay on the groundsheet enjoying the feel of the cool plastic against her forehead. Then, she slowly struggled to her knees where she waited a full minute making sure nothing was moving, before getting up. Oh God, she'd have to apologise to Gus. Unless the girls had told him some bullshit story, he must have wondered what happened to her.

Trent had rescued her last night. He might be a proper condescending arsehole at times, but he had helped her find her tent, and put her to bed, even taken her shoes off for her. No matter how much of an arse he'd been, he deserved an apology. When she checked the time on her phone, she discovered it was still early, only seven-thirty, definitely not a respectable time on New Year's Day to be waking anyone up – even if it was with a peace offering. Awakening him would be another sin to add to her long list of sins.

After making a quick dash to the long drop, Sal tiptoed back to her tent. The campground was unnaturally quiet. Sitting under her awning, killing time, she thumbed through her 'Moving on' book but she couldn't concentrate. She rubbed her forehead, bloody eyebrows, who knew they could hurt? How could they hurt when they were just sitting on your forehead doing nothing? Finally, she heard noises that suggested some of the campground residents were stirring. Small children squealed, and people carrying toilet paper and phones passed by.

She made coffee, then gathering the remnants of her dignity, headed over to Trent's tent. She coughed loudly as she knocked on the awning pole.

"What?"

He sounded grumpy.

She felt like retreating but that would be cowardly. "Um, it's me, Sal. I brought you a coffee."

Silence.

"I hope you are dressed because I'm coming in." She put down the cup and unzipped the tent. Crouching to get through the entrance, Sal held the cup outstretched before her and tried hard not to spill a drop. "Peace offering."

"Nice of you to knock," Trent said dryly. Cocooned in his sleeping bag he looked bemused as she sheepishly handed him the cup.

"I'm sorry for disturbing you last night," Sal humbly began. "I know you probably won't believe it, but I think the champagne was off."

Trent shook his head. "I'm surprised you remember anything at all. Do you remember calling me an arsehole?"

"Yes, but that wasn't because I was drunk, but because you have been a complete dickhead."

"A dickhead. Gone from arsehole to dickhead. You have a way with words. Have you been reading that book how to win friends and influence people?"

Ignoring his sarcasm, she said, "I feel bad enough, I don't

need you to make me feel worse." She rubbed her forehead.

He blew over the top of the coffee cup and keeping his eyes on Sal, slowly took a sip.

She felt awkward and thought she best go. "Well, yeah, ah, thanks for looking after me last night."

"I am pleased you didn't die," he said.

"Really?"

"Yeah, you make a good coffee."

"See ya." Sal backed away leaving him in peace.

Sal couldn't wait to brush her teeth to get rid of that furry feeling. But first, the most pressing need right now was another visit to the long drop. As she approached the hill her phone pinged.

HAPPY NEW YEAR, LOVE YOU, MISS YOU. CAN'T WAIT TO SEE YOU XXX.

Arrgh! Gone Don! Bloody stalker! Frustrated to hell, she felt like throwing her phone in the dunny.

Everyone started packing up. Wendy and Sarah came across to say goodbye.

"Hope you're not mad, we just didn't want to see you get hurt," Sarah said, hugging Sal tightly into her shoulder.

Sal winced. Being a people pleaser, she tried hard to be upbeat. "Nah, you did the right thing. I don't want to be another notch on anyone's bedpost." What about you, Sally Gelee? A wee voice inside her head needled, Aren't you a serial dater? Don't you think you're being a little hypocritical?

Sarah smiled, "Good girl, you are worth more."

Despite her best efforts, the corners of Sal's mouth sagged. So much for being a woman of the world. She was an absolute failure as a wanton. She wanted to be recklessly irresponsible and wildly passionate with a stranger she may never see again. Ah well, it wasn't meant to be, at least she would have the memory, unless all that alcohol she had in her system killed off her brain cells and she lost her memory. Fortunately, she had managed to take one sneaky pic of him at the rock pools. If she didn't have evidence no one was ever going to believe her. They would think she was making it up.

Wendy said, "Next time you are in Tauranga come visit us."

Sal promised she would pop in next time she was in the Bay of Plenty. The cousins waved goodbye and left. Her eyebrows still hurt. Sal felt flatter than highway roadkill.

In order to beat the traffic and enjoy a day at home before returning to work, the convoy was planning to leave around mid-morning. Sal could hear Mindy instructing Pete how to dismantle their campsite *properly*. Her high-pitched voice split Sal's head in two. It only took Trent a couple of minutes to pack down his tent, having been a boy scout, he had it sussed. Anton's igloo thingy was way easier to dismantle than it was to erect, and he was packed in a jiffy. Sal vaguely wondered whether anyone had mentioned to Anton that he might need to see a professional to get his snoring under control. God help the woman that ended up with him! She would have to be deaf or be a nightshift worker not to want to smother him with a pillow.

Trent stuffed his gear into Anton's car, while Anton hooked the cycle on the towbar rack and secured it. Meanwhile, Ethan and Jayne methodically packed their car in a silent but uneasy truce. Kat and Rob were nowhere to be seen. Jayne said that the happy couple had gone for one last walk to the waterfall to snog.

Although Sal knew she must get cracking and pack the car, it was way too hard. She sat in her deck chair; a can of cold coke pressed to her forehead. Sooner or later, she was going to have to drag her sorry butt out of the deck chair and get organised, or they would leave without her. To lose the others would be the final straw. If that happened, she would probably sit by the roadside and cry. With no cell phone coverage to be able to access google maps, she didn't know if it was possible to find the way out of the forest alone.

Through her heavy-lidded eyes, she saw Gus coming over the hill and her throat went dry. What was she going to say?

"Hey," he called loudly, making her wince. "What happened to you last night, Cinderella? Midnight and boom, you disappear."

"Sorry, I wasn't feeling well," she mumbled to the dewy grass.

Giving her the once over, Gus said, "Mm, you don't look so good."

Nice of him to say so. Stick the knife in when I'm feeling down, why don't you.

"We are leaving this morning," she told him. Just the thought of driving along the windy road around Lake Rotorua made her stomach queasy.

"Aww shame," he bent down and touched Sal's knee. She could feel the warmth of his hand through her three-quarter jeans. Did he know about the thigh test? Was he checking to see if her thigh felt right?

"We were just starting to get to know each other. Do you have to go?" he raised a suggestive eyebrow. "Stay," his hand moved a little higher, "here, with me."

No, he was interested in way more than just her thigh. She pretended to use his thigh as a support as she stood up. No, his thigh didn't feel right, it felt muscular and strong but not right. Her head swam, little fishies were going around and around in what was left of the jelly blob she once called a brain.

Sal hurriedly apologized, "No, I'm afraid I have to. I'm heading back with friends, we came together, and we're leaving together. It's been great, but sadly it's time to go."

He raised himself off his haunches. He towered over her. She had to raise her head to look at him and the sun burned her eyes.

"Come to Tauranga," Gus said. "There's plenty to see and do." He licked his lips. "And you can always stay at my place."

Sal gave him a waxy smile. "Next Christmas perhaps."

"Let's keep in touch on social media, or by email," Gus suggested. He grinned, "I bet your insta page is something like gorgeoussexyhotchik@paradise."

More like washed-up old hangover hag, Sally thought ruefully. "Nah, nothing so exotic, I'm afraid."

How come Gus appeared like a sexual deviant in the sobering light of day? The cousins had been right, the man was a player and she had almost fallen prey to his charms. Despite the warning in her head, she scribbled her email address down on a piece of paper and handed it to him.

Gus's grin spread wider. "Well, sexy chick, I guess this is see ya later." He went in for a kiss.

Trent loudly cleared his throat just before Gus's lips made contact. Sal jerked her head away in surprise. Gus scowled at Trent, annoyed. She put her hands to her head to stop her brain swirling.

"Are you ready, Sal?" Trent asked, giving Gus the evils. We're all done, we're just waiting for you."

Sal looked at her tent in dismay. The thought of trying to stuff her family-sized tent back into the Mini was more than she could bear.

"Um, do you need a hand with your tent, Sal?" Trent asked.

"That would be nice," she replied.

"Anton has gone for a last-minute pee before we leave but I can help you," Trent offered, and started ripping out the tent pegs.

Not to be outdone, Gus started unpegging the other side. They loaded her car and Sal hiffed the rest of her gear in.

"Thanks so much," she said with genuine gratitude. They stood there awkwardly while the other campers piled into their respective cars. Anton returned and rounded up the others.

Rob and Kat left first, then Jayne and Ethan, then Mindy and Pete. Anton jumped in his car and revved the engine. "Come on," he called to Trent.

Trent dallied by the passenger's side door, his hand resting on the door handle as if unsure they should leave Sal alone with Ironman. "If you get too far behind us, we will be stopping for coffee at Starbucks in Rotorua."

Anton yelled out the open window. "Message one of us if you get lost."

The guys waved goodbye, then Anton's station wagon slowly drove away until there was nothing to see but a lingering dust cloud.

"I guess this is it," Sal said.

"Guess so." Gus put his arms around her, his hands slipping lower than they should, and he kissed her hard.

A tremor of desire rippled through her making her shudder.

Breathless, she said, 'Bye, Gus."

Freeing herself from his grasp, she quickly slid behind the wheel of her little yellow Mini, and set off leaving Gus behind. Half a kilometre up the road she was tempted to go back but resisted. As she drove along the dusty gravel road, she thought, damn that was close. She was just as hot as the weather and there were cobwebs on her lady parts. Darn it, why did she have to be born with a conscience?

Chapter 17: Volunteer Fear

Sal often reflected on the New Year's camping trip and what might have been. She printed off the sneaky photo she had taken of Gus and added it to the box of exs. She was sure Gus would have been a red-hot lover, but she consoled herself that she'd made the right choice and wouldn't die of a sexually transmitted disease. Since New Year's she had only seen Trent and Anton once, in the driveway, and so far, had managed to skilfully avoid both of them. She didn't want to be reminded of how drunk she'd been that night and she was sure Trent and Anton would milk it for all it was worth.

It should have been a year filled with possibilities, but nothing had changed. Even with all the walking she'd done over New Year's, she hadn't lost any weight. Sal sat on her bed and emptied out the box of exs. Heart sore, she forced herself to pick up each photo and take stock. Except the letters tucked under the lining, she couldn't go there – that was too painful. Her avoidance ostrich was well and truly alive. She wondered if there would ever come a time where she could deal with those emotions and not feel the pain? With a heavy sigh she put the photos back in the box and snapped the lid shut.

It was the beginning of the year and back to life as she knew it; back to the normal routine. The stupid photocopier was working fine. She had all the wrong men targeting her; either too young, or too old. Why even Cecil, who must be all of ninety, said something entirely inappropriate the other day, the old rogue.

Work filled in most of the day and there were the usual entertainers coming in to add cheer. But Bozo the Clown was an absolute standout. He had a wicked sense of humour and made everyone, including the staff, balloon art. He made Sal a pink and purple spotted butterfly which she proudly displayed behind her desk. It was the highlight of her day.

Alice was on the warpath. The residents' laundry was mixed up and people were wearing items that didn't belong to them. Some two sizes too big, some too sizes too small. Even labelling the clothes didn't seem to work. Ann was defensive and said, she was doing her level best. It wasn't her fault that some of the carers couldn't read. Vikki needed packs for her new admissions, Harold was grumbling away fixing lights in the stairwell, and moaning that the last fire drill had been a complete disaster.

By lunchtime, things had settled down. Pearl had taken a van load off on a day trip and wasn't expected back until late afternoon. Andie arrived at the front desk in a panic. He hadn't seen Costas since mid-morning. It wasn't like him to roam, and he'd never normally missed lunch.

Andie checked the register. "Have you seen him, Sal?" he asked flicking through the pages.

Sal hadn't seen Costas leave, and he wasn't on the list for the day trip.

Daisy deposited the latest grocery order in Sal's in-tray. "He'll not be far away," she said confidently. "It's his favourite today."

While they were still discussing him, Costas appeared, strolling through the glass doors as calmly as can be.

Sighing with relief, hand on hip, Andie demanded, "Costas, where have you been? I've been looking all over for you." He waggled a painted finger at Costas, adding, "Everyone has been worried sick."

Surprised by all the fuss, Costas replied. "I went for a walk. I've had a chat with Saint Peter, and he's taking me to heaven very soon. He's Greek, you know."

"I've never been to Greece," Sal told Costas.

"I'll take you there, darling." He grinned. "You'll love it."

Sal patted his arm. "How about we start with lunch in the dining room first. It's your favourite and there's ice-cream sundaes for dessert."

Costas poked his tongue at Andie and let Sal lead the way.

***

Aside from Rob, Kat seemed to have a new interest and kept harping on about joining the volunteers. To shut her up, Sal reluctantly agreed to go. Besides, training may help her shift some of the weight she'd put on over Christmas and New Year's. But how was she going to avoid Trent and Anton if they were at the same station?

The girls arrived at the station ahead of time. Kat bounced in the door while Sally followed, dragging her heels. She knew Anton, Rob and Trent were all volunteer firefighters, but she wasn't aware that Trent was the officer in charge.

Trent told the girls to line up for the parade along with the uniformed firefighters and other new recruits. Sal said "Hello," to Trent as he went down the line calling out their names. The others yelled 'present' when they were called. Trent was enjoying bossing them about and it was irritating the heck out of Sal.

The brigade was doing medical checks and the nurse was due to arrive. It was a hearing test, blood pressure, cholesterol test, and eye check-up. A free medical was too good an opportunity to pass up, so Sal waited her turn to see the nurse. Trouble was, the vintage fire station lacked privacy. It was an old fifties style brick building with single-pane windows and it housed the paid firefighters, whereas the volunteers had to operate out of a port-a-com on site. The nurse saw each of them individually in an office that had a large window facing the vehicle bay and it was far from soundproof. Unable to distinguish between the beeps, and whistles from the trucks during the hearing test, Sal kept raising her hand at the wrong time. She was sure the nurse was going to suggest hearing aids. When the nurse asked if she had any health concerns, Sal decided to describe her last mammogram experience and didn't notice the fire truck move out of the vehicle bay. When to her horror, she glanced out the window only to find the brigade waving to her while she was squishing her right boob flat as a pancake on full public display.

She heard Trent say, "Say hi to Sally, guys." Face instantly red, she let go of her boob. God, she'd always had lousy timing.

"Do you think they saw that?" she asked the nurse.

"I'd say definitely," the nurse nodded.

After the medical, the firefighters did truck checks then they broke into groups. The recruits had to see if they were physically fit enough to do the job. First up, was running hoses.

"You'll be good at this, Sal," Trent commented as he passed by the officer in charge of the drill, "you being such an excellent runner and all."

Arse, she thought, hefting the hose over her shoulder and squeezing the end like she was wringing his neck.

The hoses were heavy and awkward, and after they had been full of water, they were tricky to roll up again. Perhaps she should quit trying to be a firefighter. There was no way she was ever going to pass basic training, and not when she could barely lift a dry hose, let alone one filled with water.

Meanwhile Kat was loving every minute. "I can pole dance," she proudly told the brigade training officer.

"That won't be necessary," he said, his face deadpan. "For health and safety reasons poles have been removed from our stations as they caused too many accidents." He went on to explain that one firefighter would slide down the pole but before they were out of the way, the next would land on top. He was so dry he could make the best comedy boring. Kat rolled her eyes.

The minute they got home; Kat flopped into the big comfy armchair. "That was fun," she said kicking off her shoes.

"You reckon? I'm absolutely knackered." Dripping with sweat, Sal longed for a nice hot shower.

"Yeah, but it was fun. You'll come next week with me, hey? We are going to look good in uniform, chick."

"You didn't tell me Trent was in charge."

"He's alright, he means well. He just seems to rub you up the wrong way. Besides, the other guys are nice, aren't they, and who knows maybe you'll find your Mr Right in the fire department."

"Have you found yours?" Sal asked, suddenly serious. "Do you think Rob is the one?"

"Maybe," Kat replied, sounding a little unsure. "Time will tell. I don't have a thigh test but his hose is pretty good," she laughed.

Sal threw the fluffy cushion at her, hitting Kat smack in the face.

Chapter 18: Obscene

Saturday was a perfect summer's day. Kat suggested they go for a walk at the beach, and maybe next door might like to join them.

Sal groaned. "What about Rob?" she asked, surprised Kat hadn't mentioned him.

She shrugged her shoulders. "Says he has to work; there's a big project that he needs to complete before the deadline."

Although she wasn't dead keen on seeing Trent, the cuddly tyre around her middle reminded Sal that she needed the exercise. And besides, as he lived next door there was only so long that she could avoid him. "Ok, I'm in."

They popped next door and knocked. Anton was already booked. He was meeting his cycling friends and going for a bike ride, but said, he would meet up with them for a coffee and just to message him when they were done.

Trent agreed to join the girls, and for more of a workout, suggested they walk down to the beach rather than drive there. Trent wore his cap low, sunglasses, his blue fire service t-shirt, and blue shorts. Sal wondered if he had fire service undies to match. Did he ever get sick of wearing blue? Sal had thrown on her leggings and sweatshirt that she normally wore around the house, had her hair tied back in a ponytail, and her scruffy old sneakers on, whereas Kat looked like she had stepped out of a Vogue magazine: designer sunglasses, black t-shirt, 3 quarter length leggings, and Nike shoes.

The three of them walked down the road towards the regional park. Although Anton had initially rubbed her up the wrong way, he was easy going and she found it hard to stay mad at him. Trent, on the other hand, always seemed to make her feel awkward. She never knew when he was being serious, or just teasing, so rather than give him any ammunition, she let Kat do all the talking. Kat nattered away to Trent while Sal quietly followed behind. First, they walked through the park. The place was crowded with children running free, swarming the playground like bees, their excited cries blending in with the shrieks of the seagulls. Sal sighed wistfully; life was complicated. It would be so much easier to be a kid again.

Sal loved living so close to the beach. Enjoying the fresh air and sunshine, they walked to the end of the park. When they reached the historical homestead, they decided to turn back but this time instead of going back through the park, they would walk along the beach. The crossed the creek where the old sunken log poked one branch up in the air like a swimmer mid-stroke.

As they walked near the water's edge, little ruffles of water raced up the sandy shore attempting to lick the soles of their shoes. Trent and Kat had long legs while Sal had to take two steps to their one but she managed to keep up and was now happily walking alongside them rather than behind. Suddenly, out of the blue, Kat said she'd been reading the latest Cosmo magazine, and had stumbled across an advert for butt plugs, and wondered if Trent knew how they worked.

Trent coughed in surprise and assured Kat he didn't. Sal didn't want to show her ignorance, so kept her mouth shut. What was Kat up to? Young kids and families were walking on the beach, people might overhear their conversation. But Kat refused to let it drop, and went on about butt plugs until finally, disappointed by their lack of knowledge, she made up a new game. They had to come up with alternative names for penis or vagina.

"I'll start," Kat said, "Mink."

"Willy," Sal jumped in. And then quickly added, "Roger, Peter."

"We are not naming all your exs, Sal," joked Trent.

"Dick," Sal said poking her tongue out at him.

"Growler," Trent said, joining in. "Muff."

Kat added, "Weapon."

"Rocket," Trent replied.

Kat laughed. "Wanger."

"Chubby," Trent replied. "Twanger."

Sal said, "The One-Eyed Trouser Snake."

Kat grinned, "You have to watch out for them."

"Jumbo," offered Trent.

"You wish," kidded Kat, jolting his arm.

"Beaver," said Trent.

"Pussy," Kat countered.

"Now we are onto animal names," giggled Sal.

Loosening up, Sal laughed most of the way back. In no time at all they had walked over the bridge and reached the carpark.

Trent messaged Anton and arranged for them to meet him at the Scout Café in half an hour. As they climbed the steepest part of the hill Sal's calves were starting to feel the burn, and she was trying not to puff. Still kitted out in full Lycra, Anton had grabbed an outdoor table and was waiting for them. Sal felt virtuous after all her exercise, so figuring she had earned it, she ordered a muffin to go with her trim latte.

A poster on the window took her eye. DanceFix promised fun, fitness and friendship. She liked a good boogie and if she was going to be a volunteer firefighter, she was going to need to get fit and get rid of this spare tyre. She decided to give it a go. She liked dancing, it should be fun, right?

***

Since diets always start on a Monday, she decided she'd start her new exercise regime on a Monday. She arrived a little late and hid in the back row of the dark hall with disco lights flickering. Sal tried to keep time with the music, and the peppy instructor was so bouncy she was like the energiser bunny on steroids. She looked vaguely familiar but it was hard to tell in the darkened hall.

Sal felt so uncoordinated. The up-tempo beat and high energy chorography meant she was still facing the front when the others were facing the back. She went right when they went left. They were like swans while she felt like she was a seagull. Sal had no idea what a massive cardio workout it was going to be, she was exhausted and drenched in sweat by the time the class finished.

The energiser bunny instructor bounded over and introduced herself as Lisa, and wanted to know if Sal had enjoyed the class. Sal wanted to say it was one of the longest hours of her life. Instead, she said, yeah, it was great.

"Hey, I remember you!" Lisa cried with enthusiasm. She chuckled. "You were throwing your scales in the rubbish bin when I was running past your place one morning."

Sal sheepishly replied, "Oh yeah. They're the reason I'm here."

The next day every muscle in her body hated her but her eyebrows didn't hurt. She was grateful her car was an automatic and she didn't have to battle a clutch with sore calf muscles. She groaned and moved around the rest home at snail's pace, even those residents with sticks or on walkers were getting around the place faster than she was.

Sal was distributing the mail and as she entered the large lounge, she noticed the physio was taking a music and movement class.

Clive shouted, "Hey Sal, come join our hip operation class. It's hip hop for us oldies."

"Yeah," agreed Marvin from his wheelchair who was enjoying watching the ladies. "It's bloody marvellous!"

"Thanks, but no thanks. The way I feel today I need a hip operation; you lot would run rings around me. Have fun."

She hoped her muscles came right by brigade training night. If they were running hoses again, she'd be struggling for sure. What had Kat got her into? And why the hell did she agree to go? Why couldn't she say no?

Turned out training night was a simulated search and rescue operation at North Head. There were members of the public trapped in a tunnel, the fire crew had to find them, perform first aid if necessary, and get them above ground. It was a shambles.

Unable to locate the victims in the dark, the stranded victims had to yell clues to the recruits so they could find them. In the end, Trent stepped in and pulled it all together so they could get home on time.

Sal beat Kat to the shower, then dressed for bed. She was exhausted but for some unknown reason she was drawn to the box hiding under the bed. She got down on her hands and knees and pulled out the box of exs. Kat had lost interest in Sal's box of exs since she had started going out with Rob. Sal could now look at the photos without Kat putting in her two cents worth in. Spreading the photos out on the bed, Sal sighed. They were a catalogue of her failures. She took a good long hard look at her rejects reminding herself that she must not make the same mistakes again. That night she dreamed of flooded tunnels, the Titanic, hip operations, and Gone Don.

After what had been a restless night's sleep, the next day's work was surprisingly relaxing. Summer helped improve everyones' mood. The residents and the staff were enjoying themselves. A wonderful pianist was entertaining in the lounge, and from the front desk, Sal could hear them singing along to the music. When she went down to check how things were going, she got roped into dancing with Norman, who although he couldn't remember his own name, could still remember how to do the foxtrot. Elsie was singing beautifully and Natalie was playing an invisible piano, her fingers moving deftly mid-air.

"Take it easy, Norm, I'm still a little stiff and sore from my DanceFix class," Sal told him as he twirled her about.

All in all, it had been a great day. The hairdresser had been in earlier so the ladies were sporting nicely washed and set dos. Sal logged off her computer and headed home feeling happy and content. She prided herself on the fact she must be getting fitter for at least today she could move without grunting.

When she got home, she saw a familiar car parked in her spot. Damn, Rob was there. He was seated on the comfy couch holding the TV remote, a tattooed arm wrapped possessively around Kat.

"Hey," Rob acknowledged her as she entered the living room.

"Why don't we go out for a drink? Be good to catch up with everyone."

"That's a great idea," Kat agreed, sparking into life. "It's a lovely evening and we haven't been out for ages." She glanced up at Sal. "Want to come?"

"Why not," Sal answered, as Rob flicked between TV channels. "It's not like there's anything on telly."

"Good, I'll pop next door and see if the guys are keen," Rob said, slowly getting to his feet.

Sal frowned, she still tried to avoid Trent but it was becoming impossible. "Anyone else coming?" she asked hopefully.

"Ethan and Jayne split up," Kat told her.

"Figured as much," Sal said. "It looked inevitable."

"Yeah, Ethan will come, he's up for anything," Rob casually replied, heading for the door with his phone in hand. He stopped as he reached the door. "He probably won't if Jayne does."

"Remember Pete and Mindy?" Kat said to Sal. "They split up too. Mindy ran off with the carpet layer."

Rob laughed. "Seems he did more than lay carpet."

"She," corrected Kat.

Rob gaped at Kat. "Really? She?" He shook his head. "Didn't see that coming."

Kat's eyes gleamed dangerously. "Yeah, so Pete's available and he's super-rich. He could be a good prospect for you, chicky," she patted Sal's arm. "Take your mind off that stupid photocopier guy."

Rob rolled his eyes to the ceiling, as he closed the door, and went next door to ask the guys.

"Come to think of it, there are four single men right there," Kat said. "Pete, Ethan, Trent, and Anton."

"Such hot prospects," Sal said sarcastically. "No thanks, I'm off men. I'm seriously considering becoming a lesbian." She hadn't heard Rob come back in and glanced up to see him looking gobsmacked. She could tell by the look on his face he thought she meant it.

On duty, Trent and Anton offered to drive and took their own cars. Sal, Rob and Kat, and Ethan went in Rob's car. They met Pete at The Shack. Set in a commercial area of Albany, The Shack resembled a rustic seventies-style bach, cluttered with iconic furniture. It was spacious enough and had a good band playing and a bit of a dance floor. The guys went to the bar and ordered drinks. Anton and Trent had a bottle of light beer each, and ordered a glass of bubbles for the girls. Kat disappeared outside to make a phone call.

The bar was full. Sal was nervous that Gone Don might randomly appear, he was the last thing she needed right now. Ethan wasn't sitting about moping – he was ready to party!

Apart from being told he was a wealthy businessman; Sal didn't know a lot about Pete. All she really knew was what she could see; he was nicely dressed, his hair was slightly greying, he was a little paunchy around the middle, and very, very down. He reminded her of a Bassett hound.

Pete sat silently brooding at the table with Sal. Feeling awkward, Sal didn't know what to say. She couldn't say, 'Never mind, I bet your new carpet looks nice'. The best he could hope for was that Mindy was poisoned by accidentally eating fish. Pete looked so sad. Mindy running off with a woman had definitely dented his ego.

Finally, he spoke. "I hear you're a lesbian. My wife's a lesbian," Pete said miserably.

Sal spluttered, "Who told you that?"

Rob stood behind her, nodding. "It's ok, we are all-inclusive around here."

Ethan came back from strutting his stuff on the dance floor. The others returned and Sal scooted over to make room for them. As Rob rehashed the highlights of their holiday, Sal hoped nobody mentioned Gus; she didn't want them to hassle her. Anton and Rob went to try their luck on the pokies.

"Come on, mate." Clapping a hand on Pete's shoulder, Ethan said. "There's plenty more fish in the Pacific." Raising his bottle in a mock toast, he wandered over to a table where a couple of pretty young ladies sat. Pete took up his beer and followed, his head low.

Kat passed Sal a fresh glass of bubbles, accepting the glass Sal took a blissful sip, "Ah, I love bubbles."

Trent raised an eyebrow. "Hitting the bottle again, Sal."

Sally snorted with indignation. "You make it sound like I am a raging alcoholic."

Why did she always feel the need to defend herself around him?

Trent wore a navy-blue shirt and faded blue jeans. He looked good in his jeans but she was feeling peevish.

Sal asked, "Don't you ever get sick of wearing blue?"

"No," he shrugged. "As a matter of fact, it's my favourite colour. Why? Do you have something against blue?"

She snorted. "Anyone would think you were a smurf."

"A smurf? That's rich coming from you when you're the height of one. You look like Smurfette. From now on, I'm going to call you Smurfette."

Sal glared at him.

"Right, I can see it's going to be a long night." Trent stood up. "I'll get you another." As he took a step, he got tangled up in the straps of her handbag, tripped, and stumbled a couple of paces, but managed to stay upright.

"Is that your man trap, Sal?" he accused.

"Yeah, I just leave it lying around, hoping eligible men will fall for me. Don't worry it wasn't meant for you."

He frowned. "I heard you'd changed sides. I've been told," he paused, "that you are now a lesbian."

"Yes, that's right," Sal snapped giving him a steely look. She put her arm around Kat. If there was going to be a rumour circulating about her, then it might as well be a good one. "I've had to as it's impossible to find a decent man."

Kat giggled, and blamed it on the bubbles.

Trent returned with the drinks and carefully stepped over Sal's handbag.

Sal gasped. Heart flipping, she grabbed Kat by the arm sinking her nails in. "Don't look now, but it's Chase."

"What!" Kat exclaimed.

"It's him," Sal squeaked. "It's Chase."

Trent turned and stared. "Who is Chase?"

Chase saw her.

"Oh, God. He's coming over. How do I look?" Sal asked, wishing she'd fixed her hair and makeup.

"Crazy," Trent replied with a quick shake of his head. "Stark raving mad."

Sal poked her tongue at him, retracting it just in the nick of time as Chase approached.

"Fancy seeing you here," Chase said. Yes, he did look better in his salmon pink shirt and stonewashed jeans than his work gear, and so distinguished with his salt and pepper hair.

"Hi," Sal murmured staring dreamily up at him. "Nice to see you again."

"You too, and not a photocopier in sight," he replied.

"Hi – Trent Powell," Trent said, shattering the moment by thrusting out his hand.

"Chase Downy," Chase shook Trent's hand.

"Oh, sorry," Sal mumbled. Damn, she didn't want Chase to get the impression Trent was her boyfriend. "Chase, this is my neighbour ... er ...friend, Trent," she finished lamely.

Kat coughed loudly.

"And, my friend Kat."

Kat stared bug-eyed at Chase. It was as though she hadn't really believed he was real.

"Please join us," Trent offered.

Suddenly tongue-tied, Sal couldn't think of a coherent word.

"Don't mind if I do," Chase replied, squeezing in beside Sal. "Are you here with anyone?" Sal asked, desperately hoping he wasn't going to say his girlfriend.

Chase smiled his warm, easy-going smile, "My family."

"Your family?" repeated Sal.

"Yeah, Mum, Dad, and my little sister, Jess," he qualified.

"Close family," muttered Trent.

"Yeah," Chase agreed, not seeming to notice Trent's sarcasm.

"How are you?" he asked Sal.

"Great, thanks," Sal quickly replied. "And you?"

"Great," Chase replied.

There was an awkward silence. Congratulations Einstein, Sal muttered to herself, that was a conservation killer.

"Your boss...she's..."

Sal could feel herself going red. "Yeah, um, sorry about that," she blurted.

Chase was about to reply when a fluttering hand caught his attention. "Oh, there they are now. We're going out for a meal, I popped in here for a quick drink first," Chase told them. Sally held her breath. It was the perfect opportunity for Chase to ask her out for dinner.

"Well, better go," Chase said. "Nice bumping into you, Sally, and meeting you Trent, and Kat. Take care, and go easy on that photocopier, Sal."

"Bye," she said sighing wistfully. Sal watched as Chase wandered over to the far end of the room and joined an elderly couple who were talking to a gangly woman dressed in a breezy red floral dress.

"What are you doing to the photocopier?" Trent asked, eyebrows raised. "Sitting on it?"

Sal flashed him a warning look.

Incredulous, Trent spluttered, "That's your photocopier man? He looks like a complete womble. The Ironman I can understand, but this doorknob? I mean, really? Where's the attraction?"

Sal whacked his arm, spilling his ginger ale. "Sssh, he might hear you."

Annoyed, he flicked the drips off his fingers. "Only if he's got bat hearing," Trent replied. He found a napkin and wiped his hands. He swivelled around to take another look. "Come to think of it, his ears are a little pointy."

Sal hit him again.

"Oww!" he complained. "That's abuse. And do I have to remind you I'm your commanding officer and I can make you pay for that on Monday."

Ignoring his threat, Sal said, "Chase is really nice, he's got lovely kind blue eyes, and he's big and morish." She wanted to add and he's got a really nice bum but she didn't want Trent to think she was a pervert.

Sal watched the Downy family leave. She turned to Trent. "Ok, Mr Big Shot, what spins your wheels?"

He smiled. "A brain."

Sally rolled her eyes. "Oh please, come on, don't tell me you're into intellect."

He grinned naughtily and cupping his chest said, "Well, I like personalities too."

"Men!" Sal exclaimed in exasperation.

"Ok, expert, so if I liked someone should I tell her?"

"You're asking me for relationship advice?" She shook her head in disbelief. "I'm the girl that ends things before they begin, remember? I'm the one who keeps a box of exs in my garage."

He laughed. "Yeah, you may be crazy but you are still a woman, so come on, enlighten me."

Sally flipped a hand. "Every woman wants to feel special. She wants to feel like she's the most important person in her man's world."

He stroked his moustache. "Are you sure?"

Kat, who had been silent up until now, agreed, chipping in. "Yeah, pretty much."

"Really?" Trent said. "Who knew it could be so simple?"

"Why, because men are simple and want a good-looking, thin young chick with big boobs and a nice arse?" Kat said.

Trent laughed. "Yeah, but you forgot great in the kitchen and even better in the bedroom. But to be fair I think you pretty much nailed it."

He frowned disbelievingly at Sal. "Are you sure that's all women want? It seems too easy. I've heard they're complicated."

Sal was adamant. "I'm telling you, most women just want to feel loved, and, that they are the most special person in their man's world."

"It's true," Kat agreed. "Most women will put up with anything if they feel loved. But not violence though, that's not ok."

Curious, he asked, "So what happened in your past, Sal? Who didn't treat you right?"

Sal squirmed. This conversation was becoming too personal. She turned the tables. "Why are you single?"

He rubbed his chin. "Haven't found the right one, I guess. There was someone once but well you know…" he broke off. A shadow crossed his face. As if chasing the bad memory away he shook his head and raised his glass in salute. "It's nice to know we are friends as well as neighbours."

"Well, I had to say that. I didn't want him to think we were together, did I?" Sal replied. Why was she justifying herself again?

He put down his glass and looked at her like he thought she had spaghetti for brains. "Ok, I don't get it."

She frowned at him. Why was he always contradicting her and what didn't he get? "What? What don't you get?" She was growing frustrated.

"The attraction! What can you possibly find attractive about a middle-aged man who hangs out with his parents? Don't you find that kind of … pathetic?"

"No, actually, I find it rather…" she fished for the right word, "endearing." Sal could feel her heckles rising. "And he's not middle-aged, he just has grey hair."

Trent snorted. "I bet he hasn't even left home yet. He looks like the type."

She was about to give him a piece of her mind when the others arrived. Turned out it was Pete's birthday but no one had remembered or acknowledged it, until Pete had drearily admitted, "it's my birthday today," with as much enthusiasm as a wet mop.

It was Ethan who suggested they head over to The Whole Hog for a bit of a sit-down meal to celebrate. The place was a meat lovers paradise. Hardly a vegetarian dish in sight. It didn't just serve pork; it served a variety of meat, but every portion was hog-sized large.

Trent barely spoke to Sal throughout dinner. Ethan and Trent chatted about sport, fishing, and skiing, and not knowing much about any of those topics, Sally couldn't contribute anything to the conversation. Something must have happened between Kat and Rob because Kat was in a right mood. Her face was as dark as a brewing thunderstorm, and she got darker throughout the evening.

The service was slow, when the waitress finally arrived Sal ordered the chicken parmigiana.

"Ok" Sal whispered to Kat, "What's going on with you and Rob? You have barely said two words."

"Mm, where do I start?" Kat folded her arms tightly across her chest. "He's turning into a right workaholic. He can't hang out with me tomorrow as he's got to work on the 'big project' again." She emphasised the word 'project,' with her hands.

Careful what you say, Sal reminded herself. Keep your mouth shut, and listen. She'd been caught out before when her friends had bagged their boyfriend to her and she'd agreed they were total dropkicks only to have them get back together a day or so later. Sal zoned out and let her mind wander while Kat raved on.

"Trent thinks he's gay."

Sal refocused, "Who's gay? Is Trent gay?" Sal asked, surprised.

"No silly, Trent thinks Chase is gay. He says any guy that could see you were that mad keen on him, would have asked you out."

Infuriated, Sal said, "He's just shy, and Alice, bloody Alice, scared him off."

"You know I love you and I mean this in the nicest possible way," she paused, "but I just don't think he's that into you."

"I'm telling you he seriously flirted with me. He's just scared, that's all. Because of what Alice said he thinks I'm the kind of chick that may wrestle him to the ground and force a wedding ring on his finger."

Kat lifted a sardonic brow. "And aren't you? Oh yeah, that's right. If you don't want to marry them then they end up in a box

141

in the garage."

The waitress placed Sal's main in front of her, and carefully backed away.

"Great, now the waitress thinks I'm a serial killer," Sal hissed stabbing at her chicken.

Three quarters of an hour had passed and they still hadn't been offered the dessert menu when Sal began to feel light-headed. She was sure it wasn't the bubbly; she had only had had two glasses. By the time the girls went to the bathroom to fix their makeup, nausea started rolling over Sal in thick waves. She got down on her hands and knees and hugged the toilet bowl thinking that maybe if she threw up, she'd feel better. But nothing happened.

When Sal emerged from the cubicle, Kat was busy checking herself in the mirror and didn't notice Sal turning various shades of green. Sally didn't tell Kat she was feeling ill. After all, it was Pete's birthday, and she didn't want to ruin his night. As the girls made their way back through the crowded lobby and into the busy restaurant, Sal suddenly felt like she couldn't breathe. She ducked outside for some fresh air. Minutes later Kat found Sal slumped against the wall looking grey and deathly pale.

"What's wrong?" Kat cried as Sal slowly slid down the wall and sat on the footpath. Sal was having trouble focusing as all the colours merged into one, like some crazy Austin Powers movie, psychedelic patterns spinning before her eyes.

Kat crouched beside her. "Are you ill?" She peered worriedly at Sal's pasty face.

"I feel sick," Sal moaned, clutching her cramping stomach.

"Stay there, I'll be right back," Kat promised as she disappeared into a heaving sea of people.

But Sal couldn't wait. She lurched forward, staggered past the bouncers, and threw up in the garden. Feeling immediately better, Sal promised herself that she would never, ever, ever order chicken at a restaurant again. A pair of dark trousers appeared to her right.

"Sorry," she mumbled to the trousers as she wiped her mouth with the back of her hand.

Unamused, the bouncer said, "Lady, I think you've had enough, it's time you got a ride home." Built like a brick shithouse, the man didn't budge but loomed over her, looking down at her with condescending eyes.

"I've either got a tummy bug or food poisoning," she said pathetically, remembering the latest gastro outbreak at the rest home. Maybe it wasn't The Whole Hog's fault.

Arms folded across his heavily muscled chest like he'd heard it all before, he said, "Have you got someone who can drive you home? You going to order an uber, or do you want me to call you a cab?"

"You don't understand, I've got to get back inside. It's a friend's birthday."

Trent appeared. "Come on, Smurfette," he said placing a hand under Sal's armpit and hauling her to her feet." Let's get you home."

"But," she started. "What about Pete's…?"

He held up his hand. "No, not another word."

"Your Missus will feel better when she's slept it off," the bouncer told Trent, a hint of sympathy in his deep rumbling voice.

"Kat can take me home," Sal protested.

"She came with Rob remember, and they aren't ready to go home."

She definitely didn't want Rob to take her home.

"But I only had a couple of drinks and the chicken," she wailed.

He gave her a look. "Have you eaten anything else today?"

"No, not really," Sal admitted. "Wait, I had a chocolate bar."

"How old are you? Five? You should know better. No food and alcohol are a lethal combination."

Anxious that he didn't think the worst of her, she said, "The chicken must have been off, or not cooked enough, or it could be a gastro bug. There's been a bug doing the rounds at the rest home." She could hear herself babbling.

Opening the ute door, Trent gave Sal a little shove so she landed in the passenger seat. Then he tucked her legs in and put her seatbelt on. Now she really did feel like she was five. Humiliated, Sal hunkered down, slouching like a sack of spuds. Trent started the engine, driving in silence for a few minutes.

"But I feel ok now, honestly," Sal argued. She checked her reflection in the sun visor mirror. She looked as pale as white linen.

"Wait! I haven't got my handbag and I haven't paid for my meal." She grasped the door handle but he locked it from his side.

"Don't worry, I'll message Kat, she'll bring it home and I'm sure someone will cover your meal. Just don't puke in my ute." He sounded like a grumpy old schoolteacher.

"And no," he told her. "I'm not going to put the lights and siren on to get you home any quicker."

Sal cast a glance in the rear vision mirror. Was that Gone Don following in his distinctive Holden? The damn laughing gnome was everywhere. Trent swerved to miss a pothole. Sal clapped her hand across her mouth to muffle a scream. She might not feel well but his driving wasn't helping any.

"Warn me if you are going to puke and I'll stop," he said tightly.

"No, I'm fine, really," she muttered, picking at an invisible thread on her jeans. She wanted to say, your driving is scaring the shit out of me, do you drive a fire truck like that? But she didn't dare, in case he dropped her at the side of the road and told her to walk. The silence was so loud she could hear herself breathing.

Sal groaned. "I feel like dying."

"Could be arranged," he muttered darkly.

She thought he blamed her for ruining his night.

They completed the rest of the journey in silence. Trent pulled into the driveway and parked his ute outside his place. He came round and opened the car door for her.

"I can walk," she assured him, waving away his hand.

She bumped into the gate, bruising her leg, and fiddled with the latch. The gate was stuck. Stupid thing, must be a dropped hinge or something. She tried forcing it but it wouldn't budge. Trent sighed, lifted it and pushed it open.

"Thanks, Superman," Sal murmured begrudgingly.

"You should ask the landlord to fix that for you girls."

As they neared the front door, they realised Sal didn't have her keys. They were in her handbag which was back at the bar.

"Now what, Einstein? We will have to go back and get my handbag."

"Do you keep a spare key anywhere?" His eyes flicked to the pot plants by the front door.

Sal sighed in despair. "Nope, Kat's all about safety first. I told you I should have got my handbag." Sal burped. Horrified, she held her tummy in case her insides evacuated.

"Plan B. You'll have to stay at my place until Kat comes home." They walked across the courtyard. He unlocked his front door and flicked the lights on.

Kat would be so jealous. She was dying to see the inside of Mrs Robinson's old townhouse. Mrs Robinson always popped over to theirs with fresh baking but they'd never so much as put a toe in her front door. The inside was dated. This place was so stuck in the seventies it was like the Brady Bunch were still living there. The olive leaf patterned wallpaper, the brown lino and dark cabinetry, made the place feel small and dark.

Trent asked, "Are you ok? Do you need anything?"

Sal took off her shoes and wriggled her toes, relieved her feet could finally breathe.

"No, I'm fine," she assured him, but she felt as limp as boiled spaghetti. "I'll just crash on the couch. You get back to the others, I don't need babysitting and they'll be missing you." Dumping her shoes, and denim jacket on the floor, she fell back like she fainted onto the soft couch.

Reluctant to leave, Trent hovered in the doorway. "Are you sure you'll be ok?"

"Of course," Sal flapped a hand. "You'd better get back to the restaurant, they'll be missing you."

"No, I don't want to leave you until I know you are going to be alright." He got a bucket and placed it beside her, then went and got a pillow and blanket off his bed. "This feels a bit like déjàvu."

Sal lifted her head and tucked the pillow beneath. Trent spread the blanket over her.

"I'll live." However, she wasn't really sure she would. Sally peeped at him through her laced fingers. He hadn't budged an inch. Oh, for a moment to daydream about Chase without interruption. Trent seemed to have a hate on Chase and she didn't know why; Chase was a lovely guy. She wished Trent would stop teasing her. He always made her feel like such a flake.

"No more lectures, ok? I feel bad enough as it is." Sally stared at the peeling paint on the ceiling. "I know you don't believe this but I'm not a big drinker."

He raised a sceptical eyebrow. "Whatever!" he snorted. "Pretty much every time I've seen you you've been hammered."

"It's just been a set of unfortunate circumstances; no wait, series." Sally exclaimed, "You didn't get to finish your dinner and it's Pete's birthday. The service was super slow but if you hurry you might get dessert. Go on, I'm fine, really, I am."

"It's alright, there's ice cream in the fridge," he said taking a seat.

"But what if there's a fire call?"

"I have my pager."

Trent rubbed the arms of the chair and studied Sal. There was a bit more colour in her sallow cheeks, but she still didn't look at all well.

She opened one eye. "What are you still doing here?"

"Looking after you. It seems someone's got to as you are not very good at taking care of yourself. Besides, I want to make sure you don't damage any of our furniture."

"Looks pretty old and cruddy," Sal said.

"That's a new couch," he told her.

Damn, her filter wasn't working. That's the trouble with having a couple of drinks – no filter. Sal closed her eyes and felt herself succumbing to the lure of sleep.

Trent covertly watched her. He found the rhythmic rise and fall of her chest mesmerising. She was the strangest, craziest woman he'd ever met. She sparkled. Instead of smelling like someone who had thrown up, she smelt like green apple shampoo. To complicate matters further, she wasn't the slightest bit interested in him, but was infatuated by an oversized womble who hadn't detached from his parents. Trent couldn't for the life of him figure out what Sally saw in that loser? There were absolutely no redeeming features as far as he could see. The guy was a big boof-head with the personality of a telephone pole. Go figure – it had him beat.

Like a cat, she stretched and settled, curling in on herself again. What was it about her that intrigued him? She drove him nuts. She continually needed rescuing. She said and did dumb blonde things. Kat had warned him Sally had terrible taste in men but now he'd seen it first-hand. Fancy falling for that Mummy's boy!

Ethan may have been putting on a brave face after his separation but he genuinely seemed to be enjoying his newfound freedom. Pete, on the other hand, was miserable. Anton was happily single, and more into his health, conspiracy theories, and cycling, than girls. Rob and Kat had had words tonight which made him grateful he was single. Man, Trent thought, it was easier and a whole lot less stressful to remain single. It was no wonder he'd not got involved in more than two serious relationships; they were too much like hard work. And, Sonia, the last one, she'd been a real heartbreaker. He had loved her with his whole heart and she smashed it into a million pieces when she cheated on him with Jude who was supposed to be a mate.

Damn it, he had to save Sal from herself. If she went out with that idiot, she'd be stuffing things up and he couldn't let that happen. She'd be ok, she just needed to sleep it off. He'd head back and join the others, but he would just sit here for a few minutes to make sure she was alright.

Trent heard the key in the lock and the front door open. Instantly awake, he rubbed at the crick in his neck and saw Sal was still asleep on the couch. Anton tiptoed past.

"I think she's in a coma but at least she doesn't snore like you do," Trent told Anton. "Is Kat home? Sal didn't have her key to get in."

"Yeah, Rob and Kat had a bit of a barney at the restaurant, but seemed to have patched things up by the end of the night. They had had too much to drink to drive so I dropped them off. Damn," Anton smacked his forehead. "I left Sal's handbag in the car. I'll be back in a tick." He returned shortly and carefully placed Sal's bag down by the couch.

"What do I owe you for dinner, mate?" Trent asked.

"Nothing – Pete paid. He shouted all of us. He said he might as well spend it before Mindy took it all." Anton frowned at Sal's sleeping form. "Shall we wake her, or just leave her be?"

"Leave Sleeping Beauty be." Trent turned off the lights and went to bed.

Chapter 19: Falling

It was daylight when Sally rolled off the couch. Dazed, she shook her head and tried to figure out where she was. She was on the floor of Trent's apartment. She still felt a little seedy, but much better. The events of yesterday came back in a horrible rush. Holy moly! She had managed to embarrass herself yet again. Why was it, whenever she was around Trent she acted like a complete moron? Sal folded up the blanket, gathered her bag, jacket, and shoes, and crept to the front door. Hoping not to wake anyone, she fiddled with the lock, turned the handle quietly, and carefully closed the door behind her.

At home, all was quiet. She went straight to the shower to freshen up. Apart from being embarrassed, she felt loads better. It must have been a twenty-four-hour gastro bug. After she dressed, she headed to the kitchen to make a coffee. She hadn't heard them come in, but there they were, large as life, seated at the table, eating McD's for breakfast. They must have kissed and made up. Bugger! Just when she was looking forward to having the couch and the TV remote back. Lucky, she didn't bare her soul and tell Kat what she really thought of Rob.

"Morning sunshine, how are we feeling this morning?" Rob goaded. "We popped out to get breakfast and then boom you appear."

"We would have got you breakfast if we'd known you were home," Kat apologised.

Sal flicked the jug on. "Don't mind me, I just need a coffee."

"Was it a good night?" Rob wanted to know.

"Fine," Sally replied coolly.

"You feeling better, hon?" Kat asked, genuinely concerned.

"Thought I may have had food poisoning but it was probably just a gastro bug. It's doing the rounds at work," Sal said.

"Sure, a gastro bug, sure." Rob gave Kat an exaggerated wink.

Sal wanted to throttle him.

"Did you guys enjoy yourselves?" Sal eyed Kat wondering how she would answer, if she would mention their fight.

"Not as much as you did," interjected Rob.

Sal stared at her coffee and wished Rob far, far, away.

When Rob left, Kat told her they hadn't been happy with their meals either; she reckoned their food was average and cold. Ethan didn't mind as he was busy chatting up the barmaid, but Pete had an absolute meltdown over the service being so slow. "Still," she added, "it was nice of him to pay for all of us."

"So, what happened after I left that Rob's back in your good books?" Sal asked, confused.

"He apologised for being a dick, promising he'd spend more time with me, and then we had great make-up sex."

Sal covered her ears. "Too much information."

After getting Pete's number from Kat, Sal sent Pete a text message, apologising for bunking early and telling him she'd caught a tummy bug, and thanked him for paying for her meal. Then, she sent a 'Thank you for looking after me last night' text to Trent.

He replied, 'See you at training, you are on extra drills.'

She thought, he's still mad and going to make me pay.

Sal sat on her bed, opened the box and picked up the photo of David. Her first love. She couldn't believe it when he cheated on her. She had thought they would be together forever. The memory of lost love made her sad, and she put the photo away. Then she saw a photo of Gone Don. He was wearing a slick black suit, white shirt and tie, and his shoes were highly polished, shining like mirrors. He was smiling. She willed herself to hold onto the photo and analyse it further. She vividly remembered the evening out. They had gone to a stage show in Melbourne – 'Mama Mia.' The show had been fantastic and she felt very spoiled. All well and good, she told herself, that's how she felt about the event but how did she feel about Don? Numb really, and irritated that he didn't believe she meant it when she said, it was over.

She dropped the photo as if it burned her fingertips and shut the lid. Perhaps she should hide the box back in the garage where it wouldn't constantly remind her of her past failures. She'd wait until Kat was out then sneak it back to the garage so no questions would be asked. For now, it could be tucked safely back under the bed. Sal hid it away, and then went to the window to see what was going on outside.

Sal peered out her upstairs bedroom window to see if the fire service ute was still parked in the drive. It wasn't.

Sal checked herself in the dresser mirror and thought her face looked a little less chubby. She ran her hand under her chin and down her throat. Although the tummy bug had helped her lose a couple of kilos around the middle, she knew it wouldn't stay off for long. She was still going to her DanceFix classes and finally starting to be able to complete a class without feeling like she was going to die of cardiac arrest. A bit of extra exercise might be beneficial and help her lose some of the blubber, so Sal decided to volunteer to take Mrs Mac's dogs for a walk. She went over to Mrs Mac's and told her she'd take her little darlings for a walk tomorrow when she got home from work. Mrs Mac seemed surprised by the offer, but accepted it with a 'as you like' kind of shrug.

Penny was a miniature schnauzer and looked like a cross between a grumpy old man with her bushy eyebrows and whiskers and an Ewok. Penny acted like a superior being, and would have been happy to stay on the couch indefinitely. Whereas Bonny was a cross between a papillon and a Yorkshire terrier. She had Dumbo-sized ears, a long body and bounced along like her paws had springs. Bonny thought she was a husky, tugging on the lead like they were sledding across the Arctic Circle, while Penny was like the pokey little puppy who had to stop at every lamp post and blade of grass to have a sniff.

Sal thought she must look like a mad dog lady, as one arm was jerked one way with Bonny bounding ahead and the other stretched in the opposite direction with Penny lagging behind. When they met other dogs, Penny changed from aloof princess to thinking she was part Alsatian and would bark and growl at dogs two or three times her size. Meanwhile, the energiser bunny Bonny, bounced excitedly around them like a happy rabbit. Amused, Sal thought they were quite sweet dogs really, and she enjoyed their company.

She walked them down to the reserve then back up the hill when the clouds began to gather with the sky looking menacing. It had been fine when Sal left home, so she hadn't thought to bring a jacket. As she turned the last corner, the wind picked up and it started to rain. First a few spots, then the heavens opened and it bucketed down. Tugging Penny along, Sal started to run. She turned into the shared common area and was almost home when she stepped into a pot hole in the courtyard, and fell on her hands and knees, grazing them. She yelped, and dropped both leads. Instead of the dogs taking off, worried, they turned back to see what had happened, and licked her face to make her feel better.

Sal managed to grab the leads, but when she went to stand up, she realised she had not only grazed her hands and knees, but she had turned her ankle as well. To top it off, she was kneeling in a puddle. She felt like howling.

Trent was in the kitchen buttering a piece of toast when he happened to glance out the window and he saw Sally fall. He saw her try to get up and fall back on her hands and knees. He quickly donned his jacket and ran across the courtyard.

Sal was saturated. Her wet hair stuck to her face. She looked a sorry sight. The dogs barked as he approached.

"Are you ok?" he called out as he ran towards her.

She sniffed. "No."

Puzzled, Trent asked, "What happened?"

"Stepped in a hole," she said, trying to keep the tears at bay. "I think I've turned my ankle."

Bonny and Penny barked louder as Trent came closer. He knelt and let them sniff him.

The rain was relentless. Sal felt lower than the puddle she had landed in. "Can you help me by taking these two back to Mrs

Mac?"

Trent put the dog's leads on his wrist, bent down, and told her to lean on him.

"Owww!" Sal cried as she put weight on her bad ankle.

Grimacing, she hobbled along with his arm about her waist. Her grazed knees and her hands stung, she was soaked, but grateful for his help.

She was still leaning against him when Trent knocked on Mrs Mac's door. Mrs Mac opened the door to find Trent and Sal and her very wet dogs on the doorstep. Mrs Mac shooed her dogs inside telling them to wipe their muddy paws on the mat before they took their places on the couch. Sal apologised saying she probably wouldn't be up to walking the dogs for a few weeks as she'd damaged her ankle. Mrs Mac thanked Trent and Sal for bringing them home and closed the door abruptly to stop the rain getting in. Sal had expected more appreciation for her good deed. Mrs Mac could be a cranky old biddy at times.

"I'm taking you up to the medical centre to get that ankle checked," Trent told her. Sal squealed as he hefted her over his shoulder in the fireman's lift, and carried her across the courtyard. Opening his ute door, he put her in the passenger seat, hopped in the other side then started the engine.

Sal was intrigued by his radio beeping and blipping constantly as calls came in as they drove to Shore Care, but the throbbing pain in her ankle distracted her from asking what everything on the dashboard did. Her ankle hurt badly. Sal was certain her foot would swell to the size of a watermelon when her shoe came off.

As they neared the Northcross intersection, Sal suddenly ducked down.

Trent threw her a sideways glance. "What are you doing?"

She had seen Gone Don's car approaching in the adjacent lane and ducked by reflex.

"Sudden pain," Sal said rubbing her ankle.

Sal breathed a sigh of relief when Gone Don drove through the traffic lights and turned the corner. Trent indicated, and they pulled into the Shore Care carpark. They found the waiting room crammed with people. The receptionist told them to take a seat. As expected, they were in for a long wait. Trent went to the toilet, and while he was gone a guy who had a bandage wrapped around his head like a turban, came over and introduced himself.

"Hi, my name is Jay," he told her, easing himself in beside her.

"Hello, Jay," Sal replied, shifting further down. Jay continued to stare. He was creeping her out.

"I think if you like someone you should just come right out and say so, don't you?" Jay said.

Typical head injury. No filter. "Umm." Uncomfortable, Sal moved further away. Ouch, she winced as her damn foot hurt. Trent returned and sat between them. Sal was happy to use him as a human shield.

The nurse called, "Jay West?"

Jay rose, and obediently followed the nurse into another room.

"Poor guy," Sal murmured. She told Trent what Jay had said. "Can't blame him for inappropriate behaviour. He's got a head injury."

Trent snorted. "Might have nothing to do with that and more to do with that low-cut wet t-shirt you're wearing."

Shocked, Sal glanced down to see her t-shirt was low and practically see through. She yanked her t-shirt higher in an attempt to cover her cleavage.

More people arrived and filled the waiting room. Bored, Trent flicked through fishing magazines while Sal picked up the Women's Weekly. She noticed an advert for the life insurance company, Sovereign Assurance. Sal told Trent about the insurance broker and the gazillion questions that she had answered as part of the medical questionnaire, casually dropping in, that Andrew had said, he was surprised she was single.

"What a slimy mackerel," grunted Trent. "Fancy hitting on customers just to get business."

Sal declared, "No, he wasn't. He was just doing his job."

"Do you have to defend everybody?" he asked.

She felt very defensive lately and didn't know why.

"No, but do you have to hate on everybody?" she retaliated.

"Why do you say that? I don't have a hate on everybody, just jerks."

"You put people down." Sal argued. "You put me down."

"No, I don't," he disagreed.

There was a pointed silence.

"Not Gone Don, I'm not defensive of him."

Trent glanced sideways. "Who's Gone Don when he's at home?"

"An ex who won't leave me alone." Why did she bring up Gone Don? Now Trent had more ammunition to tease her with.

"Should be called Not Gone Don then, don't you think?" Trent said.

Their conversation was interrupted when they were sent to x-ray, and then to see the doctor.

"Just strained," The doctor said cheerfully. "I could give you crutches, but it's probably easier if you hop around on your heel until you can bear weight."

"That's good, but means you won't be able to come to training tonight and probably not for a few weeks until your ankle is better," said Trent.

Every cloud has a silver lining. Unfortunately, it meant no DanceFix either. Still, she would have a valid reason for a rest. "That's a shame, I was just getting into it," she lied.

"On the up side, it will stop you from doing runners."

Ignoring him, Sal whipped her phone out of her back pocket and paid the bill.

"Don't trouble yourself, I'll hop to the car," she said before he could throw her over his shoulder.

It had stopped raining. She felt like a drowned hedgehog. Her hair was still plastered to her face, and her jeans were dirty where she'd fallen, and now she felt exposed like she was in some sort of wet t-shirt competition. She couldn't wait to get home and have a hot shower and get changed.

Kat wasn't home when they returned. She had texted Sal earlier in the day to say she was going to the movies with Rob. Trent followed Sal inside and told her to go ahead and have a shower, he'd make her a hot drink and leave it for her. "What would you like? Cup of tea?"

"Yes, please, tea, please, just milk."

She went straight to the shower, got warm, then quickly dried off, and dressed in some fresh clothes. Trent had left her tea cooling on the coffee table, a packet of painkillers and a glass of water lay beside it, along with a note saying, "Hope you're ok. Finishing cooking dinner. Hop over if you are hungry. T."

She flicked him a text. "Thanks, but no thanks, going to call it a night and go to bed early." Sal negotiated the stairs as best she could then hobbled to her bed and lay on top of her quilt. She hugged her teddy bear tight feeling genuinely sorry for herself. The box of exs was still under the bed. The ghosts of the past were haunting her. Courage, she told herself, as she leaned over the side and pulled it up and onto the bed. Sal opened it, and lifting all the photos out, she pulled up the lining and took out the memories hidden there.

Showing double lines, was the positive test, she felt the tears prick her eyes and swallowed the lump in her throat. She wished things were different, but Hemi had deserted her, and, being a teenager who could barely look after herself, the decision to terminate had been the worst, most horrible decision she had ever made. She wondered if one day she would ever get her happily ever after, or have children. What if her biological clock had stopped? She tucked the painful memory back under the lining and sighed, full of regret.

Her phone beeped. Trent sent her a message. *Hope you ok. Meant it about dinner. Anton's out and I've made too much. Help! T.*

Sal thought for a minute before replying. Her stomach growled. She'd checked the fridge this morning – empty! They weren't due to do the shopping until tomorrow either. She messaged, *Thanks for rescuing me, Superman. On 2nd thought, can*

I change my mind and come over.

Phone beeped. *Sure. See you soon.*

Then again, *Do you need a lift?*

Sal texted, *Ha ha. Very funny.*

Searching the far recesses of the pantry Sal found a bottle of red. Probably cooking wine, but it was better than going empty-handed. Thinking this was probably going to be a mistake, Sal timidly tapped on Trent's front door. He opened the door and grinned. He'd changed out of his uniform and was wearing a dark blue hoodie and blue jeans. Still damp from the rain, his hair smelt like soap; perhaps he'd showered.

"Peace-offering," Sal said, presenting him with the wine.

"Thanks," he said, graciously accepting the bottle.

"Sorry, didn't have any light beer or ginger beer at ours. It's kind of a soft drink free zone at our house."

He grinned. "All good, I'm not on duty. Thankfully I've got the next four days off. You are just in time for spaghetti Bolognese."

"Smells great." The rich aroma of spaghetti sauce filled the room.

"How's it feel? Does it hurt bad?"

"Yeah, when I put weight on it, but my grazed hands and knees really hurt."

His mouth turned up at the corners. "Nothing worse. Take a seat and put your foot up."

Sal glanced around, chose the closest kitchen stool and tried to hoist herself up on it without causing more pain. "Where's Anton?" she asked, resting her foot on the bottom rung of the neighbouring stool.

Trent had his back to her as he rummaged in the cupboard for a glass. He poured the wine with a practised hand. "Working late. There's some big lighting expo in the city." He handed her a large goblet generously filled with wine. "Where's Kat?

"She went to the movies with Rob. Can't remember what they went to see. They seem a bit up and down at the moment," she casually remarked while watching him stir the spaghetti sauce.

He shrugged. "Yeah, makes you glad you are single, right?"

Sal bit her tongue. She wasn't going to let him tease her about her dating disasters.

They chatted over dinner, and for once Trent didn't upset her. Sal attempted to gather the plates and offered to help with the dishes. Waving away her good intentions, he told her to make herself comfy in the lounge while he tidied up and popped the dishes in the dishwasher.

Feeling slightly awkward Sal waited for him. She couldn't help thinking it wasn't long ago that she fell asleep on this same couch. She vividly remembered the humiliation of that night, and insulting his taste in furniture.

"Want to watch a movie?" Trent asked, wiping his hands on the back of his blue jeans.

"Ok, but aren't you tired?"

"Yep, that's why we'll have to watch something that's action packed so I will stay awake."

Trent flicked through the movie titles. She waited for him to be smartarsed and suggest they watch Runaway Bride, but instead, he found a Marvel movie, called Black Widow.

"I know you like superheroes and you'll like this one, it's real girl power. And," he added with a devious grin, "I like it because it's easy on the eyes."

She laughed. "Bet they have good personalities."

Trent topped up her glass.

"Between the painkillers and this I won't be able to feel my leg soon."

"Medicinal purposes are allowed," he smiled.

"Then why are you drinking?"

"Because I can feel your pain." He clicked the remote. The movie was action-packed, with a few laughs, and a little emotion thrown in for good measure. She enjoyed it.

As the movie ended and the credits rolled, Sal said, "Those widows would never have sat in a puddle and cried."

"No, probably not, but then they are superheroes and you are only Smurfette."

Sal limped to the kitchen and put her glass on the bench.

"Thanks for dinner it was yummy, and the movie was pretty good too."

"You're welcome." He put his glass down and followed her to the door. "Hang on, I'll walk you home in case you find another hole to fall in."

"Thank you, Sir Galahad, but I'm sure I'll be ok."

He walked alongside Sal as she hobbled down his path.

"I could just throw you over the hedge."

Sal pushed the gate open, giving it a good shove. "Stupid thing keeps sticking," she muttered.

"Tell the landlord to fix it." Trent followed her to the door and waited while she found the key. "Take care now, and don't make me rescue you again tonight."

Sal promised she'd be careful.

"And, by the way," he began, his voice growing serious. "Your landlord should be shot. There aren't enough smoke detectors in your house, I'll get some for you."

"Thanks. Night."

"Catch you later," Trent replied, as he walked away.

Sal got ready for bed, thinking apart from her sore foot, tonight had been surprisingly pleasant, not at all what she had expected. She felt like they had reached a truce. Maybe Kat was right, maybe Trent was ok after all. He eventually may even become a good friend.

Chapter 20: Bad Loser

True to his word, Trent came over and put the smoke detectors in; one in the dining area, one in the hall, and one in each bedroom. Kat thought it was overkill. She reckoned every time she put the toaster on, the smoke alarms would go off.

"Better safe than sorry," Trent told her from the top of the ladder.

"Yeah, safety first," Sal agreed, impressed by how quickly he'd scrambled up the ladder.

Kat pointed at Sal's ankle, and repeated, "Yeah, safety first, right Sal?"

Trent organised a card night at his place. Sal was reluctant to join in, but this time nobody was going to let her off the hook. Besides, Trent told her they needed her to make up the numbers. There was Kat and Rob, Pete and Ethan, Trent and Sal. Sal and Kat arrived first. Being nosey, Kat asked Anton to show her around the rest of the house so Sal tagged along for the tour. The bedrooms were decorated in the same loud print as the kitchen. The main bathroom and the ensuite were mustard and brown with an olive-green hand basin, Trent's bedroom was the master while Anton had the smaller room down the end of the hall. Both rooms were decorated with large orange geometric print wallpaper. Mrs Robertson must have liked the seventies era and never moved on from it.

They ordered pizza. Cards were cutthroat. Competitive, Sal always played to win and the others were determined not to let her. They played cards well into the night, accusing each other of cheating. Sal had an absolute shocker. She lost five games straight and the guys teased her mercilessly insisting on a *down trou*. She adamantly refused. Not that she would have dropped her jeans regardless, but that particular night she had on a giant-sized pair of underpants that her grandmother would have been proud of. Come to think of it they probably were the best contraceptive in the olden days. They might look unsightly but they were comfy and practical for that time of the month, when her stomach bloated beyond all reasonable proportions. No one was ever going to see her in her granny pants, ever, not even Kat.

Kat helped Sal get home; her ankle still hurt but it was improving, she just couldn't get anywhere in a hurry. They were all teasing her that the runaway bride was crippled.

As Kat hung up her coat she said, "That place makes ours look like a palace, don't it?"

"It sure does," Sal replied.

"Weren't the bathrooms simply hideous." Kat shook her head. "So dated."

Sal thought if anyone ever saw her giant undies, then they would know what hideous truly was.

"Night," Kat called over her shoulder as she climbed the stairs.

"Night." Sal looked bleakly at the stairs, then crawled up them on her hands and knees.

Kat didn't have time to run around after Sal because she was too preoccupied with Rob. Bored, Sal started hanging out more with the guys next door. Then Anton started spending more time 'at work' and that just left Trent and Sal to hang out together. Since she had sprained her ankle, Trent had been super nice, telling her to let him know if there was anything she needed and he'd get it for her. And he had taken to fixing things around the apartment. He changed the lock on the back door as it was broken. He put up a sensor light that came on as you approached the gate. Her injury must have brought out the rescuer in him.

She reminded herself that David had also been nice when she first met him but he turned into a right hot head. She had to stop being so susceptible and stop trusting people at face value. Time usually showed a person's true character. When he wasn't teasing her about her exs, Sal found Trent pretty good company, it was great having a "no strings" guy mate you could be comfortable around.

Anton sent Kat and Sal a birthday party invite saying they were having a cocktail night at their place on Saturday to celebrate Trent's birthday.

"Bet Trent wears blue," Sal said. "I'll get him something to go with it."

DanceFix was starting to become enjoyable. The other girls were super friendly and no-one expected her to be a graceful ballerina, let alone a rap artist. As long as she moved to the music Lisa was happy. Sal wasn't exhausted at the end of a session now but she definitely knew she had worked out. She was thinking about Chase while singing along to 'Damn, I've fallen in love again.' Why wouldn't he call? She wondered how Andrew the insurance guy was getting on with the policy. She had thought he'd call. Maybe she was losing her pulling power.

Hopefully, a stroll around the mall would help her stretch her aching legs. She knew exactly what to get Trent for his birthday. She was tempted to pop in to see Andrew while she was at the mall, just in case he needed any additional info, although what he didn't already know she couldn't imagine. Turned out, he didn't work Saturdays.

Rob had been invited to come to Trent's party but much to Kat's disgust, he was working late – again. He had gone from spending every waking minute at their place to working late most nights. However, Ethan was in boots and all. And Pete said he'd come for a bit, but he'd not stay for long as he had to work the following morning. Pete was definitely not over his wife ditching him for a chick, and found it hard to get into a party vibe. That, and he was down that his fortune was being eaten away by lawyers' bills and a costly property settlement.

When they arrived at the party, Kat whispered in Sal's ear, "Mrs Mac and the Wrinklies aren't here."

"Probably past their bedtime," Sal replied.

"Nah, I reckon we must be the cool neighbours," Kat gloated.

"The Saffers are here too," Sal noted, glancing out the window into the backyard. "Anton said they offered to work the BBQ."

It was cramped in the small townhouse. Yelling over the loud music, Anton informed them, "Trent wanted to have a party before redecorating. Better to trash the place now rather than later," he said.

The guys had set up a bar on their kitchen benchtop and there was an array of spirits to choose from. Trent and Anton were dressed as waiters in black trousers, white shirts, and black bowties. Sal thought Trent looked very James Bond. It was nice to see him dressed in something other than blue.

Trent leaned against the makeshift bar, cocktail shaker in hand, and looked expectantly at Sal as if anticipating her order.

Handing him the tomato juice she had brought she said, "A Virgin Mary, please.

"Really?" he asked, holding up a bottle of vodka and waving it in front of her nose.

She caved. "Oh alright, make mine a Bloody Mary."

While he was adding the spice, he casually said, "'You look nice tonight."

Surprised by the compliment, she changed the subject. "Happy birthday," Sal said, handing Trent the small soft package. He did the usual, 'you shouldn't have,' before opening it.

Finding a pair of navy-blue superman socks, he laughed.

"You're always rescuing me so I thought this gift was appropriate, and what's more, they are blue so they should go with absolutely everything in your wardrobe."

"Thanks. I'll wear them with pride," he told her. "Might even tuck my trousers in my socks so people can see them."

Kat remembered they had some mint growing in the garden which would be perfect for mojitos and nipped back home to get it. Moments later she returned with a bunch of mint and a cocktail recipe book. Cracking up at some of the outlandish names, Kat flicked through the cocktail book, trying to make up her mind. Ethan cranked up the music in an attempt to get others to dance. Sal's foot still wasn't a hundred percent so she opted for the backyard and joined the huddle around the BBQ. Sal started to mingle. She introduced herself to Suzette, Josie, and Julie, friends of the guys, who had brought their peace-loving hippy friend, Aurora with them. Aurora was a vegetarian; she might be dairy-free and gluten-free, but she certainly wasn't alcohol-free. Sal immediately liked her and thought her interesting in a quirky happy-go-lucky kind of way. Julie was attractive and single, and Sal noticed Ethan making a bee line for her. He asked Julie to dance and she half-heartedly agreed and followed him inside. Josie and Suzette were a couple, and good fun. Sal immediately thought she must introduce Andie to this lot as she was certain they'd get on well.

A little while later Trent came outside with a tray of drinks. He popped them on the table, and lifted his trouser leg to show Sal that he was wearing his new socks. "They suit me, don't you think?"

"Yeah." Sal grinned. "I'll get you the cape next birthday."

Sal drifted inside to see what Kat was up to. She saw Ethan and Kat talking to a gorgeous leggy brunette. The mysterious brunette in the far corner wore faded Levi's and a leather jacket. Leggy was drinking some fancy-looking concoction with a cocktail umbrella and cherry on top. Mrs Saffer arrived at Sal's elbow and steered her to the table insisting Sal try the special milk tart she had made for dessert. Obediently, Sal ate the tart which was pretty good and decided to quiz Kat later to get all the goss on who Leggy was, and how she fitted in.

It was a fabulous party, the vibe was good, the music was great, and if you wanted to you could dance. Ethan was having a lovely time, although Pete had gone home early citing a headache. Sal believed it was because he found out Suzette and Josie were a couple and it brought up negative emotions for him. Anton and Trent were playing host and refilling glasses. Sal enjoyed herself, and it was the first time Trent hadn't had to come to her rescue. She also didn't have to worry about Gone Don popping up and ruining the evening.

When Sal left at midnight, Kat was standing on the kitchen table drinking tequila shots. She reminded herself to ask Kat who that leggy girl was. As Sal lay in bed drifting off to sleep, she thought that the guys moving in next door had been quite a good thing really. Maybe it was the cocktails, but she had the weirdest dreams that night. All her ex's escaped from under the bed and were holding a cocktail party in the lounge and discussing her. They said she had a commitment problem. No Commitment Sally Jelly, they called her. She woke up in a sweat.

"Hey, who was that tall brunette you and Ethan were talking to last night?" Sal asked when Kat stumbled to the breakfast table in the morning.

Kat groaned, and made herself a coffee. "That's Trent's ex. I don't think she'll stay an ex. Look at her – she's stunning, and nice. He'd be mad not to try to get back with her, don't you think?"

"She must be an ex for a reason," countered Sal.

Chapter 21: Surprise Guy

Work was a nightmare. Sal felt like she was being pulled in a million different directions. That particular morning had been more demanding than usual; everyone needed something. The cleaner needed stock, the nurses needed medical supplies, Daisy needed a food order and new menu charts printed, the staff needed new uniforms. The residents wanted bills paid and Sal to check their accounts for them, or show them how to work their phone – again. And then who should walk in – none other than Chase.

Surprised by his sudden appearance, Sal wondered if someone had lodged a service call. She hadn't noticed anything wrong with the photocopier. Was Alice trying to set her up?

"Morning," Chase smiled. "I was in the neighbourhood and I wondered if you had time for a coffee?"

She swallowed and tried to play it cool. "Here or ...?"

"Um...," he glanced nervously about like he expected Alice to pounce.

Fortunately, due to staff shortages, Alice was busy helping out in the secure wing.

"How about a café?"

Flustered, in a breathy rush, Sal said, "I'll just see if someone can cover."

Vikki yelled from her office, "I'll cover. Go!"

Wow. Wow. Wow! She couldn't wait to tell Trent and Kat they were wrong.

"Where shall we go?" She asked, grabbing her handbag.

"Your choice."

How chivalrous.

"Somewhere close would be good." God, she was such a control freak. Surely, work could manage for an hour without her. She was acutely aware of his presence as they went out the back way into the main street and crossed the road.

As it was the closest café, Sal chose White Flower. Chase was so tall she felt like a hobbit standing next to him. After asking what she'd like, he ordered the coffees and two large pieces of chocolate cake. She didn't want to ruin the moment by telling him she was supposed to be on a diet. They settled themselves at a table and waited for their coffee and cake to arrive.

Sal glanced out the window and happened to see a familiar Holden on the other side of the street. Crap, it was Gone Don! She could hardly hide under the table so she strategically placed the menu against the window to block his view. Luckily Don didn't see her and drove off none the wiser.

Sal breathed a sigh of relief, put the menu down and gazed into Chase's mesmerising blue eyes. "So, tell me a little about yourself. I only know that you can fix photocopiers."

A smile teased the corners of his mouth. "And I know that you are really good at jamming them," he returned.

The waitress brought their order to the table. They thanked her and she disappeared again.

Chase slowly stirred his coffee. "Tell me about your family. Do they live local?"

"My sister does, but my Mum, and my brother, live down in the deep south."

"Let me guess, they hate Aucklanders and want to cut the cable and all that sort of carry on?"

"Yes, well, a little," Sal admitted. Her voice softened as Sal told him, "Sadly, my dad passed away a few years ago."

A shadow clouded his handsome face. "I'm sorry." He looked as if he didn't know what to say.

Sal picked up the conversation. "Mum's in a new relationship. It's sweet, and it's more than companionship." Remembering the debacle in the music shop she stopped before she said too much.

"It's nice that love doesn't have age limits," Chase said.

There was a bit of chocolate icing on his lip and she longed to reach across and wipe it away with her finger and kiss him very softly on the mouth.

"Tell me about your family." She picked up the last bit of cake, relishing every delicious mouthful.

"There's only my immediate family here in New Zealand," he told her. "We came out from England ten years ago. The rest of our relatives are back in the old country so we are a pretty tight unit."

"That's nice."

Chase asked, "Do you like working in a rest home?"

She nodded. "Yeah, it's a bit hectic at times but I love it."

"Rest homes freak me out," he admitted. "They are full of people waiting to die."

Sal swallowed her coffee. "It's busy, a little crazy and challenging at times, but I love working with the staff, and the residents."

A frown wrinkled his forehead. "But you must hate it when one of the oldies passes away."

"Yeah, that's hard," she shrugged. "But we do our best to make their last years' happy ones. We all want to live our best lives."

Sal wished she could ask him all the questions on the insurance questionnaire but that would be a bit too intimate, and as she didn't have much time to glean the info she needed. She rushed in a few important questions and managed to find out, that no, he'd never been married, and no, he didn't have any kids, and that he had recently holidayed in the UK before returning to New Zealand for good.

As their empty plates and coffee cups were taken away, Sal mentioned she needed to get back to work.

Chase glanced at his watch. "Yes, we can't have your crazy boss going off, can we? She's scary."

"You're right there," Sal agreed feeling vindicated. She had been right all along. Alice had scared him. Her chair scraped noisily as she rose and thanked him for the coffee and cake.

"My pleasure," he beamed. Damn he was cute!

As they wandered back to the rest home, Chase asked, "Do you fancy going for a walk at the beach this weekend?" Adding, "We could get ice cream."

Sal nodded. "Sounds perfect." Bugger the diet. She was never going to lose that stubborn cuddly tyre round her middle anyway.

He grinned. "Great."

Back at the office, Chase asked for her mobile number, and promised to call her on the weekend. There was no quick peck on the cheek, just a slightly awkward, see you, and then he was gone.

Back at her desk, Sally resisted the urge to shriek with delight. Trent was wrong. Kat was wrong. They were all wrong. Chase did fancy her and whoop whoop they were going on a date!

For the rest of the day Sally was obsessed with her phone. She entered the timesheets, ordered the groceries for the kitchen, checked her mobile, entered the daily stats, checked her mobile, had morning tea, checked her mobile while reconciling the bank statements, checked her mobile, and sent the statements out. To stop herself from checking again, she threw her mobile in the top drawer in disgust and closed it.

She couldn't wait to get home to tell Kat and Trent the news. And as luck would have it, Trent was driving out as she drove in. She pulled up alongside him and leaned out the window. "Hey."

Trent let down his window. "Hey, what's up?"

Unable to contain her excitement a second longer, she blurted, "I've got a date! Chase and I are going for a beach walk on the weekend and we're going to get ice-cream."

He looked shocked, then muttered, "He's cheap."

"No, he's not," Sal declared. "That's romantic."

He looked sceptical. "What's changed? Why is he suddenly interested?"

It was hardly a discussion to have between vehicles, and what was his problem? Why did he have to go and burst her bubble?

"Had to work up the courage to get past Alice, I guess."

"You are unbelievable," Trent said, shaking his head. He closed his window and drove off.

Fuming, Sal went inside, closed the door with a bang and

dumped her bag on the kitchen table.

Kat had suddenly turned into a domestic goddess and had been baking, she slid the muffins into the oven and closed the door.

She told Kat what happened. "Stuff him." Sal huffed. "He's gone back to being a dick."

For once, Kat didn't say anything. Instead, she quietly picked up the washing basket and carried it out back.

Sal followed her out to the washing line. "What do you think? Do you think ice-cream and a walk on the beach sounds romantic?"

Kat was particular about the washing, it had to be hung just so, colour coded to match the pegs, and folded correctly. Kat didn't answer straight away, instead she unpegged a pillowcase and gave it a shake, before folding it and neatly putting it in the basket.

Sal repeated, "Do you think that's cheap?"

Kat plucked the last piece of clothing off the line and turned to Sal. "It doesn't matter what I think. What do you think?"

"I think it's romantic."

Kat murmured, "Well, that's all that matters then isn't it."

"Trent doesn't like anyone I like. We were getting on fine, and now he's being a total jerk again," Sal complained.

"That so?" Kat replied. "Do you think there may be a reason for that?" The basket balanced on her hip, Kat headed back inside.

Sal hurried after her. "Yeah, it is like he doesn't trust me to choose a good one."

Kat shook her head. "Well, your track record isn't great, is it sweetheart, but, no, I don't think that's it."

"What then?"

Kat was to say what she thought when Sal heard her phone.

"That's my phone! It might be Chase." Sal sprinted to the kitchen to find her phone, leaving Kat shaking her head. It was Andie wanting a lift to work in the morning. His car had broken down.

Chapter 22: Feast Or Fleeced

When Saturday finally arrived, it was overcast and drizzly. Not a good day for a walk at the beach, Sal thought glumly. Still, she hadn't received a text, or call from Chase yet, so maybe his weekend meant Sunday. She rubbed her ankle; it was still a little tender but was much better.

Kat was grumpy because Rob was working on his big project again. Kat asked Sal if she wanted to go out for brunch and she'd ask the guys next door if they wanted to come too. Sal said she was busy, but really, she was still mad at Trent and didn't want to see him. All she was really busy doing was checking her phone. Kat told her Trent said he was busy as well so Anton and Kat went out for breakfast.

Kat wasn't gone long when there was a solid knock on the front door. Sal opened the door to find Ken standing on the stoop with a spade over his shoulder looking like a garden gnome.

He was the last person she expected to see. "Ken!" Sal exclaimed, her eyes popping in surprise. "What are you doing here?" He looked good; he had lost a ton of weight. Damn him.

Ken wiped a finger under his Roman nose. "I promised you I'd dig out that tree stump you were rattling on about when we were seeing each other, and I mean to keep my promise."

Blindsided, Sal spluttered. "What! That promise was moonbeams ago. Forget it, that's not necessary." However, a tiny voice in her head said, it would be great to get rid of that stump.

"No, Sal, a promise is a promise, I may be late but I always keep my word." The garden guy had cut the rotting tree but not removed the stump and it bugged the heck out of Sal that the job wasn't finished. Ken promised he'd dig it out for her when they started dating, but being a procrastinator, he'd never gotten around to it. But why now?

Sal tried to protest but he wasn't wearing it. He stood

stalwart, on the step, all bandy-legged and determined not to let her sway him from his mission. Shovel across his shoulder, Ken went round the side of the apartment and walked out to the small back garden looking like one of Snow White's dwarfs off to work. He located the offending stump. Unable to stop him, Sal grabbed her raincoat and watched him dig. Ken began to dig as a man possessed. It began to pour down but Ken was as relentless as the rain, and kept digging. Finally, the stump was extracted and the muddy tangled roots lay on the ground. Puffing with exertion and shining with sweat, Ken looked absolutely triumphant.

"There you go, mission accomplished."

"Thank you."

He wiped his hands on the back of his ripped jeans. "I'd like to take you out for lunch, but I need to shower and change first."

"Lunch?" Sal squeaked. "No, no, not necessary, thanks for the stump removal I really didn't…"

"Do you mind if I take a shower and change my clothes here? I've got a bag in the car. I'll shower, and get changed and we can pop up the road for a cheap and cheerful for old times' sake." He gave her that lop-sided endearing smile of his that she found hard to refuse.

Sal's mouth went dry. She couldn't think straight.

"We're still friends, aren't we?" Ken had the best puppy dog eyes.

Sal was struggling but she could feel herself caving. "Yes, but…"

"I know, I know, you are in love with someone else." He said as if he knew it was a line. "I won't be long," he promised, putting the spade in the back of his car and picking up his backpack. "Oh, and by the way," he called over his shoulder "I've fixed the gate. Did it before I got to your front door."

"Really?" she squeaked and went to check. Sure enough the gate swung open without sticking. Why couldn't he have done that a year ago? Sal went inside.

She could hear the shower running and Ken singing loudly,

"Hey, hey, hey, get your gear off." How had this happened? And why was he here – naked in her shower? She was still trying to figure it out when there was another knock at the door.

On the doorstep stood an elderly man of Asian descent holding a large bouquet of red roses in his hand. He was a thin little wisp of a man who looked like a wise old soul that should be a martial arts instructor. She half expected him to bow and then use the flowers as a weapon.

"Sally Jelly?" he asked gruffly.

"That's G-e-l-e-e. Yes," she replied.

"These are for you." He handed her the flowers.

She read the card. It was addressed to Sally Jelly and read 'You are too hurt to be single – Conner Andrew.

She frowned. "Hurt? Conner? Who is Conner Andrews?" she asked the man, puzzled.

"He said, you too hurt to be single, conner, Andrew. I wrote what he said." The old man bristled, stabbing a bony finger at the card.

"Hot?" guessed Sal. "Comma as in punctuation? You are too hot to be single, comma," she drew a comma in the air, "Andrew?"

The man grunted. "Sounds same. Stupid English language."

Sal saw Trent walking down the shared driveway. He glowered at the delivery van parked across his driveway blocking him in, and came across. "Hey mate," he called impatiently jangling his keys. "Can you move your van please? I need to get out."

Scowling, the man barked. "I go now." He marched up the path, hopped in the van, slammed the door, and reversed up the drive at great speed.

"Bet he spreads sunshine wherever he goes," Trent muttered as he approached.

Sal didn't reply. As far as she was concerned Trent certainly wasn't full of joy either. In fact, she knew him to be positively rude.

"I have to go up to the Station," Trent told her. He shuffled his feet. "Look, Sal, I'm sorry I...," he broke off. His lips pressed in a thin line. "Are those flowers from Chase?"

"No, Andrew."

"Andrew? Who's Andrew?"

"My insurance broker."

"What? The sleaze?"

"He's not a sleaze! He's a really nice guy," Sal retorted. Why the hell was she explaining herself? It was none of his business.

"You certainly play the field; I just met a guy who told me he was your boyfriend and he wasn't Chase."

"I don't know what you are talking about." She could feel her blood pressure rising.

"Hey, doll!" Ken called, his head poking around the corner of the bathroom door, "I forgot a towel, can you chuck me one?"

"Who's that?" Trent asked, trying to catch a glimpse.

Although Ken's muscular bare arm was held aloft, thankfully the rest of him was hidden behind the bathroom door.

"The gardener," she replied. "Oh, and he fixed the gate too."

"Hey, I can't take you out in nothing but my birthday suit, I need a towel. Now's good," Ken hollered. "I'm dripping water all over the floor."

Sal hurriedly put the bouquet on the table and ran to the linen cupboard. She threw a towel down the hall. Ken caught it deftly in one hand, then closed the bathroom door.

"The gardener?" Trent repeated, eyes bulging.

Sal stiffened. There was no way she was going to try to explain why Ken was in her shower – it was nothing to do with him. Besides she still couldn't figure it out herself.

"He fixed the gate as well."

Trent was still focused on the bathroom. "How come your boyfriend doesn't know where you live?"

It had to be Gone Don. Sal smacked a hand to her forehead. "Oh no, you didn't tell him this is where I live, did you?"

Sal's phone beeped. She prayed it wasn't Don saying, 'Hi gorgeous, I'll just pop by and say hello." She closed one eye and swiped. The message was from Chase. '*The weather will be better tomorrow. Meet you at Beach Café in Browns Bay at 10:00am. Looking forward to seeing you, Chase.'*

Seeing the gooey look on Sal's face, Trent said, "Let me guess, Chase?"

Sal shrugged. "What can I say – it's either feast or famine."

"Unreal!" Trent stalked off, pushed open the gate, and slammed it behind him. It reverberated as it clicked shut.

She wanted to shout, 'Oi dickhead, don't break my gate.' Suddenly aware of a presence behind her. She turned to find Ken. They watched Trent storm off and get in his work ute. "Who's that?" Ken asked. "Is he your new boyfriend?"

She turned slowly, relieved to find Ken was dressed in a nice shirt and clean jeans. "No, he's my neighbour. He wasn't happy about the florist van parking across his driveway."

"Uptight kind of dude," Ken remarked. "That's the trouble with apartment style living. If you get a neighbour from hell, it can make your life an absolute misery," he said, shaking his head.

Sal felt a tightening in the pit of her stomach. "Up until recently, he's been a pretty good neighbour."

"Right then," rubbing his hands together, Ken said, "let's go grab a cheeky Indian for lunch, shall we?" He laughed at his own joke.

Sal put down the flowers. "Just give me a minute. Wait here, I won't be long." She stalked up the drive. Don was lurking at the letterbox grinning like a Cheshire cat. She had had enough. Enough hiding, avoiding, and making up excuses. She lost it; and launched herself at him shouting obscenities.

Shaking, she screamed, "Will you feck off and leave me alone! I'm not your girlfriend! Stop telling people I am."

Mouth dropping, Don stumbled a couple of steps backwards but recovered his footing in time to stop himself from falling.

She screeched, "When will you get it into your thick skull that I never want to see you again. Go away and leave me alone!" she cried, shooing him. "Don't bother me ever again!"

Thinking she had gone completely mad he stared at her like

she was possessed.

She stamped her foot. "Go!"

Glancing nervously over his shoulder, Don retreated to his car. "You'll regret this," he told her as he hastily climbed in, closed the door, and sped off.

Sal felt completely spent after venting and would have liked nothing more than a cup of tea and a lie down but knew that wasn't going to happen. She returned to find Ken waiting for her.

"Just a minute," she sighed. Trying to salvage the flowers she popped them in a vase.

It was only a short walk to the Curry House. They found a seat near the window. Sal was relieved to see it was close to the door. Over a cheap curry, Sal listened to Ken brag about his new girlfriend, Nevada. It was like some sort of revenge, Ken wanted her to believe he was ecstatically happy without her and living his best life. It was as if he wanted payback by telling her that she wasn't the only one in love with someone else. He kept going on about how wonderful Nevada was until Sal wanted to gag. She almost wished she had food poisoning and couldn't wait to get home.

She thanked him for lunch, for digging out the stump and fixing the gate, and excused herself. But he insisted on walking her home in the rain. Besides he had to get his car. Finally, he left.

Why had she agreed to go out for lunch with him? Why couldn't she tell people what she really thought or felt? What was wrong with her? At least she had told Don where to go. It was a start.

On Sunday morning, Chase met her at the Beach Café where he ordered coffees. They chatted as they sat outside watching people strolling, cycling or walking their dogs pass-by on the boardwalk. The conversation didn't flow but Sal didn't care. She was happy to have snagged her man. She was proud to be seen out and about with him. He didn't have many good work stories – not like she did. There were a few water cooler stories but nothing of any substance. She thought about how Kat had broken the ice with Trent by suggesting they come up with names for the reproductive parts, but Sal didn't think that would be a suitable icebreaker for Chase.

They finished their coffee and then Chase suggested they walk up and down the beach to get a little exercise. Sal assured him it was fine. But her ankle began to ache a little as they came up the bank. Chase offered to buy ice-cream from Gingersnap. Delighted to sit down, Sal agreed, besides she had done some exercise and the diet wasn't working anyway, so, what the hell. Ice-cream sounded great.

While attacking her boysenberry ice-cream, she stole sneaky glances at Chase. He caught her eye. She blushed and looked away. Licking a few drips of orange choc chip off the back of his hand, Chase happened to notice the time. He hurriedly apologised telling Sal he'd have to go as he was meeting his folks, and was running late.

They returned to the carpark and Chase promised he'd call her soon to tee up another time to meet. He waited until she was in her car, before closing the door, and waving goodbye. Not even a kiss goodbye. Disappointed, she drove home. She thought, perhaps Chase believed you shouldn't kiss on the first date. Yes, that was it; Chase was a gentleman.

The policy documents arrived by email from Andrew. Trying to keep things formal, Sal thanked him for the flowers and for sorting out her insurances for her, ending her email, with kind regards, Sally Gelee. There, that wasn't an invitation. She didn't need Andrew scaring Chase off, not now when she had finally nabbed her man.

That week, Chase took her out for dinner, but his Mum, Dad and sister came too. Sal thought that was a bit weird unless he thought she was a keeper, and he was confident enough to let his family meet her right off. However, she'd have preferred the date being just the two of them. Over dinner Chase mentioned that he'd met her neighbour, the fireman, when he'd pulled into the driveway to pick her up, and the guy asked him if he'd met all Sal's other boyfriends?

Sal was livid. Was Trent deliberating trying to sabotage her happiness?

When Chase dropped her home, he brought up the topic again.

"Would you care to elaborate about these other men?" Chase asked, one eyebrow arched.

No, she wouldn't. She did her best to explain, but it sounded lame. Chase looked like he wasn't quite convinced. She was so annoyed with Trent she wanted to kill him.

Chase leaned down to kiss her. She closed her eyes and waited for the starbursts, but they never came. It was a nice kiss but hardly your Mills and Boon bodice ripper. Disappointed, she said goodnight, and tiptoed inside hoping Kat was asleep. She wasn't.

"How was it?" Kat asked before Sal could sneak past.

"Nice."

Kat frowned. "Nice? Not toe-curlingly great?"

"It was nice. Night. I'm off to bed."

Sal wearily climbed the stairs. Life wasn't going according to plan.

Chapter 23: Therapy Blues

Sal hadn't seen or heard from Trent all week which suited her fine. And when Kat suggested they go over to see the guys, Trent was either out, or just heading out – which was perfect. Yet the most annoying thing about the whole situation was – she missed him and that infuriated her even more. Why was he being such a jerk? What made him feel like he had the right to tell Chase about her past? Every time she thought about it the more her blood boiled.

Monday night, the Fire Brigade was holding an AGM. Kat went to training determined to have it out with him on Sal's behalf. The team sat around discussing the fire service business over a drink and fries at the local pub. Trent was in charge of the meeting, and kept avoiding eye contact. Kat tried to engage him in conversation but he brushed her off saying he had another meeting with the officers to go to and would catch up with her later. Sal went home angry. Even though she was furious with him, like it or not, she felt like she had lost a friend.

Fortunately, Chase didn't bring up the other guys again. He phoned most nights and promised they would go out on the weekend. Sal hoped that meant just the two of them but couldn't bring herself to ask.

Alice finally noticed that Sal was snowed under at work and hired an assistant to help her. Unfortunately, it was Alice's niece. Cherry was young, pretty, and bubbly, but not used to office work. She was courteous, lovely with the residents, and could type, but her accounts knowledge was limited.

Sal didn't have the time or energy to put into training Cherry, and found having an assistant difficult. Cherry was easily distracted and talkative and instead of the pile of paperwork shrinking – it grew. There was no point complaining to Alice –

Cherry was her niece and therefore untouchable.

The moment Sal came in the door from work, Kat said, "Did you know Trent's dating his ex?"

"No! Why would I?" she retaliated. "He's not talking to me. Ridiculous, isn't it, when I'm not the one who has done anything wrong. He should apologise to me; he threw me under the bus."

Kat gave Sal that look that said if you want me to agree I will, but I won't really mean it. Kat searched the pantry for a snack, pulled out a tube of Pringles chips and popped the top. Kat seemed to be eating constantly lately, and to Sal's surprise had put on some weight. "You got worms or something?" asked Sal.

"Yeah, maybe, can't stop eating.

Crunching on a chip, Kat said, "Thought you would be happy – about Trent."

Other than curious, Sal wasn't sure how she felt. Surely an ex was an ex for a reason. "Doesn't he know the no going back rule? When did that happen?"

Kat shrugged her shoulders. "No idea."

"What's she like?

"She's an interior designer. She's got a cool car; a black Mustang. Seems really nice. She was at the cocktail party, remember. Tall, brunette, super good-looking."

"Oh yeah, now I remember Miss Leggy. Good on him."

"Her name is Demi." Kat finished the Pringles and threw the empty container in the rubbish bin. "I was out in the driveway talking to the guys when Demi pulled up. She gushed all over Trent, then she told him to hop in the car because she was taking him somewhere special and he just *had to* see it."

"That doesn't mean they're dating again."

"Anton told me Demi was Trent's ex and suddenly she's at his house every day, I'd say that means they are back together, wouldn't you?"

Sal didn't respond.

"So, what are you and Chase up to this weekend?" Kat wanted to know.

Sal rolled her eyes. "I expect we will be hanging out with his family – again.".

Kat shook her head in disbelief. "Man, that's one super close family."

Too close, thought Sal.

"Hope you are going somewhere nice," Kat said.

Sal doubted Chase had thought of anything like a romantic getaway. It was probably just his parents' place and they would be sitting around drinking coffee. She longed to go somewhere like lunch in a vineyard, or the movies, or a restaurant but didn't feel as if she could suggest it. And when they kissed, it was ok but there was no magic, no bewitching cherubs flying around them with undeniable irresistible attraction.

Chase looked cute but he was turning out to be a real bore. The last time, she suggested they go on a picnic, Chase said, he'd check with his folks, and he came back to her saying, yes, they'd love to go. How romantic – not. And when she squeezed his thigh, it was a nice thigh, nothing wrong with it but it didn't feel right. For someone who had a hot bum, Chase had a very average thigh.

She was sitting on the balcony pondering how she was forming more of a relationship with Chase's parents instead of Chase when he sent her a message. Sal ignored it. He rang. She ignored it. She went for a walk and purposefully left her phone behind. She recognised the familiar pattern of avoidance.

That night, the girls had takeaways for dinner. Kat stopped mid-bite of her chip and studied Sal.

"You happy, chicky?" Kat asked, immediately realising Sal wasn't.

"No," Sal admitted. "Chase is a bit boring. Not at all like I'd hoped. You were right, he was pure fantasy."

"What are you going to do?" Kat asked, licking the sauce off her fingertips. "The usual?" She reached for a serviette to wipe her mouth. "Are you going to tell him you are in love with someone else?" How did Kat do that? Nail her in a few words.

No, I'm being an ostrich. I'm probably going to get real fit going for long walks to avoid him, thought Sal.

Sal didn't respond to any of Chase's calls or messages and hoped like hell that the photocopier didn't break down. What was she going to say? "I'm sorry but I find you incredibly boring, and the fact that you still live at home with your parents is a real turn-off." No, she couldn't say that – that would be mean. It riled her that Trent was right; Chase was a Mummy's boy still tied to the apron strings.

The following morning Sal asked Vikki if she could recommend a local counsellor. Vikki seemed surprised but found Sal a business card of a friend of hers, and said "You'll like Liz, she's a lovely lady and really good at what she does."

"How do you know it's for me?" Sal asked.

Vikki grinned. "Lucky guess."

It had been a particularly trying day. Ignoring the guidelines Cherry had hole punched the invoices leaving five centimetres of paper trailing out the bottom of the files. All the residents' medical labels were printed on the wrong side of the label paper. Cherry had entered a large bill twice under two different numbers and Sal not realising they were for the same invoice, paid both. Now she needed to contact the supplier to get the money refunded.

By the time she got to the counsellors' office, Sal was fuming.

"Hello," said Liz brightly. In her early forties, Liz had her black hair tied up in a messy bun. She wore huge round glasses that made her look intelligent and colourful red beads over a rather loud purple pantsuit. She looked like a cross between a librarian and Gok Wan.

"Please make yourself comfortable." Liz waved to a comfy chair. Sal was relieved it was only a chair, not a psychiatrist's couch, she didn't have to lie down and spill her guts from the date of her birth, or thank goodness re-enact her birth. Hers had been a nice childhood. Everything had been nice up until she'd met Hemi. Sal sighed. That's when things started to go wrong. Perhaps she really should become a lesbian. Men obviously were her problem.

"Now, Sally, why are you here?" Liz had a high sing-song voice that grated on Sal. She doubted that they would click. This had been a mistake. She should leave now.

"I've come about my commitment phobia. But I think I'm here for the wrong reason because right now I want to kill my assistant," Sal admitted.

Liz's face clouded with concern. "Whatever you tell me is confidential, however, if it's outside the bounds of law I will have to disclose it."

She was nice, but her high-pitched voice made it difficult for Sal to concentrate on what she was saying. Liz drew balloon circles on the whiteboard and drew connecting lines to them. She was unable to focus when a couple of words were misspelled and longed to rub them out and correct them. When they finished, Sal wondered if it was worth the money she'd spent on the session. She hadn't dealt with anything and she still wanted to kill Cherry.

Monday evening Sal spotted Trent pulling into his driveway. She waited until he'd parked before going over.

"Hi, how are you?" Sal asked, striving to keep it casual. She hoped he'd apologise for his bad behaviour and they could go back to being friends again.

"Fine," he replied coldly, and locked his car.

Sal tried again. "What've you been up to?"

"Been busy." He glanced at his phone, still not looking at her.

"Doing what?"

He shrugged. "Nothing much."

"Ok, I've had enough," Sal snapped. "What's your problem?"

He looked up sharply, his eyes blazing. "You drive me crazy. Do you know that?"

"I drive you crazy? You drive me crazy," she retaliated. "And what's the deal telling Chase about all my exs?"

"You are absolutely oblivious to how you affect others by your behaviour."

"My behaviour? I don't know what you mean," she retorted. "It's your behaviour that I have a problem with. You are positively rude."

He threw his hands in the air. "I'm not the problem – you are! You play with guys emotions; you don't realise the affect you have on guys and don't seem to care. I wish I'd never met you." He turned and walked away, shaking his head.

"I wish I'd never met you," she called after him.

Still muttering to himself he disappeared inside his apartment.

***

Sal felt like she had been bitch-slapped. Did he really mean that? The bastard. What the hell had she done to deserve that? She stomped home and slammed the door. Stupid man, how dare he! She curled up on the sofa with a book and tried to relax but it wasn't working, she had read the same page three times, and none of it had sunk in.

Kat already had her jacket on and her hand on the doorknob, when she asked, "You coming to training?"

"No, can't."

"Why?"

"Trent doesn't want to see me."

"Oh, come on, don't be silly."

Sal cast the book aside. "No. It's mutual, I don't want to see him either."

Kat eyed Sal suspiciously. "What happened? What have you done to upset him this time?"

"Nothing. What do you mean what have I done to upset him? Why are you taking his side?"

Kat frowned. "So, nothing happened but neither of you want to see each other. That's going to be pretty much impossible when he lives next door, don't you think?"

Kat was right. Of course, she was.

"Go ahead, Kat, firefighting isn't for me, I'm more treasurer material than action hero anyway."

"We'll talk about this later," Kat promised as she left, quietly closing the door behind her.

It was well after nine thirty when Kat returned and demanded Sal tell all.

Kat stared in disbelief. "Really? He really said that?"

Sal nodded.

"Jeez, the big nob. Shall I have a word with him?" Kat offered.

"No, no, just leave it, please," pleaded Sal.

Kat gave her a sideways glance. "How do you feel about him?"

"He drives me crazy," Sal told her. "I can't believe he can go from being nice to being a total jerk. He's like Jekyll and Hyde. He's a dick. In fact, I could call him all those names we came up with for that appendage."

Kat smirked. "Have you tried the thigh test?"

"No, of course, I haven't – he doesn't like me like that, we were just friends. Oh God, this is a right mess."

"Yeah, that's your firefighting career down the toilet."

That was the one thing Sal wasn't worried about.

Snuggling down, she pulled the sheets up round her head and willed herself to sleep but deep down a large worm of worry grew. Somehow, she had started to develop feelings for Trent. She couldn't understand the attraction. He really wasn't her type. She didn't usually go for moustaches. He was good-looking in a rugged way, and up until now had been quite caring but still he wasn't the kind of guy she normally went for. No, he was just a bit too normal.

Chapter 24: Losing The Compass

The weather was turning, and everything felt melancholy. Although she was still mad as hell, Sal missed him. When something funny happened at work she longed to share it with Trent or when something sad had happened she'd wanted to call him. She hadn't noticed how close they'd become; it had been gradual and had snuck up on her like a hungry tiger.

Everyone at work tried cheering her up. Daisy popped little treats on her desk but she didn't feel like eating. Pearl asked her if she wanted to go out on the town with the oldies when they were next going to cruise the streets in the van.

Andie did his darndest to help, even offering to give Sal a makeover. "Think Kardashian, honey," he told her. Thinking that she would end up looking like a drag queen with a trout pout, Sal politely declined. Ethel offered to share her meds. Cherry tried to improve the quality of her work, but nothing cheered Sal up.

Misery loves company and Sal had plenty of it. Kat finally split up with Rob. Turned out his working late – wasn't because he was working. He was working out with a work colleague. Kat had an inkling but it was confirmed when she staked out the office dressed as security personnel and saw through the window Rob in action with a pretty petite little blonde she assumed to be the secretary. Under the cover of darkness, Kat spray-painted his lawn with weedkiller writing Cheating Dick in the grass outside his flat. She sent him a final text message then blocked his number. Rob got the message his calls weren't wanted and neither was his presence.

When Sal asked Kat how she felt, Kat shrugged it off, saying she knew Rob was a dick and wasn't in too deep anyway, and to prove it she took Sal with her to the jewellery store to buy a new necklace as a cheer-up present to herself.

Mesmerised by the pretty sparkly pieces of jewellery in the glass cabinets, Sal and Kat were unable to make a decision.

Sal pointed to a large square solitaire diamond on a white gold band, and whispered to Kat, "If I ever get married, I want a rock just like that."

The well-dressed middle-aged sales lady with a perfect blonde bob and carefully manicured nails came to help them. Her name badge read Diane.

Kat told Diane that she was treating herself because her boyfriend, now ex, had cheated on her. "Wish I'd pinched his credit card. I'd like him to really pay," she said.

Perfectly groomed Diane didn't bat an extended eyelash as she replied, "Dear, men are like compasses, they go whatever way it's pointing."

Kat and Sal chuckled.

Diane was an excellent salesperson. Kat blew the budget and bought an enchanting tear-drop diamond necklace and matching earrings.

"And what about you?" Diane said, eyeing Sal speculatively.

Sal wanted to say I want to buy something to celebrate my friend breaking up with the cheating dick but instead she said, "My neighbour's mad at me."

Diane's tinted eyebrows rose. "Any reason is a good reason." She smiled. "I have the perfect thing."

And just like that, without meaning to, Sal bought a silver bangle.

Later that night, at a loss, Kat absently scrolled through her phone. "Wonder what Ethan's up to? Maybe he'd like to hang out, you know like buddies. Like you and Trent used to. I don't need a relationship right now, but I could do with a guy mate to hang out with. Could be nice…and since you aren't speaking to Trent, I'd feel a bit like a traitor if I hung out with him. And Anton's so into his cycling, he's barely ever home."

Yeah, thought Sal. Would be nice to have a guy buddy to hang out with again. Why did Trent have to go and ruin things?

That week, when she arrived at her counselling session Liz

had a surprise waiting for her. There were heaps of toys on a table and a small sandpit.

"How are you?" Liz asked in her sing-song voice.

"Semi ok," Sal replied. "What's all this?" Sal asked, her curiosity getting the better of her.

Liz explained that Sal was to choose as many of the toys from the table she wanted and place them in the sandpit any way she liked. Sal thought Liz should be the one getting analysed on the couch. Sal hadn't played in a sandpit since she was five. Sal picked up several items and placed them in the sand.

Liz tapped her chin. "Now explain what or who they are and what they mean to you."

Sal looked at the circle in the corner, there was Smurfette, Poppa Smurf, Winnie-the-Pooh, Piglet, Jemima Puddle duck, Barbie seated around a spotted fairy mushroom table that held teapot and teacups. "These are my close friends and family. This is my safe, happy place." She remembered Trent calling her Smurfette.

"And this?" Liz asked pointing to the marble and ribbon. "The marble is God and the ribbon connects everything." She briefly wondered if God was ok about being a marble. The blue ribbon ran across to a plastic computer and nurse, and Lego people.

"Work."

"And this?"

Sal looked at the ballerina, and the puppy dog, and her books, and the tiny wine glass, hamburger buns.

"Things I enjoy, dancing, dogs, reading, wine, food."

Mm, Liz murmured, she touched the far corner where the ribbon didn't reach.

Sal shook her head. "No, we mustn't go there," she said decisively.

"Why?" Liz gently probed.

"That's the bad corner." Sal had placed a transformer, a snake, and a spider in that corner. "Bad stuff hides there."

"Who are they?" Liz coaxed.

Sal thought for a moment. "David." He was Jekyll and Hyde.

The snake was his mother, she was poison, broke your spirit, and the spider, he was Don, ready to jump out and surprise her.

"And who is this over here near the circle of friends but just outside the circle."

Sal stared at the tiny Superman figurine. "That's Trent."

"And he is?"

"My neighbour."

"Why is he Superman?"

"Cos, he's always rescuing me."

"Why's he on the outside of the circle?"

"He's mad at me and doesn't want to see me."

"Oh?" Liz's gaze was intense as she zeroed in. "Why?"

"Apparently, I drive him nuts. I always need rescuing and according to him, I don't realise how my behaviour affects others."

Liz pushed her glasses further up her nose and nodded in that ah-hah kind of way therapists have. "And how do you feel about him?"

"He annoys the hell out of me, he's always teasing me, but," Sal reluctantly admitted, "I like him. I'm not sure what to do about that. I mean how can I smooth things over when he's not talking to me?"

Sal jumped as the alarm beeped signalling the end of their session.

"That's our time for today." Liz snapped her notebook shut. "Your homework this week is to think about the way you have placed these items in the sandpit, and their connection to you. Good work, and I'll see you next week."

"But it was just getting interesting. Can't we continue?"

"No, I've got another client waiting. I'll see you next week." Liz ushered Sal out.

"Don't you want to know if I killed my assistant?" Sal asked as Liz closed the door. "We'll discuss that next week," came the muffled reply.

Sal drove home perplexed. She had gone there thinking she would have to open up about the box of exs. However, Liz didn't ask anything about her past relationships, or why she thought she suffered from commitment phobia.

Sandpit therapy had surprised her. She knew what she had hidden in the lining of the box of exs but she hadn't even gotten around to mentioning that, because Liz had made her arrange toys in the sandpit. The transformer, the serpent, and the spider were enlightening. They might be tucked in the corner away from the rest of her world but they obviously affected her ability to connect on a real level in a relationship. Yep, she was seriously deranged. Therapy was going to cost a fortune.

She no sooner came in the door when Kat asked, "How'd it go?"

"You're right," Sal answered. "I'm nuts."

"Did she tell you that, or did you figure it out all by yourself?" asked Kat.

"She made me play with toys in a sandpit," Sal told her.

"Sounds like she's nuts, chick."

"You were Barbie."

"Barbie? Really? That's interesting. I'll get the wine."

The girls sat outside on the front deck, the sun was sinking and beginning to hide behind the tops of the trees. Kat was re-examining everything that Sal told her about the therapy session.

When Sal started complaining about Cherry's admin skills, Kat teased Sal, saying, "Are you picking on her, chick, because she's prettier and younger than you? Is Sally Gelee jealous?"

Sal straightened as she saw a black Mustang drive into the mews and pull into Trent and Anton's driveway. Both girls edged forward and lifted themselves slightly off their chairs to see better.

"It's her –Demi," Kat hissed.

The leggy brunette got out of the car. She wore faded ripped designer jeans and a white t-shirt, she had long legs and curves in all the right places. She smiled at them. Startled, Sal turned her head away, but Kat waved. Demi tapped on the boys' front door. Anton let her in, then she disappeared inside out of sight.

"Attractive, huh." Kat mirrored Sal's thoughts.

"Why do you reckon they broke up? Did he tell you?" asked Sal.

Kat leaned in like a conspirator. "No, he must have been crazy though. Who do you think ended it? Him or her? And why?"

Sal shrugged. "Maybe he broke up with her and now he regrets it." She tried to sound nonchalant but there was a niggle of jealousy worming deep within. How come Trent could find someone and she couldn't find the right man?

"Maybe," Kat agreed. "Why don't we ask him? It would be easier than guessing."

"You ask him, he's not talking to me, remember."

"I'll ask Anton, he'll know."

"Good idea," agreed Sal. "Except he's never flipping home."

The black Mustang was still parked next door when Sal went to bed. She dreamed of spiders, transformers, and superman, and then a giant Winnie-the-Pooh sat on all of them and squished them flat, and Marvin said that it was bloody marvellous.

Chapter 25: Killer Assistant

When Sal opened the lounge curtains in the morning, she was relieved to see Demi's car wasn't parked out front of the boy's flat. Sal called in sick, mostly, because she felt unable to face working with Cherry that day. Besides, she reasoned she needed a mental health day – she was sure she was close to having a breakdown.

Chase called and she ignored it, switching her phone to silent. She messaged Cherry and sent her the password for her PC then spent the day in bed watching her favourite old movies. Sal always watched 'Pride and Prejudice' when she was feeling down, but she couldn't get the sandpit toys out of her head. Why were there no representatives of her past boyfriends in the sandpit? Chase wasn't even there. Had she already dismissed him from becoming more than an infatuation? What toy would represent him? A nice dumpty-doo kind of teddy like the Hudson's Cookie Bear? Gone Don would be a weasel. She went through her memories assigning a toy to each ex. It was good – less frightening. As toys, they didn't seem to have any power over her.

The following day when Sal arrived at work she parked her car next to Cherry's as Cherry had nicked her parking spot. Next thing she'd be taking over my chair, Sal fumed. Sal took a deep breath as she made her way inside the building.

Cherry was sitting in Sal's office chair; she flicked her long dark hair back off her face and smiled. She seemed genuinely pleased to see Sal which Sal couldn't quite fathom. She always felt grumpy around Cherry. Always felt like she was contradicting Cherry or pointing out her mistakes, whereas Cherry remained upbeat. She didn't seem to take offence which made Sal feel even worse.

"Hope you are feeling better," chirped Cherry, vacating Sal's seat.

I'll let you know, Sal thought as she logged on. She hoped no terrible disaster had happened in her absence. There were 131 unread emails.

Horrified, Sal glanced at Cherry, "Did you action any of these, or did you just mark them unread so I would know what came in?"

Cherry fidgeted, colouring slightly. "The password you gave me didn't work, and I didn't want to bother you when you were sick so I…"

"You didn't do anything?" Incredulous, Sal gasped. "All day?"

Looking rather pleased with herself, Cherry passed over the large pile of invoices. "I put all the pieces of paper on your desk in date order so you would know which ones came first."

"These are suppliers' invoices and they were in alpha order. It doesn't matter the date they arrive; they are all due on the twentieth."

The residents' files were muddled up too, the shopping list was still in the in-tray, and the roster was nowhere to be seen.

Confused, Sal logged out and asked Cherry to try and log in.

Cherry did.

The password was correct. "The number lock key must have been off." She told Cherry. "Did you not think to check that?"

Cherry shook her head.

Sal resisted the urge to scream. She sighed and strove to be patient. "So, what did you do yesterday?"

"I answered the phone. Here are your messages. Oh, and I wrote everything everyone else wanted on this to-do list for you."

Sal wanted to strangle Cherry and thought the prison term might be worth it.

Alice came out of her office and put more files on Sal's desk. "Good to see you, Sal. I'm glad you are feeling better. Cherry's been wonderful. Everyone loves her."

Sal gritted her teeth and sorted the piles into the correct order.

Ethel pushed her walker to the counter and asked for forty dollars out of her comfort account.

Before Sal could reply, Cherry leapt into action. "Sure!" she cried and punched in the code to Sid Snot. The treacherous safe immediately opened.

Cherry handed the money to Ethel while smiling her beautiful Colgate white smile, "There you go, dear," she beamed.

"Aren't you a love," Ethel said, pocketing the cash.

Sal asked Ethel to wait. "Cherry, you have to get Ethel to sign that she has received the money, you need to record it in the spreadsheet so we know how much money she still has left in her account."

"Oh," Cherry frowned. "I thought you'd do that."

"How would I know how much you have given out if you haven't recorded anything? Did you give any money to anyone yesterday?"

Cherry thought for a moment. "Yes, an old man, bald, stooping, no stick."

Sal shook her head in disbelief. "Not helpful. That describes quite a few of the males around here."

"He's forgetful, does that help?

"Norman?"

Cherry plucked at her bottom lip. "Ah, I think so."

To give herself time to breathe and get herself under control, Sal said, "Please go to the nurse's station and get the previous fortnight's roster so we can enter the hours in for the payroll."

"Ok," Cherry smiled; she bounced up the hallway happily humming to herself.

Booked for an outing, some of the residents were gathered in the lobby area waiting for the van to be brought around the front to pick them up. Norman was amongst them. There was no point asking Norman if he got any money out of his comfort account yesterday, he'd never have remembered.

The double doors opened and a middle-aged gentleman arrived to see a relative. As he was signing in, he spotted Norman sitting in the lobby and recognised him immediately.

Delighted to see Norm, he greeted him cheerfully. "Hello, Norm," he said.

Looking mystified, Norm said, "Hello."

Thinking that Norm might be vision impaired the man moved closer until they were almost nose-to-nose. "It's me, Brian, your daughter Trish's friend."

"I have a daughter?" Norman asked, astonished.

Flummoxed, Brian looked helplessly at Sal.

"It's ok, Norman's a bit like Dory from Finding Nemo," Sal explained.

"Have I upset him?" Brian's face was full of concern.

"In five minutes, he won't remember the conversation," Sal replied.

Pearl tooted and the residents waved Sal goodbye and slowly shuffled out.

"Where are we going?" Norm asked Sal.

"Out for ice-cream," she reminded him.

"Oh goody," Norm said, delighted. Norman happily waved goodbye to Brian as he trotted out the front door and clambered into the van.

"Don't worry, it happens all the time," Sal tried to console Brian who seemed a little shaken by the experience. Thanking Sal, he disappeared up the hall towards the lounge to visit his uncle Clive.

Cherry still hadn't returned. Sal was about to go in search of the girl when Chase arrived.

He stood in front of the desk looking down at her with his intense blue eyes. "Hi, I was wondering if I could take you out for coffee?"

Flustered, Sal glanced around seeking an excuse. "Oh, sorry, I'm super busy. I was sick yesterday and took the day off so now I have to catch up. I'll call you later, ok?"

Cherry finally appeared and overhearing the conversation, she volunteered to man the front desk so Sal could take a break.

"Off you go," Cherry insisted.

Sal eyeballed Cherry and hoping Chase wouldn't notice she

gave a barely perceptible shake of her head. "No, really it's ok, I can't."

But well-meaning Cherry wasn't having a bar of it. "No, don't worry, go," she gestured. "I've got this. I've got the password sorted now, so don't worry."

Sal wanted to clap her hand over Cherry's mouth, but couldn't. She continued to argue. "No, I'm too busy, I can't."

Sal could feel the sand shifting under her feet as Chase put down the pen and waited, a look of expectation on his handsome face.

Daisy arrived in reception ready to give her monthly menu to Alice to peruse and she suggested that Chase and Sal stay in and have a coffee in the dining room as she had made chocolate Afghans for morning tea.

Daisy winked. "They are delicious even if I say so myself."

Alice must have been eavesdropping and agreed. Shouting from her office, "Yes, Sal," Alice said, "You two go have a coffee in the dining room. Cherry will cover."

Cornered, Sal couldn't figure any way out. Reluctantly she took Chase to the dining room. She made them both a coffee from the urn.

"Those Afghans are bloody marvellous, they are," called Marvin from the other side of the dining room.

Sal gave Marvin the thumbs up.

Determined to get her attention, Chase persisted, "I've been calling and calling you but you haven't returned any of my calls," he said, looking wounded. "Have I upset you?"

Sal squirmed. "Ah, no, of course not. I wasn't feeling well yesterday."

"You should have told me. I would have brought you something."

"But why haven't you answered any of my calls?"

"I've been busy, is all."

He frowned. "What have you been busy doing?" He took a bite of his biscuit and chewed thoughtfully, studying her. Could he see the truth hidden in her face? That she was freaking out and needed to get away from him – and fast.

"I've been going to therapy," she blurted.

"What? All weekend?" he asked, astonished.

"No, I've…I've just had a lot on my mind. I needed to process a few er…things."

"Such as?" Chase blew across the top of his coffee cup.

Andie, bless him, came up the hallway with a trolley full of incontinence pants.

Pleased for the diversion, Sal called out, "Andie, come and meet, Chase."

"Hello, darling," Andie trilled. Grinning mischievously, Andie turned to Sal and flapped a painted hand. "Oh, you are so right, he's yummy."

Chase didn't know how to respond.

"Lovely to meet you, heard so much about you," raved Andie. "But must scarper, got important business to attend to." He motioned at the trolley and its contents, then whisked them away leaving Sal alone with Chase.

"Interesting bloke," Chase commented as he finished his coffee.

"He's a treasure." She bit her biscuit and slowly chewed while wondering what else to say. In the uncomfortable silence that followed, Sal glanced out the window and saw a familiar face peering in the window and almost dropped her cup. Millie was standing in the garden on the outside of the building looking in. Oh God, what if she had a fall?

"Millie!"

Sal leaped to her feet and rushed to the side exit. She punched the door code in and flew outside.

"Come on, Millie," Sal gently coaxed as she brought Millie back inside.

Bewildered by Sal's sudden departure, Chase was still sitting in his chair, coffee cup tightly clasped in his hand wondering what the hell just happened.

"I'm sorry Chase," Sal apologised. "I need to take Millie back to the secure wing."

Chase nodded. "I can see you are busy." He put the empty cups and plates on the tray and took them over to the kitchen slider. "I'll call you later, alright?"

"Alright."

Chase disappeared up the corridor. Stalling until she was sure Chase was far enough away, Sal slowly buttoned Millie's pink cardy, "I owe you one, Millie, thanks." Sal kissed Millie's soft cheek. Millie smiled placidly and let Sal take her hand leading her back to the TV room in the secure wing.

***

Thursday's counselling session couldn't come soon enough. Sal desperately needed to talk to Liz. She couldn't keep avoiding people forever. Liz listened patiently as Sal explained what happened, Chase, Cherry, Gone Don.

"I haven't heard from Don since I gave him a piece of my mind. Still, I keep expecting him to pop up at random."

"Mm, your avoidance is a pattern," Liz murmured scribbling in her notebook.

"How do I fix it?" Sal asked.

The alarm went signalling the end of the session.

Liz closed her notebook, "Your homework this week is to tell people the truth. Tell them how you really feel. You have made a good start with Don. Admittedly, the delivery could have been more assertive and less aggressive but you seemed to have got your point across."

Sal left the building with a sinking heart. Wasn't she supposed to be cured or something? She had see-sawed between feeling like she had been interrogated by a terrorist to feeling like she was as bland as a bowl of rice. Obviously, this therapy thing wasn't working.

Chase phoned and she ignored him. She deliberately left her phone behind and went for a long walk alone to the beach and back. When she got back, she picked up her phone to see she'd missed three calls from him. Liz had challenged her to speak her truth, she needed to do that. Was it ok to do it by text or was that a major cop-out?

He rang again. Sal took a big breath and answered. "Hi."

"What's up? What have I done wrong?" Chase asked.

"Chase, it's not you, it's me. I'm in love with someone else. I'm sorry."

"What?" He was stunned.

She repeated, "I'm in love with someone else."

"Who?" he demanded.

Sal floundered. "It doesn't matter who."

"Is it one of the other guys your neighbour warned me about?"

Sal was silent.

"Is it him? Your neighbour?"

"It doesn't matter who," Sal replied her stomach knotting in shame. He hung up.

Phew! It was over. She could hear Trent chanting in her head, another one down, another one down, another one for the box. Bloody, bloody, bloody Trent.

Less aggressive more assertive she reminded herself as she bailed up Trent later that evening. He had just put the key in his front door when she stalked up his path. "I've got a bone to pick with you. Why did you think you had the right to say what you said to Chase?" She demanded.

"Thought he had a right to know that you were seeing a bunch of other guys. It's not right to lead a guy on. Who is it today, the gardener, the insurance broker? The butcher, the baker, or the candlestick maker?"

Her jaw clenched. Why was he always trying to provoke her? "No, no, no, no, and no." There was a lump in her throat and she was finding it difficult to speak.

He saw her lip tremble and hastily apologised. "Sorry. I don't know why I said that. It was dumb of me. I don't know why I say stupid stuff around you. I'm sorry. Forget it, forget what I said – I've been a total dork."

"You are a dick, and I can't forget it." Sal turned on her heel and ran.

"I mean it, I'm truly sorry," he called across the hedge as the door of Sal's flat banged shut.

Sal threw herself on her bed and cried. He was being so cruel. She had broken up with boyfriends before but this was the first time she had broken up with a neighbour. So far, she had told Don to take a hike, Chase she wasn't into him, and Trent he was being a dick. And while she was on a roll, she might as well talk to Cherry. Yep, she was going to have to move and she might as well look for a new job.

Chapter 26: Telling The Truth

Sal tried palming Cherry off on Pearl, telling her that Cherry was great with the elderly and could be a real help with craft activities, or driving the van. Pearl flatly refused, saying "She's a nice girl, Sal, but I don't need her help." Pearl suggested perhaps some of the carers could do with a hand.

Dismayed, Sal looked at the growing pile of paperwork. Ever since Cherry started Sal never seemed to find the bottom of the in-tray. The only thing Cherry was good at was opening Sid Snot, the capricious safe.

"Morning," trilled Cherry, her infectious smile lighting the room.

Cherry was punctual, Sal had to give her that – but admin just wasn't her thing. She needed to be useful, and she wasn't. Sal swallowed the anxious lump in her throat. She needed to do it now before she wimped out.

Alice had gone to a meeting in the city and wasn't expected back until lunchtime. It was an opportune time to address things. "Cherry, can we have a little chat in Alice's office?"

Sal sat at Alice's desk and waited. A full ten minutes passed but still Cherry hadn't arrived. Sal went back to reception and found Cherry still at the front desk seemingly in no hurry to join her.

Sal cleared her throat. "Excuse me, Cherry, I'm waiting for you in Alice's office."

"Oh, sorry, I didn't hear you," Cherry pointed at the earbuds in her ears. She was listening to her playlist! How was she ever going to hear the phone with earbuds rammed in her ears?

Cherry put her earbuds into her handbag and followed Sal into Alice's office. Sal closed the door and, hoping to feel more official than she felt, took a seat in Alice's chair.

"Look at you sitting in the boss's chair all business-like,"

Cherry said.

Sal strove to keep on point. "Cherry, I want you to consider this as a formal meeting. I need to talk to you about the quality of your work."

Cherry lowered herself into the chair on the other side of the large desk and looked at Sal with her big beautiful soft doe eyes. "What's wrong with it?" she asked.

Sal took a breath. "Cherry, you're supposed to be my assistant."

"Yes, you just tell me what you want me to do and I'll do it," Cherry assured Sal.

Sal sighed. "I want you to hole-punch paperwork in the correct place, if you can't use the paper guide fold the paper in half if you have to, but I don't want to find a page five centimetres below the bottom of the file. I want the staple in the top left-hand corner of the page, not in the bottom right so you can't turn the page. I don't want to find pages upside down and back to front in files. I don't want to find packing slips entered as invoices. In short, I want you to get the basics right."

"You only had to say," Cherry replied, looking wounded.

"I have, over and over again, and I'm feeling very frustrated. Cherry, you are a nice person, and great with the elderly, but your admin skills need improvement. I don't want to assist my assistant; I need my assistant to assist me." There, the words were out – she had said what needed to be said. So why didn't she feel better?

Cherry's eyes began to swim with tears. "I'll try harder," she promised.

Sal felt like she was the biggest heel on the planet. Relieved that the talk was over, Sal was keen to get back to work. "Good, then let's get on with it and I'm sure we will have a great day."

The next day Cherry phoned in sick. She was sick the following day and the one after that. By Friday, Sal wondered if Cherry would turn up on Monday.

"I've got a dental appointment first thing on Monday morning," Sal told Alice, "I'm not sure if Cherry will be here or not."

Alice shrugged. "Poor girl must have a terrible tummy bug. Don't worry, off you go, I'll cover if she's not here."

"Thanks, Alice." Sal would have rather cancelled the appointment.

That night, Sal glumly poked her food around her plate while thinking about how dire her life was. Chase. Trent. Alice. Cherry. And to top it all off she was going to the dentist on Monday. She hated dentists, they always made her feel like she was five and off to visit the murder house to be tortured.

"Are you going to eat your dinner or play with it?" Kat knew how good Sal was at avoiding things she found unpleasant, and knew how worked up Sal had been about having to talk with Cherry.

"How did it go? Did you talk to Cherry?" Kat asked.

"She looked at me with big puppy dog eyes. She's so sweet it's like telling My Little Pony off."

But has she improved?" Kat wanted to know.

"She hasn't been to work since."

"So, a win-win," Kat replied.

Sal hadn't thought of it that way.

Kat looked really down. It was like she had the weight of the world on her shoulders.

"Are you ok, chicky?" Sal asked, giving Kat a pat on the shoulder. She felt really bad she had been so preoccupied with her own problems lately that she hadn't even asked Kat how she was doing. Come to think of it, Kat had been a bit depressed lately and that wasn't like her at all.

Sal hedged a guess. "Are you still upset about Rob?"

Tears welled up in Kat's almond-shaped eyes.

Alarmed, Sal rushed across, threw her arm around Kat and hugged her tight. "What is it? What's upsetting you?"

"I'm pregnant," sobbed Kat.

"Pregnant?" Sal repeated, aghast. "To...Rob?"

"Who else?" Kat blindly searched for the tissues. "Yes, to the cheater." Finding the box, she yanked out a handful of tissues and blew her nose.

"Oh, God." Sal handed Kat more tissues so she could dry her eyes. "What are you going to do?"

"I'm keeping it," Kat declared through her tears. "How could you think otherwise?"

"I...I'm in shock." Sal replied, internalising. A prick of memory stabbed her.

Kat told Sal that she had texted Rob that he was going to be a father and he hadn't replied. "Guess I'll be doing this on my own." Kat sighed.

"How many months are you?

"Three."

"Three? Wow. Was it that night we went out for dinner?"

"Yeah, I drank too much. Guess the pill didn't work because I vomited." Kat looked stricken. She clasped Sal's hands in hers. "What if my baby is damaged? I was drunk at the time of conception." Kat agonised.

Sal didn't know what to say.

"I don't have my parents anymore and my old aunt can't help me. You'll be there for me, won't you? If I am doing this alone, I'll need you. Will you come to ante-natal classes with me?"

"Of course, I will," Sal promised kissing Kat's tear-stained cheek. "And be at the birth if you want me to."

"Thanks, babe," Kat sniffed and dabbed her nose with another tissue. "At least I can count on you."

Sal desperately wanted to confide in someone who knew Kat and who would look out for her. She really had to smooth things over with Trent. She didn't like things ending this way – she may have ended numerous relationships but she had never willingly lost a friendship. And weirdly, them not speaking to each other felt a lot like a break-up. She wished he'd make the first move and apologise but if she had to be the bigger person then so be it.

Sal spotted Anton in the driveway from the kitchen window. He had his helmet in hand, leathers on, and was about to hop on his motorbike. She hurried outside to catch him before he disappeared. "Hey stranger, how are you doing?"

"Good," he replied, clipping on his helmet. "Can't stop now, I'm on my way out."

"Is Trent home?"

"Yeah," Anton answered. "But I wouldn't go in there if I were you. Demi and he are ripping it up in there. That's why I'm keeping well out of the way."

Sal blanched. Oh God. Thank God, he'd warned her. "Oh, ok, thanks."

Sal practically slunk inside like a wet dog.

There was a loud bang then a crash. Whatever was happening next door was very physical. She tried not to think about Trent and Demi having rough and tumble sex but thoughts kept popping unbidden into her brain. She went to bed early only to endure a restless night's sleep. She pictured them slamming hard up against the wall having wild, hot, 'Fifty Shades of Grey' passionate sex. Then in her dreams, the dentist morphed into Cherry who told Sal all her teeth were rotten and had to come out. As the dentist shoved his cold hard extraction instruments halfway down her throat, he said, "That's what you got for being mean and saying nasty things – you lose all your teeth."

Sal's dental appointment was first thing Monday. As she drove there Sal tried not to think about Trent but Charlie Puth was on the radio singing, *I'm only one call away, Superman has nothing on me...* A lump rose in Sal's throat. Chase hated her. Cherry hated her. Nothing was right in her world. Damn therapy. Wasn't therapy supposed to make life better not worse?

Haunted by her dental nightmare, her knuckles were white as she clung to the chair. Resisting the reflex urge to bite the hygienist, she endured the torture as her teeth and gums were attacked. Then the dentist filled a tooth. Feeling as if her mouth had been violated, Sal arrived at work to find Alice sitting at the front desk, all smiles.

"No Cherry?" asked Sal as she dumped her bag under the desk. The anaesthetic hadn't worn off and Sal could feel she was dribbling from the corner of her mouth.

Alice was beaming. "First things first," said Alice. "Look," she pointed at the brand-new photocopier. "We finally got approval."

Sal could barely believe her eyes. "Awesome, thank you," Sal high-fived Alice. Sal ran her hand gently over the new machine. It was twice the size of the old one. It smelt new. There were more trays. Ecstatic, she hugged the copier.

Wondering if Cherry mentioned anything to Alice about their little chat, Sal tentatively asked, "Is Cherry still sick?"

"No, I'm sorry Sal, but Cherry's decided administration isn't where she wants to be."

"Has she resigned?" Sal squeaked in a mixture of horror and delight.

Alice smiled smugly. "No, I've utilised her skills elsewhere."

"Really?"

"Follow me," Alice beckoned with a crook of her finger. Sal followed Alice down the corridor's long dark throat towards the salon. Ethel, Natalie, and Ruth were in the salon with their hair in curlers and getting their makeup done by none other than Cherry. The ladies looked delighted with their Hollywood hairdos.

"I love this job," Cherry grinned at Sal as she dabbed Sophia blue eye shadow on Ruth.

Ruth said, "Do you like my eyebrows, Sal? They've been threaded." She whispered. "Cherry even plucked my chin hairs for me, isn't she a dear."

Andie arrived in their midst. He was wearing a new shade of coral pink lipstick, his eyelashes had been extended, and his hair was freshly curled by a styling wand.

"What do you think?" He gave a little twirl and patted his hair. "So Sophia Loren, don't you think?"

"Gorgeous," approved Sal. Giving Cherry the thumbs up, she said, "Great work, Cherry, everyone looks stunning."

"Don't worry, Sal, I'll come help you when you need me." Cherry said in a patronising voice as she backcombed and teased Ruth's hair.

Sal swallowed her panic. What did Cherry mean by that?

Cherry said, "I know how much trouble you have with the

safe."

Sal breathed a sigh of relief.

Chapter 27: Confessions

Trent was on his way back from a run when he saw Sal waiting at the letterbox. He knew he'd been a dick and he knew he'd hurt her. He could see the wounded look in her eyes when he'd teased her about dating a tinker, tailor, baker, candlestick maker. Why couldn't he keep his big mouth shut? Should he go for another lap around the block so he could avoid her, or should he man up and run past? He couldn't muster the energy to run any further so he opted for ignoring her. But she stopped him as he ran past by tapping him on the shoulder with a piece of junk mail.

"Oi, you got a minute? I want to talk to you."

He kept jogging on the spot. "What about?"

She frowned at him. "Want to take your ears off first so you can hear what I have to say?"

Reluctantly he took them off. "Yeah, what is it?"

She heard Liz inside her head, saying tell the truth, Sal. She sucked in a breath and then said in a rush, "I've decided I won't come to training anymore." There she'd said it. The words were out.

Trent stopped jogging. "Don't do that because of me," he said, feeling guilty. He was breathing hard and trying to catch his breath.

It wasn't easy but she managed to find the words. "No, it's not because of you; it's not really my thing. I would offer to become the treasurer as I'd like to help the brigade but you don't want me there." She willed herself to look him in the eye so she lifted her chin. She met his eyes head on.

He ran his hand through his dark hair and knotted his fingers behind his sweaty neck. "That's the whole problem, Sal, I do," he said puffing. Still catching his breath, Trent continued, "So, it's best I don't have anything to do with you, but if you want to be a firefighter, I can suck it up, don't let me stop you from doing what you want to do."

Sal was speechless.

Confused, she stared at him, unable to comprehend what he had just said. She deflected. "Demi looks like a nice girl, I'm sure you'll be very happy."

He frowned. "Demi? Yeah, she does great work."

Sal coughed in surprise. Was Demi some sort of high-end escort? Was that why she had a fancy car? "What do you mean?" Then tried to gobble the words back; but it was too late they were out there.

"She's doing a great job of redesigning the house," he clarified. "You knew that, right?"

"No, I didn't know, I thought…," she broke off, not wanting to say what she thought. Sal was slowly processing. "So, you aren't going out with Demi?"

"Whatever gave you that idea? Demi's a great interior designer so I asked her to help me redecorate. Her partner, Dan, is in the army and is away a lot so she's not worried about working late helping me sort my place."

"She's not the one that broke your heart?"

"No, but that's hardly a discussion for the driveway." Trent glanced over his shoulder and saw Mrs Mac peering out her front door watching them.

Feeling humiliated, he plugged his earbuds back in. "Well, guess I better go and have a shower while I still have one, the bathroom is getting demolished tomorrow night."

In shock, Sal watched him jog up the drive and disappear inside his apartment.

Sal gave Kat the junk mail to read and tried to keep herself occupied but she couldn't settle. The truth struck her with the force of a sledgehammer. Trent liked her! More than just as a friend. She decided to go for a walk to clear her head, walking blindly, placing one foot in front of the other and without realising it she had walked to the beach. The sky was cloudy and dull like her mood. The troublesome wind buffeted her from behind pushing sand along in front of her. She half expected a tumbleweed to roll past. There were only a handful of diehard people on the beach braving the stormy weather.

Head down, Sal walked along the shoreline wondering how things got so messed up? Trent didn't want to get his heart broken by a heartbreaker like she was, a crazy chick that goes around breaking guys hearts because they don't have the right thigh. 'All by myself' was playing loudly in her ear. Appropriate, she thought. God, she needed to see her shrink. She really was screwed up.

Sal didn't see him at first. Hands shoved deep in his jean pockets, he was mooching along the beach kicking at shells and didn't notice her until they were only a couple of feet from each other. Trent's eyes widened in surprise and he tried to sidestep to allow her to get past. Sal stepped the same way and they collided.

They both said sorry at the same time.

It was awkward. Her breath hitched. Squirming, she pulled her earbuds out and turned them off in case he heard the roaring music and recognised her theme song.

The wind was whipping along the beach forcing her sideways. Her hair lifted and blew around her face and in her eyes. She mumbled, "No, I'm sorry."

"No, I'm sorry," he said, looking ashamed. "I shouldn't have said anything. I shouldn't have said what I said to Chase…it's none of my business."

Sal put up her hand and stopped him. "We broke up."

"What?" He asked stunned. "Why? I thought he was your dream man?"

"You were right. He failed to launch and I'd made him perfect in my imagination, and he wasn't perfect – he was dead boring."

Tell the truth, Sal, said a little voice in her head. "I miss you."

"Yeah, I miss you too. I'm sorry for being a total jerk. Can you forget what I said and can we go back to being friends?" Trent's hopeful look gave her courage.

Sal pulled herself up by her big girl knicker elastic and said,

"No, I don't think so."

Trent bit his lip.

Sal added, "Because unfortunately I think I've fallen for you."

His jaw dropped. "Do you really mean that?"

"Yeah, I must do because half of me wants to rip your balls off and shove them down your throat for being mean to me, and the fact that I'm not doing that must mean I like you more than as a friend."

He shook his head like a dog with water in his ears.

Bewildered, Trent couldn't make sense of anything. "But you think I'm an arsehole."

"More than an arsehole…" she paused, before adding, "sometimes you can be a real dick."

He nodded as if to accept the accuracy of her description.

Having finally told the truth, Sal was on a roll. "You think I'm impossible, you think I can be a real ditz, and that I'm a player."

His face softened. "Yeah, I do." Trent shifted uneasily from foot to foot. "Truth is, it freaks me out because I don't want to become just another statistic, just another ex in your box of exs."

"I'm going to therapy to get over my commitment phobia," Sal blurted. "What are you going to do to get over yourself?"

Trent gave her a half-smile. "How about we sit down and talk about it up there where we are a bit more sheltered from this god-awful wind," he suggested. He motioned to the covered wooden BBQ shelter up on the grass area.

"It would be nice to get out of the wind," agreed Sal.

They climbed the dune embankment and walked to the shelters, sitting at the BBQ table on the same side and stared at the view. Both were aware of each other's close proximity. It was cold and Sal longed to hunker closer for warmth. They sat close, but not quite touching. The air was heavy with words unsaid.

Attempting to lighten things up, Sal said, "Tell me you weren't walking along the beach thinking about butt plugs."

He chuckled. "I have been trying to rid my mind of such things ever since Kat brought up the subject." He glanced at her and smiled shyly. "No, I was thinking about you. I can't get you out of my head and I'm not sure what to do about it."

Unable to meet his eyes, Sal fiddled with the ties on the bottom of her windbreaker. "And I was thinking about you and feeling sad because I was going to have to move." Her trembling mouth curved into a smile and she lifted her gaze. Trent ran his hand around the back of his head. "What are we going to do about it?" he asked, adding, "It's costly to move."

"For the record Gone Don is Long Gone Don, if he hasn't got the message now – he never will."

"And there's no one else?"

"No one," she assured him.

He was silent.

"So, where to from here?" she asked looking expectantly at him.

"Here," Trent said, kissing her.

Touching her lips, she giggled, "I knew your moustache was going to tickle.

Chapter 28: The Great Knicker Caper

Sal arrived home hand-in-hand with Trent. "We made up," Sal told Kat exuberantly.

"So I see," Kat replied, a grin splitting her face.

"Yeah, she apologised," Trent cut in.

Sal shot him a warning look.

"The good news is I don't have to move, the bad news for you is that you will have to put up with me a bit longer."

"Move?" Kat's eyebrows rose. "Were you considering it?"

"Never mind, that's not important now. Just like the book says, I'm moving on and getting on with my life."

Of course, when her workmates heard about Trent, they gave Sal heaps, teasing her by taking bets, wondering how long this one would last before she dumped him. Miffed, Sal thought bugger the lot of them, she'd prove them all wrong.

Kat was blooming in pregnancy. Her hair was luscious and her skin glowing. Trent mentioned to Sal he thought Kat was stacking on the weight. Sal longed to tell Trent that Kat was up the duff but it wasn't her news to tell and she'd promised to let Kat do it in her time and in her own way. Ethan and Kat had become great mates and spent a lot of time together. Sal expected Kat would tell Ethan before the others.

Anton finally confessed to them that he'd met someone online. Her name was Yulia, and she was the reason they'd hardly seen him lately. He was keeping up his fitness regime either spending most of his time cycling, or out running with Yulia. He hadn't brought her to a social occasion yet but they'd heard a fair bit about her so thought it wouldn't be long until they met her. Pete drifted off the scene and they didn't hear from him again. Someone reckoned he went to Oz to get away from bumping into his ex and her girlfriend.

Sal still kept the box of exs under the bed at her place, and there were times she thought she should hide them back in the garage, but while hers and Trent relationship was fresh, she thought she should keep the box near – just in case. So far, she hadn't felt the familiar feeling of not being able to breathe. Sal also noticed that she hadn't given him a letter of the alphabet. And when she introduced Trent to people, she'd immediately referred to him as her boyfriend. This was a huge shift, and Liz noticed the change too. Liz thought Sal was making great progress and asked her what she thought about speaking her truth to Cherry, Don and Trent.

Sal reflected. "It wasn't easy but nobody died," she said.

***

They were having a courtyard neighbours BBQ dinner with the Saffers, the Wrinklies, Mrs Mac, and her two dogs, Penny and Bonny. The Dinklahs were away cruising again. Mrs Saffer was busy filling up glasses, and loading plates with food, making sure everyone was comfortable and full. Meanwhile, Anton was being instructed on how to correctly cook boerewors by Mr Saffer, Trent was sitting at the BBQ table telling fire brigade stories, when Kat suddenly reached across and squeezed Trent's thigh.

Surprised, he asked Kat, "What are you doing?"

"I just want to see what a good thigh feels like."

"Here, have a drumstick then," Trent said, passing her the plate of barbequed chicken. "Cos if you squeeze my thigh again, I think Sal will blacken your eye."

Kat laughingly told him to ask Sal to fill him in about the thigh test. Eyebrows raised, he turned to Sal who said she'd tell him some other time.

For the good of the brigade, Sal gave up trying to be a firefighter and volunteered to be their treasurer instead. She was way more suited to that role. Kat had to give up firefighting because of her pregnancy and said if they weren't told soon, they might think she had swallowed a basketball or had a massive stomach tumour, or something. Sal gave up trying to lose the 3 kilos she'd gained and decided she'd be fat and happy, much to Trent and Kat's relief. Neither of them wanted to be around a hungry lettuce muncher. Besides, Kat told her, they might as well be fat together.

One warm evening, Trent asked Sal if she wanted to stroll down to the little cove not far from where they lived. A small hidden beach only the locals knew about. They walked hand-in-hand down the hill and came to the cove. To their delight they were the only ones there. They rolled their jeans up, and carrying their shoes they walked across the soft sand to the bendy Pohutukawa branch that grew sideways from the shore over the water like a long bench seat. They sat on the branch gazing out across the horizon towards the cityscape where the lights were beginning to flicker in the distance.

It was such a warm romantic evening as the first stars began to pinprick the night sky and the golden globe of the moon began to rise behind Rangitoto. Solid dependable Rangitoto Island was a comforting blot on the landscape. As it got darker, it grew colder and the stars more plentiful. Sal started to shiver and cuddled closer, leaning back against him for warmth.

Feeling happy and relaxed Sal leaned into Trent's embrace and sighed. Everything was picture-perfect. He nuzzled in, tenderly kissing her neck, gentle, long soft kisses that made her purr. He offered her his dark blue hoodie. When she put it on it drowned her.

"Tell me," she said gently, "about her. What happened?"

He spoke quietly, his voice distant and strained as he shared with her his heartbreak. How he'd been engaged to Sonia and it was only a month before the wedding when Sonia cheated on him with a guy he used to think of as one of his close mates, a guy called Jude. "He's no longer a friend," he added bitterly.

"What about you and Demi? Why didn't that work out? She's nice." Demi was everything Sal dreamed of being. Good-looking, with great taste, height, legs to her armpits, money, and a great car. What wasn't to like?

Trent shook his head. "Demi said I was married to the job. She said she didn't like being abandoned when I rushed off to a call out. Funny that, since she is with Dan who is in the army and away most of the time. So, I guess that wasn't the real reason. Guess we were just better as friends than as a couple. Demi and I – it was nice but not... well you know...," he drifted off unable to find the words.

"Right." Sal finished for him.

"Yeah, guess so. Demi was a long time ago, she's with Dan now. We are still friends, it works." His face clouded, "But Sonia was different, I truly loved her."

Trent explained since his having his heart broken by Sonia, he'd been scared of entering into another relationship in case the heartbreak happened again. He'd lost trust and that's why he was so freaked out about Sal's box of ex's. He was scared he'd fall in love and have his heart broken all over again.

Sal didn't interrupt, she listened, feeling honoured that he trusted her enough to share his heart with her, and it helped her understand him better, and why her box of many exs worried him.

It got late and they decided it was time to head back home. Sal had rolled the sleeves up on his hoodie so she didn't feel like she was flapping like an emperor penguin when she moved her arms. They walked back, hand-in-hand, without speaking. Trent opened the picket fence, forgetting Ken had fixed it he gave it a nudge with his foot. The gate swung open but Sal wasn't ready to go home yet. She didn't want to say goodnight. For the first time in a long, long time, she didn't want to escape.

"Is Anton home?" she asked breathlessly, kissing Trent.

"No."

"Good." Tugging him by the front of his T-shirt she pulled the picket gate to, then taking his hand she walked to his place, and waited for him to open the door for her.

Trent leaned down; his mouth brushing hers as he opened the door and led her inside. They kissed, mouths hungry and bodies heated. Trent led her up the small flight of stairs to his room. He turned on the side lamp so the lighting was soft, yellow, and romantic. He commanded the Echo Dot speaker to play love songs.

Intimate, the room smelled like him, like his aftershave. She noticed he had a photo of her on his bedside cabinet and she smiled and kissed him again. He ran his hands gently down her back causing her to shiver with desire as his mouth nibbled her ear. A flutter of panic made her heart beat faster.

"I want you," Trent said, his voice husky.

Sal nodded, feeling the same desire. "I don't want you to see my wobbly bits," she protested weakly.

"I love your wobbly bits," he smiled into her hair, adding, "And your great personalities."

He lay her on his bed and began to slowly undress her, all the while kissing her neck, breasts, and torso with soft butterfly kisses. He slowly unzipped her jeans. It was then Sal remembered she was wearing her granny pants.

"No," she cried slapping his hand away.

He sat back on his haunches, confused. "No?"

He smiled wolfishly. "Hello, what have we here?"

Too late, he had seen them. Granny pants just like Bridget Jones's ginormous pair when she was being seduced by the rogue, Daniel Cleaver.

Pushing him away, Sal struggled to do up her zip. She was as tragic as Bridget Jones and the perfect romantic moment was ruined. She felt humiliated. Sal resolved that as soon as she could she was going shopping to buy new lingerie. Chuckling softly, Trent kissed the top of her head as she buried herself in her shoulder, her face blood red with embarrassment.

"I love your granny pants but I'd love it more if you would remove them," Trent grinned. "Or even better if I could. Still, it might take a while," he teased.

She gave him a playful shove; telling him she was not amused.

"Oh, come here, little Pixie with the enormous unflattering granny pants. Let me free you from their evil grasp."

All thought of resistance gone, Sal allowed him to remove her jeans, then the offending undies. Trent's kisses travelled all over her naked body, then lower until nothing else in the world mattered. They fell asleep entwined in each other's arms listening to the gentle patter of rain on the roof, her hideous granny pants abandoned in a puddle of clothes on the floor.

The next day Sal floated around the rest home humming softly to herself and smiling her little Mona Lisa smile.

Andie teased her, saying, "I reckon someone got lucky last night."

Later that evening Sal burned all her granny pants. She went shopping on the way home and splashed out on some sexy lingerie. Trent would never see her in granny underpants again, and if they ever had another card night and she lost five games in a row and had to down trou, at least she'd be wearing something sexy.

Now and then, Trent saw fear in Sal's eyes. Those were the times he wondered if she might ditch him, and he'd end up being another statistic in her box of exs. The reno was going well, the bathroom was finished, the walls painted, and next on the agenda was the kitchen. Trent even asked Sal to liaise with Demi on colours and styles, and what she thought was important in a kitchen. He told Demi that Sal hated the couch he'd chosen, even going so far as to call it cruddy, and suggested she could help Sal purchase a new one. Sal felt a bit weird about teaming up with Demi. Secretly Sal believed Demi was wondering what Trent saw in a short, fat blonde when he could have had someone like her.

While they were in a lighting shop, Sal tentatively tried to broach the subject of Sonia with Demi to see if she had any dirt she could share, but couldn't figure out how to bring it up without looking totally obvious. She fished a couple of times, but gave up when Demi didn't take the bait. She refused to talk about it, saying that's in the past.

Demi flicked her long hair back over her shoulder and smiled, "I'm pleased he's happy now, looks like he might have found the right one, don't you think?"

Sal's stomach clenched. She was excited and frightened at the same time. She was convinced as long as Trent didn't ruin things by saying something stupid like "I love you," everything should be alright.

They were having dinner when she felt Trent's eyes on her she raised her gaze to see a strange look on his face.

"I love..."

She quickly put her finger to his lips and warned him. "Don't say it."

His face fell. "What you have done with your hair. It looks really nice."

She hadn't done anything with her hair and she was certain that wasn't what he was going to say. Still, she felt like she had dodged a bullet. Anytime anyone had ever said, 'I love you', it had ended in tears.

As usual, work was busy but without Cherry's help Sal felt more in control. She loved the brand-new photocopier and was happier being sole charge of the office than having an assistant, so didn't mind the days being hectic.

Poor Ann in laundry was under pressure and stressing out. To give Ann a break so she could take some time off, Alice decided to send the laundry off-site. Soon afterwards they got a new respite admission and Mrs Butcher needed her washing done. Her family had gone away for the week as they needed a break and weren't expected back early. They hadn't packed enough clothes for Mrs Butcher's week-long stay. Sal offered to take Mrs Butcher's washing home and said she'd return it the next day. Alice was grateful for the offer and took Sal up on it.

"What are you doing?" Kat asked. "It's not washing day. I do the washing. You know I can't stand the way you hang things all willy-nilly and you don't colour code the pegs to the washing."

Sal promised she would throw it in the dryer then Kat would not have to watch her hang it out wrong. Kat relaxed.

"I don't know why we just don't get all pink pegs," Sal complained.

"Are you pre-empting that I'm going to have a girl?" Kat

asked, lovingly rubbing her growing belly.

That night was going to be their first ante-natal class. Kat was nervous as anything, and Sal was feeling protective and vulnerable. It brought up painful memories and made her heart ache. She admired Kat's strength. Kat was determined to parent on her own. Being a single mother wasn't going to be easy but if anyone could do it, Kat could. She would make a great mother. After all, she had plenty of experience; she mothered Sal all the time.

The other couples in the group assumed they were a couple, and neither of them corrected the assumption, figuring what did it matter anyway. It would stop people asking about the father, and any other questions that Kat would rather not answer. Sal practiced how to massage Kat's back during contractions and they learned breathing exercises. Nervously excited, Sal was looking forward to meeting this little baby and felt honoured to be Kat's support person.

Saturday night Trent and Sal decided to have a big night in at his place, cuddling on the couch and watching a new TV series. Anton was out again and they appreciated the time they had alone together. Trent's long legs were propped up on the coffee table while Sal was curled up beside him with her legs across his lap and head tucked under his arm. She wondered what he would do if she told him she was pregnant. Would he bail, or insist she abort the child? Trent noticed she was quiet, and seemed distant, and asked what was up.

She swallowed. She felt like she was walking on broken glass.

He asked again, turning off the TV and waiting patiently. She hesitated.

Finally, she asked, "What would you do if I told you I was pregnant?"

His mouth fell open. He took his arm away and sat up straight looking her dead in the eye. "Are you? Pregnant?"

She watched him carefully, studying his face for any tell-tale signs. When she had told the deserter the same news he had fled, wanting nothing to do with her, or his offspring. "Answer first."

"Wow," Trent said thunderstruck. He ran his hand round the back of his head tussling his dark hair, and frowned. "I know the decision would ultimately be yours, but I would love a kid."

He was so sweet. Sal swallowed the lump in her throat, bit her lip, and tried to fight back her tears. She finally managed to speak.

"Relax," she told him. "I'm not preggers, but Kat is. She has asked me to go to ante-natal classes with her as her support person."

"Phew!" He blew out his cheeks. "Can't say I'm not relieved as I would like to be more prepared and plan for such a major life change, but then going by what other folks have told me about becoming a parent, I expect you never really are – ready." He settled back and put his arm around her shoulder and drew her close. She put her head on his chest and snuggled in listening to the steady beat of his heart.

"Does Rob know?" Trent asked.

"Kat doesn't want to involve him," Sal replied. "She's prepared to parent on her own."

He didn't like the idea of Rob being excluded but understood Kat's reasons. Trent told Sal that he and the other guys would be there for Kat if she needed anything; all she had to do was ask. Then he fell silent as if he was internalising things. Sal thought he was thinking about what their kid would be like if they had one.

Then he said, "You know they are going to assume you guys are lesbians, right."

"They already do." Sal tapped his nose. "Just as well you know better then, isn't it?"

Chapter 29: Man Traps

The weekend ended too soon. Sal was running late for work. She got in the car then remembered Mrs Butcher's washing. Worried that Mrs Butcher might run out of knickers, she ran back inside to get the laundry, then raced back to the car throwing the bag on the back seat.

The minute she arrived at work Sal handed the bag of laundry to the carers to put away.

Shortly after, Carla arrived at the reception with Andie in tow both in hysterics.

"What's so funny?" Sal asked, wanting to be in on the joke.

Clara tried to get herself under control. "I was dressing Mrs Butcher and when I went to put her underwear on, I found this little scanty red lacey G-string in the drawer. I asked Mrs Butcher, if they were hers? To which she replied no, they most certainly were not. Alice tells me you took Mrs Butcher's washing home. Are these," Carla twirled the panties around her finger, then went to use them as a slingshot, "yours, Sal?"

Not wanting the whole world to see her sexy new red undies, Sal snatched them from Carla's hand. "Give them here."

The jokers dissolved into fits of giggles.

Andie said, "Darling, I could recommend a G-string that would look great on you. Make you look two sizes smaller, hon."

"Shut up," Sal hissed, as she hurriedly stuffed the panties in her handbag.

Sal had just changed out of her work clothes when Trent arrived. She was trying to improve her wardrobe so that Kat didn't tease her about looking dowdy and she did want to look nice for Trent.

"What do you want to do tonight? The kitchen has been completely demolished so it's either takeaways on the floor, dinner at yours, or I take you out for a slap-up dinner. Your choice."

Looking forward to being wined and dined, Sal chose dinner out. Trent drove as he was on call and wouldn't be drinking. Sal hoped there were no call-outs tonight. They could be out somewhere and next minute his pager would go off and he would race away to whatever emergency might be happening. Sometimes it was a false alarm. She was getting used to Trent being there one minute and gone the next but she really didn't want to have a nice dinner out ruined by a call-out tonight.

Sal chose the little local Italian restaurant near Waiake beach. The food was good and the place quiet, the waiter pleasantly attentive, and the wine rich and full-bodied. During dinner, Trent casually told her that there had been some incident up north and he would be leaving at four-thirty am so he couldn't stay out late as he still had to pack. He had been deployed to help with the peat fire burning in the Far North. But she wasn't to worry he'd call her every day.

While she was digesting this news, Sal ducked down to get her phone out of her handbag to check what the time was and, in the process, knocked the bag over spilling its contents.

Trent crawled under the table to help pick up her things. His eyes widened at the sight of her scanty little red G-string lying on the carpet. She scrabbled to pick up everything and chucked the G-string back in her bag and zipped it closed.

They resumed their places at the table. Hoping he wouldn't mention it, Sal drained her glass of wine and tried to catch the waiter's eye to signal she wanted another.

Cracking up, Trent said, "That really is your man trap; it has certainly caught my attention." He grinned. "Were you in the girl guides? Always be prepared and all that?" His eyes lit up. "Are you wearing any? Or do you just carry them in your handbag in case of an emergency?"

Humiliated, Sal told him her work story. Trent laughed until he had tears in his eyes.

He leaned across and whispered. "I'm wearing my undies, underneath my pants mind, and I've got my superman socks on." He stuck his leg out from under the table and pulled the hem of his trousers up. "I reckon these are my lucky socks."

Sal gave him the look. "So, you think you are going to get lucky, do you?"

"I hope so. Well, that's certainly the plan," Trent said giving her a sly wink.

Trent explained that he and Anton were going to assist the crew up North as the fire was out of control and the fatigued firefighters there needed a rest. As they drove home Trent said she was not to worry about him because he knew his job. He added, "I'd say stay the night at mine but I don't want to wake you at four am when I get up so its best if you stay at yours tonight."

Sal nodded, feeling suddenly lost that he was going away and they wouldn't be together the night before he left.

He walked Sal to her front door and kissed her goodnight.

"I'm going to keep thinking about you wearing that little red G-string while I'm away," he said with a devilish grin. Then blowing her kisses he hopped the hedge and disappeared inside his front door.

Sal climbed the stairs and made her way to her bedroom. Maybe she could lose three kilos while he was away so her arse wouldn't be the size of twin moons hanging out of her little red G when he finally did get to see her wearing it. But as soon as her head hit the pillow she panicked. She felt like she was drowning and couldn't breathe.

The old fear was back. It was still there in the morning. Sal had shut down. She ignored her phone, went for long walks, and didn't answer when he called. How was she going to avoid him when he returned? He lived next door – it would be impossible. She'd have to move. She reminded herself never to date a neighbour again.

The phone rang, she saw it was Trent. It was the fifth time he had called that day. She closed her eyes and swallowed down the panic, took a deep breath, blew it out, and swiped. "Hi."

"What's up, buttercup? Why are you avoiding me? Have I

done something to upset you?" he asked. He sounded shattered and worried.

She felt stink. She really needed to grow a pair, put her big girl panties on and tell the truth. She could hear Liz's singsong voice in her head saying, tell your truth. Explain what's happening for you.

Sal launched into a long-winded ramble that even she didn't understand.

There was a long pause, followed by a puzzled, "What?"

Sal tried again. "I panicked when you said you were going away because I suddenly realised, I would miss you, and if I missed you, then I was in too deep. It means I care, and if I care, I could get hurt so it's easier to bail before you break my heart."

She expected him to say, "I knew this would happen. I was going to be another ex in the box of exs." But he didn't.

Trent said, "You think I'm going to break your heart? I'm scared shitless that you are going to break mine. You're a silly little pixie."

And boom, just like that, she realised she was overreacting. She was thinking of ending something good for no other reason than because she cared. And wasn't caring necessary for a loving relationship?

"Yeah," she agreed sheepishly. "I am."

"Right, good I'm glad we got that sorted. Now, I want you to know, you are not to worry, I have my superman socks with me."

"I need a hug." What was she – five?

"I promise to give you one as soon as I get back. I'll be there as soon as I can, babe. Hang on, I'll just get my cape."

Sal laughed. "Now who is being silly."

Trent called every day. He told her he was tired, but unscathed and so far, had suffered no more than sunburn and blisters.

Sal checked the news and social media for updates. The fire was huge, the small township of Kaimaumau had to be evacuated while the crew attempted to stop the spread of the fire. But the peat was burning underground and the only way to contain it was to dig around the perimeter and drench the ground with water to stop the fire spreading. Just as they thought they had it under control, the tree roots would ignite and the flames would flare up again.

Instead of avoiding Trent's calls, now she anxiously waited for him to call to tell her he was alright, and assure her that he would be home soon. It was the end of a very long week when Trent called and told her the crews were swapping over. They were all exhausted.

He messaged when he'd left to say he was on his way but it took him three long hours to drive home. Sal breathed a sigh of relief when his ute drove into the shared drive and rushed out to greet him. As he got out of the vehicle, she threw her arms around his neck and hugged him like she would never let go.

Then she noticed he was alone. She glanced about. "Where's Anton?"

"He'll be back tomorrow. He had to stay another day."

"Great!" Sal beamed. "Hope you not too exhausted, I plan to welcome you home in style." Smiling she tugged his hand and led him towards his front door. "By the way I'm wearing that little red G."

"Holy cow! I can barely raise my eyebrows little one, but I'll do my best."

Chapter 30: Step-By-Step

Sally was freaked out that she was so happy to see Trent. Weird things were happening to her. She was definitely changing – evolving. Perhaps those expensive therapy sessions were paying off after all. Maybe she was moving on and getting on with her life for real. She still had the occasional flare-up where she panicked and couldn't breathe. He seemed to recognise the signs and he would back off giving her some wriggle room and then she came right again. Sal would remind herself that she was overreacting. And when Trent kissed her lightly on top of her head, she melted, and the world felt like a better place.

One evening, Sal put the box of exs on the dining table and cautiously opened the lid as if a cloud of bats might fly out and bite her.

Kat was drying the dishes. She had become a complete nester and nurturer and was cleaning and cooking all the time.

Curious, Kat watched Sal carefully sift through the photos.

"What are you doing? Kat asked, putting the tea-towel down and coming closer.

"Just checking."

"For what?"

"Feelings."

"You are a strange one, Sally Gelee."

Sal stared at the photos. Amazed, she declared, "You know, I don't feel anything. I don't feel anything when I look at these old photos now."

Kat frowned at Sal like she thought she had grown three heads. "Babe, I'm worried about you. Are you still seeing the shrink?"

"Yep. This is homework."

Kat chuckled and gave her a side squeeze. "You really are

crazy chick, but I still love you."

"Have you ever been in love?" Sal suddenly asked.

Kat stared at her blankly for a moment as if she didn't comprehend.

"I don't mean head over heels infatuation but real love," Sal clarified.

"Twice," Kat said quietly as if remembering the pain.

"Rob?"

"No." Kat paused. "Aidan and Lee."

"What happened?"

Kat rubbed a protective hand over her baby bump and sighed. "They didn't reciprocate."

"If I was lesbian, I would definitely be into you. Look at you, you are smart, funny, gorgeous and kind," Sal said in an attempt to wipe the sadness from Kat's memory.

Kat gave Sally a small smile.

"Are you scared?" Sal asked, as she put her hand on Kat's baby bump and felt the little life within move.

"Yeah, of course I am. I'm worried that my baby won't be ok. I was drunk at the time of conception, what if he or she has foetal alcohol syndrome, or if something is wrong with the baby because of me, because of something I've done."

Sal couldn't think of anything to say to reassure Kat everything was going to be alright.

Kat's eyes misted. "I'm not really doing this alone, am I? I've got my bestie, and Ethan, and the other uncles. We'll still love our little one, no matter what, won't we?" It was as much a declaration as a plea and Sal knew it.

"Course we will," Sal promised. Sal enveloped Kat in a hug. "Don't you worry, we will all be there for you and your little one."

***

Alice was ropable. Due to staff sickness, she was having to hire staff from the agency, and she wasn't happy about the extra cost. She glowered over Sal's shoulder at the price on the agency's invoice.

"Are you still seeing the fireman?" Alice unexpectedly asked.

"They are called firefighters these days. And yes, I am," Sal replied. Everyone questioned her like that. Are you still seeing… uh…what's his name? And then waited for her to fill in the blank.

Alice whistled through her teeth. "Goodness, that must be a record."

How rude! Sal gritted her teeth.

Vikki called out, "Sal hasn't brought him in to see us, so I'm not sure he really does exist."

"He's real," Sal assured them.

"He must be because she's had a dopey grin on her face for ages. When are we going to meet him then, darling?" Andie wanted to know.

"I can show you photos." Sal started flicking through the gallery on her phone.

They could hear Harold approaching, his toolbelt jangling as he walked. Earwigging, Harold plucked a screwdriver out of his belt, and was trying to fix a latch that had come loose on the window nearest Sal's desk.

"Let's hope we don't have the fire alarm go off and he turns out for that," grumbled Harold. Each time he pushed his glasses higher they slid further down his nose.

Andie was curious and leaned over her shoulder to get a better look at the photos. "Ok hon, he's handsome but what's this one got that makes him a keeper? Is he a keeper, babe?"

Sal thought for a moment. "Well, he makes me laugh."

"Oh, so a whole lot is going for him then," quipped Alice.

"I wasn't finished," Sal bit. "He brings me a coffee every morning before he goes to work. And he makes me breakfast or dinner if I am at his house."

Vikki laughed. "You like him because he meets your dietary requirements."

Ignoring the dig, Sal continued, "He calls me during the day for no other reason than to hear my voice."

"That's sweet," Andie sighed wistfully. Then giving Sal a

meaningful look, he said, "But is he good with his hands?"

Purposefully ignoring the innuendo, Sal continued, "He fixes things to make my life easier. Checks the oil in my car and my tyres before I go on a journey."

"That's good." Howard nodded hitching his toolbelt a little higher. "A man needs to be able to do those things."

Sal continued, "He buys little things, practical things, and big things and never makes me feel like I owe him."

"Sparkly things?" Andie wanted to know.

Sal ignored Andie and carried on. "He tells me I'm beautiful even when I'm a dishevelled neurotic mess. He gives me freedom when I look panicked like a deer caught in the headlights. He calls it wriggle room." Sal smiled, then added, "Trent makes me feel like a hug can fix anything."

Vikki was being nosey. "What do you enjoy most?"

Sal felt a little uncomfortable by the intimate questions. It made her realise she was in a whole lot deeper than she imagined. Alice, Vikki, Andie, and Howard were hanging on her every word.

She thought for a moment before replying. "I love a kiss on the top of the forehead, cuddling up on the couch watching telly together. Being in the same space, and breathing the same air. I feel free to be myself around him. He makes me laugh, and I feel like my smile makes him happy."

They appeared impressed and that gave Sal the confidence to continue.

"I love him calling me Smurfette, or his little pixie and not putting me down when I am definitely being stupid, over-the-top neurotic."

"Sounds like this one might just be a keeper," Vikki said thoughtfully.

"I like him already," Andie said giving Sal's shoulder a little squeeze. Andie threw Harold a wicked smile. "A man who is good with his tools is so sexy, don't you think, Harry?"

Harold shuffled off, muttering something about harassment in the workplace.

"Mm, the counselling must be working, Sal," Vikki commented.

"The proof will be in the pudding," warned Alice.

Chapter 31: Surprises

Trent promised to take her out for dinner to celebrate her birthday and told her he'd pop over and get her at seven o'clock. She wore her new black leather jacket, nice white blouse, faded blue designer jeans, and heels. She matched her silver bangle with the silver hoop earrings her Mum had given her for Christmas, and a slim silver pendant. She spent time on her hair and makeup and was happy with her reflection in the full-length mirror when she heard a knock at the door.

"Romeo's here," Kat shouted, her voice muffled by the closed door.

When she opened the door, she was surprised to find Kat dressed to kill. Kat hadn't been out anywhere except ante-natal group for ages. She had gone from party girl to hermit.

"Are you going out?" Sal asked unable to contain her surprise.

Kat got huffy. "You are not the only one with a life, you know." But didn't divulge where she was going, or who with. Sal put it down to Kat being hormonally imbalanced and let it slide.

Trent was waiting downstairs for her. She had hoped they would enjoy a romantic dinner for two at the local Italian where they had their first official date but Trent told her he wasn't feeling well. He had a hell of a headache and an upset tummy, and if it was alright with her could they just have takeaways at the beach instead. Naturally, she was disappointed. She got all dressed up for takeaways at the beach. Telling herself to suck it up, she hopped in the car and they drove down the road.

"Don't worry, no pager tonight, I'm off duty," he said as if reading her mind.

Trent drove past the Torbay takeaway shop and as they reached Waiake he slowed, turned and parked outside the Torbay Sailing club.

He glanced at her apologetically. "I've just got to pop in here for a minute to see a mate. Won't be long. Come with me."

"What for?" she asked, perplexed. That's weird, she thought he said he was sick. If he was well enough to pop into the Sailing Club, why weren't they going out for a proper slap-up dinner to celebrate her birthday?

He seemed flustered. "I need to talk to..., it won't take a minute."

"Looks like there's a party going on," Sal told him, peering up at the deck. "I can see people on the balcony."

"Yeah," she didn't hear the end of the sentence as his words were lost, muffled by the closed car door. He opened her door and held it. "Come on, I'd like him to meet you. You'll like him," he promised.

"I thought you were feeling sick," Sal grumbled. She sighed. "Ok, ok," she got out of the vehicle and closed the car door.

Resigned, Sal followed Trent upstairs the noise grew louder and when they arrived at the top of the stairs, there was a hell of a din.

"After you," Trent said opening the door.

The noise stopped abruptly. The bold gold banner on the far wall read, *Happy Birthday Sally!* The room was filled with her friends and workmates. "Surprise!" they yelled in unison.

As everyone surged towards her the DJ cranked up the music to wish her a happy birthday. She was really blown away.

"Happy birthday, babe." Kat handed her a glass of champagne. "Hasn't Trent done a great job?" She clinked her glass against Sal's. "Don't worry," she said, "mine is only orange juice. Bottoms up, babe."

"But...but...when did you organise all this?" she asked Trent, amazed by how sneaky he had been.

He nodded. "A couple of weeks ago." He gave Kat a wink. "I had a little help from a friend."

The party was a wonderful surprise; she'd not had a clue. She was having trouble believing this was really happening. Frowning up at him she asked, "So, let me guess you aren't really feeling sick?"

"No, little one," he grinned. "I'm ready to party, and I hope you are too," he said twirling her around and planting a kiss on her cheek.

"You guys are super sneaky!" Sal declared, delighted.

He'd even organised the catering and the birthday cake. Anton was in charge of the bar. He and Yulia were both wearing black suits, white shirts and bowties, and were doing an excellent job of serving drinks. Sal could see why Anton had fallen for Yulia; she was exotic looking, long limbed with charcoal eyes, and flawless skin. Her straight raven black hair was pulled back off her face and secured in a tight bun at the nape. She was rocking the outfit. No wonder they had hardly seen Anton lately, Yulia was cool East European chic.

"I've still got to give you my present," Trent whispered in her ear.

She drew breath when she opened the jewellery box to find the most gorgeous delicate gold and diamond heart-shaped necklace.

"It's beautiful, thank you." She kissed him. "And thank you for the most wonderful surprise birthday."

"It's not over yet," he promised. "I'm just sorry your family couldn't be here but mine are and I can't wait for you to meet them."

Mr and Mrs Powell were hard case and couldn't wait to tell Sal about Trent's formative years. When he felt like he'd suffered enough embarrassment, Trent dragged her away so she could mix and mingle with her other guests. Over a glass of bubbles, Andie told Sal he thought Ethan was sexy. Ethan was busy helping in the kitchen and was none the wiser that he was being checked out.

Sal shook her head, "He's not gay," she told him. "And I don't think he'd turn even for you, darling."

"Aww, shame." Andie shrugged.

"Finally, we, get to meet Superman," Andie said to Trent. "He's a bit of alright, Sal." Andie flicked his long hair and puckered his bright red lips. "Just the kind of man I'd go for."

Trent played along by air kissing Andie. "Why thank you darling, but I have to tell you I'm taken. I have to warn you little Smurfette here, gets mighty jealous." He tucked Sal under his wing. "She may look wee but she's feisty."

"Oh, I know, darling, believe me I know," Andie empathised.

Sal had a wonderful night. It was well after eleven when they left. Trent had organised cleaners to go in at midnight, and Ethan and Anton stayed back to lend a hand. They insisted Kat go home and put her feet up, but she refused saying she'd stay and help clean up.

"Where are you going?" she asked when they left the sailing club and Trent turned the wrong direction.

"Where are we going?"

"You'll see," he answered mysteriously.

He drove into the city, and towards Wynyard Quarter then he turned into the Hilton Hotel.

Sal let out a low whistle. It was way too perfect. She stared up at the large white building shaped like a cruise ship and then back at Trent. "But I haven't got any clothes."

"Not necessary we are only staying the night, and I have packed a brand-new toothbrush and toothpaste for you." He tugged a scrap of material from his back pocket and twirled her G string mid-air, "And I brought these for you, however you could always go commando if you'd prefer."

"Give them to me." She snatched them from him and hid them before the valet noticed. The valet parked the car and they walked hand-in-hand into the lobby. Trent had booked the Deluxe Harbour View suite. The views over the Waitemata harbour were beautiful.

"Wow," was all she could say as they entered the room. Everything was breathtakingly beautiful. He was more of a romantic than she could have ever imagined. There were fresh red rose petals scattered on the bed. On a small table nearby was a platter of exquisite handmade chocolates, and champagne cooling in a silver ice bucket, with two chilled glasses next to it. Ed Sheeran was playing from some hidden music source. Trent joined in, singing the lyrics, 'You look perfect to me.'

Trent filled their champagne glasses and led her out onto the balcony where they watched boats criss-crossing the harbour against a backdrop of city lights that coloured the water and the sky. The weather was warm and the evening perfect.

"Happy birthday, honey," Trent said as they chinked their glasses, then he leaned in and whispered in her ear. "Just in case you are wondering, I'm wearing my lucky socks."

"I've got my new sexy lingerie on," she said coyly.

"Oh," he said pretending to be disappointed, "I'll miss the granny pants."

Cocooned in the Egyptian cotton sheets, they slept late. Fortunately, Trent had organised a late checkout. Entwined in a tangle of arms and legs they relaxed chatting about nothing in particular as Sal played with his chest hair. She put her hand on his thigh and said, "You have nice thighs."

"I hope it's the right thigh. Now, if you move your hand a little higher and slightly to the centre..." He teased.

They made love again and as they bathed in the afterglow he said, "You know I love your thighs, and your bum. You have a cute bum."

Sal giggled.

Trent grew serious. "You know you have accused me of being a dick on numerous occasions," he reminded her.

"That's cos you have been one."

He propped himself up on his elbow. "Do you still think I am? A dick?"

Chuckling, she replied, "A real dick. Still, for the record I like that and your thighs."

Trent followed her into the shower. First out, she dried herself and wrapped herself in the hotels luxurious white robe and stepped outside onto the balcony to enjoy the view. Enjoying her coffee, she sat at the table slowly sipping her coffee while overlooking the harbour and cityscape thinking, right now, life is good.

They got dressed and went down to breakfast. Sal loved the

décor, everywhere she looked made her think she was on a cruise ship. While they were ordering breakfast the waitress pointed out there were two orca whales playing in the harbour.

Sal leaned her head on Trent's shoulder and said, "It couldn't be any more special."

"Oops, I forgot," he said casually pulling something out of his shirt pocket, "here's your other present."

"Another present!" she exclaimed. Dazed, Sal opened it. Inside she discovered two return tickets to Queenstown.

"I thought you needed a holiday; I hope you don't mind if I come with you? I've already checked with Bossy Alice. She said you don't work on the weekends, and as a special favour, she'd let you have the Friday off so we can have a long weekend together."

Oblivious to the disapproving looks of the other restaurant patrons, Sal threw her arms around his neck and kissed him.

***

Three weeks later they flew to Queenstown and stayed at the Crowne Plaza on the lake's edge. Trent removed his pager and relaxed from the moment they stepped on the plane. It took Sal a little longer, yet with a little gentle persuasion she forgot about work and concentrated on having fun. They did the usual touristy things, enjoying the adrenalin rush of the jet boats, then the next day parasailing on the lake, but he couldn't talk Sal into doing a bungy jump.

They went up the gondola and surveyed the beauty of Queenstown. Trent suggested they race each other on the luge but Sal wanted a more leisurely day. He booked lunch at Walter Peak Station and then they went across Lake Wakatipu on the grand old Lady of the Lake, the steamship SS Earnslaw. The trip was vintage romantic, the food at Walter Peak sublime, the wine delectable and the view incredible.

Then the old niggle rose, like a sea monster it welled up from somewhere deep within; the fear that this was too perfect. It couldn't be real, could it? Her heart began to thump uncomfortably against her breastbone. When she put a hand to her chest, she could feel her heart thudding beneath her sweaty palm. She couldn't breathe. It was the old familiar feeling of suffocation.

Why couldn't she breathe? The toys in the sandpit sprang to mind. Maybe all the sand was about to blow up in her face because God didn't want to be a marble and didn't like his placement in the sandpit. But then, what did God look like? At least she had chosen a giant marble. She thought about where she had placed Superman in the scheme of her life. She certainly didn't enjoy it when Superman wasn't part of the inner circle.

What she was the most scared of? That it wouldn't be perfect that when everything went wrong there would be hurt and plenty of pain. She couldn't bail now; he held the tickets to get home. They'd fly home tomorrow and then if she still felt nauseous, she could run. Tonight, she'd have to make the best of things.

She was distant on the trip back across the lake, and Trent noticed.

"What's up, Smurfette?"

"Nothing," she said evasively.

"Nothing?"

"Nothing." She thought the steely tone in her voice would prevent him from asking again. But no.

"Nothing looks like something. What's wrong?"

"Everything."

"Interesting. Nothing went to everything in a nano second. Everything? Can you narrow that down for me, little Pixie?"

The SS Earnslaw reached Queenstown wharf.

The thrusters helped drown out the words, "I'm scared."

She heard Liz in her head, instructing her that fear after being hurt was a normal reaction. She had to guard her affections wisely, but did not need to shut everybody out.

After strolling along the water's edge, they sat beneath the sun umbrella at a waterfront restaurant and enjoyed the last few hours of sunshine. It cooled quickly in this part of the world, but everywhere she looked was stunningly beautiful. The majestic snow-tipped mountains rose out of the icy cold lake. The low-lying sunlight skated across the lake's surface turning it golden. Even the ducks bobbing at the lake's edge looked content.

A talented musician was playing a pan flute nearby and the music echoed across the water towards them, transporting them as if by magic, and lifting her spirits. Reminding herself to enjoy this happy moment for however long it lasted, she sipped her Pinot Gris. This holiday was incredible and not to be wasted by living in fear.

Trent interrupted her thoughts by saying, "Now do you want to try and tell me what's going on in that busy little head of yours?"

"Do you think God minds being a marble?" Sal asked.

"What?" Floored, he shook his head. "I'm never going to understand women."

Sal quietly said, "Guess I'm scared of being too happy in case it all goes wrong."

He reached across the table and picked up her hand, stroking it lightly with his thumb and forefinger, he said, "I love you."

Sal stopped breathing. Damn he'd said those fatal words. Words you couldn't take back once they were out. And those words that changed everything. She remembered back to when she'd said thank you as a reply to this statement, back to all the times when she'd turned and ran. A tumult of emotions flickered across Sally's face. She swallowed, took a deep breath, and responded by stuttering, "I...I...love you." The words surprised her. There was no way to take them back now.

Smiling, Trent kissed the back of her hand.

Their meals arrived. Sal enjoyed the entrée of oysters while he joked that she only needed half a dozen. She had succulent lamb cutlets while he had the salmon, they both choose chocolate mousse for dessert.

They strolled arm-in-arm back to the hotel. She didn't pull away but inside she was screaming, what just happened? She had fallen off a cliff and there was no going back now.

Sal woke up, her arm wound around Trent and she was curled into him, face-to-face. He was still sleeping, a small smile playing at the edge of his lips. Resisting the urge to kiss him she bit her lip. He really was lovely. He'd been so loving, and treated her like a queen. To think she had thought him such an arse when they first met. How had she lost her heart, which she had kept so guarded for so long, to this man? Here she was lying next to him, in no hurry to leave. It had to be a first. Was it a sign?

On the flight home, Sal noticed she could hold hands without her palms being sweaty. She could breathe. They were going to be ok.

***

"What are you doing now, chick?" Kat eyed Sal with suspicion.

The box of exs lay open on the table and Sal was digging underneath the photos. A candle and lighter and a metal bowl were positioned ceremoniously on the dining table. Sal lifted the lining at the bottom of the box and took out the yellowed letters buried there.

"Time to get rid of a few bad memories," Sal told her, and lighting the corner of the letters she dropped them into the metal dish and watched them burn. Sal's heart lifted as the paper flared, burnt purple and orange, and a wisp of smoke curled to the ceiling, when the smoke alarm went off.

Leaping the hedge in a single bound, Trent barged breathlessly through the front door.

"Is everything alright?" he panted, looking for signs of fire his eyes lighting on the charred remains in the metal bowl.

Sal beamed. "Perfectly."

Chapter 32: An Ex Is Back

Sal wanted to tell Trent about the cool running shoes she'd seen at the mall. They would be perfect for Dancefix but they were a little pricey so she wanted him to see them first. If he liked them then she could justify spending that much on sports shoes. His door was unlocked. Not bothering to knock she went in only to find him sitting on the couch with his arm around an auburn-headed woman she didn't know. Startled, he immediately removed his arm from the woman's shoulders.

Sal gasped. Her stomach sank. "Oh, sorry," she apologised. "I didn't know...you had company."

Trent got up. He gestured to the woman who kept her face hidden. "Sal this is Sonia. Sonia, Sal." His voice was flat.

Sonia murmured, "Hi." Yet she didn't look up.

Sonia! The name instantly registered. The ex he loved.

Flustered, Sal coloured. "Oh, hi." Panicking, she made up a lie. "Kat's baking and wondered if..." she faltered, fishing for something obscure. "If maybe you had any arrowroot."

"No, I don't," Trent replied.

He didn't even look in the pantry. "Oh, ok, thanks. Sorry, bye." She fled.

Devastated, she flew through the front door, up the stairs to her room and closed her bedroom door. She pressed herself against the wall to stop her legs giving way. Sonia! Sonia was back, and she wanted Trent. And he wanted her.

Her happily ever after was a fantasy. She should have known better. Fairy tales were just that – fantasies. Bloody Disney movies made you believe the impossible could happen.

Sal's eyes fell on the photo frame on her bedside table. It was the photo of her and Trent taken at Walter Peak Station. With shaking hands, she opened the back, took out the photo and saw the date and location written on the back in blue pen. She found a pen in her handbag and drew on the back of the picture a broken heart. Then taking the box of exs out from under her bed she dropped the photo inside, and snapped the lid closed. Sal took the case out to the garage and put it back on the top shelf. Then, as if in a trance she went back upstairs and curled up in a foetal position on her bed and cried herself to sleep.

Hours passed. There was a timid knock-on Sal's bedroom door and without waiting for an answer, Kat opened the door and came in with a cup of tea. Placing the cup on the bedside table, she sat on the bed and leaned down to give Sally a hug.

"What's wrong, chick? What's happened?" she asked her face creasing with concern.

Amongst tears, Sal vomited all the gory details and fell back on the bed hugging her pillow as she sobbed her heart out. Kat felt helpless as she watched Sal fall apart. In the end, Kat lay down beside Sal and wrapped her arms around her, holding her until Sal fell asleep. Once Sal's breathing was steady and regular and Kat was certain Sal had gone to sleep, she tiptoed out and closed the door.

Trent had been rocked when Sonia arrived on his doorstep. She had a black eye and a split lip and had obviously been bashed. He felt he had no choice other than to invite her in. Sobbing, she begged his forgiveness telling him she had made a terrible mistake. Jude was nothing but an animal and had smacked her over. Amidst a storm of tears, Sonia asked him to take her back. Sally arrived in the middle of things and he didn't know what to do. He could see by Sally's face she thought the worst and she'd fled before he had a chance to explain.

All this time he had dreamed of Sonia returning. And now she had, he was surprised to find that wasn't what he wanted. However, he still wanted to smack Jude for hurting Sonia, and to get even. But, now, he knew what he wanted – it was crazy Sally Gelee. She was cute, lovable, kind, quirky, klutzy brought out the best and worst in him but who also made him feel like a superhero.

In the morning, Sal checked out her bedroom window to see

if Trent's ute was there. Sonia's car was still in the driveway. Distraught, Sal went back to bed and pulled the sheets up over her head and willed herself to sleep. She texted Alice to say she was sick and wouldn't be in. And for the first time in living memory, she didn't care what happened at work, or how they would manage without her. She just wanted to be numb and not feel the pain that cut her heart in two.

Concerned, Kat came and checked on her. She brought Sal up breakfast but Sal refused to eat, saying she wasn't hungry. Kat said, she had to go to work but she'd come home straight after. Sal nodded mutely.

She spent the next two days in bed, texting Alice that she wasn't able to come to work, and buried herself under the blankets hoping the big bad world would go away.

Worried by Sal's withdrawal from the world, Kat waited until Saturday before going over to the guys flat to have it out with Trent. But he wasn't home so she chose the next best thing and caught Anton in the driveway.

"Hey, you got time for a coffee?" she said.

"I'm just heading over to see Yulia," he told her.

"Change your plans. Give her a call and tell her you will be a bit late." Kat told him. "You and I need to talk."

Anton knew better than to argue with a pregnant woman. His sister, Kelly was pregnant and she was nuts; she went from happy to hysterical in a nano second. Anton made them coffee and sat at the kitchen table looking like he'd like to be elsewhere. If Kat hadn't had been so focused on the task at hand, she would have admired the renovations. Sal and Demi had done a great job.

"What the fudge is Trent up to?" Kat exclaimed the second Anton sat down. "I thought he cared about Sal."

"I don't want to get involved," Anton said fiddling with the table coasters.

"Too late for that buddy, much too late," Kat warned.
"Come on, what's really going on? Spill the beans. Is Trent really seeing his ex?"

Anton looked cagey, as if he didn't know how to answer the question. "Sonia arrived at our place. She had a black eye and a thick lip. Trent let her stay the night. Other than that, I know nothing."

"Rubbish," countered Kat.

Anton was torn. He didn't like the thought of betraying his mate, but he was afraid of Kat. She ranted on about men who pointed their compasses in all directions were sure to die of STDs, or be shot and buried in the backyard by their pissed off exs.

Trying to appease her, he said, "All I know is Sonia turned up out of the blue and Trent let her stay the night, but she slept on the couch." Anton sighed. "He couldn't turn her away. She needed his help. He's a big softie. You know that. It's the rescuer in him."

"I'm so angry I could spit," Kat said. "Sal is miserable. I've never seen her so cut up."

"Look, Kat, I don't know what to tell you other than I think they need to work this out themselves, interfering really isn't going to help."

Frustrated, Kat gave him a withering glance.

"Now, if you will excuse me," he said rising, "I really must be going." He collected the cups and stuck them in the dishwasher.

***

By Sunday Kat had had enough of Sal moping about, looking like the world had ended. She pulled the bedcovers off Sal, and ordered her to get up, get showered and dressed, they were going shopping.

Like a zombie Sal did as she was told. Kat drove to the mall, parked near the main entrance and steered Sal towards the jewellery store, telling her they were going to see Diane.

Remembering them, Diane greeted them with a warm smile. Seeing the distraught look on Sal's face Diane placed a velvet tray of earrings on the glass countertop and said, "Dearie, men come and go, but diamonds are forever."

Sal had just finished paying for her new earrings when she heard a familiar voice behind her.

"Sal, we need to talk."

Kat bailed him up. "How could you?" she demanded.

"Ah, excuse me, I would like to talk to Sal alone," Trent replied keeping his voice even.

Sal had disappeared. He glanced around to see her hurrying away, a small bag dangling from her wrist. He chased after her. She broke into a run.

"Don't make me cry shoplifter," he threatened.

He saw her shoulders tense as she slowed her pace.

"I don't want to have to tackle you," he called out as he lunged and managed to grasp her arm.

"Go away!" She twisted and tried to struggle free.

People were staring at them. Trent loosened his grip but didn't let go.

"Sal, please. Sit down a moment. I need to talk to you."

"I don't want to hear anything you have to say," she argued. She could feel the tears forming and tried to keep them at bay.

Trent pushed her to a large red vinyl padded chair and placing his hands on her shoulders forced her to sit.

"Please. You need to hear me out."

She stayed seated but kept her face turned.

Kat watched them from a distance her arms tightly crossed over her chest and her foot tapping.

"Sonia turned up at my place," Trent began. "I didn't ask her to come. Jude had beaten her up, and she came to me for help. She had only just arrived and was telling me about it when you barged in and assumed the worst."

Sal turned but concentrating on an invisible spot on the wall above his head, she replied, "She came to you because she wanted you back. She came to tell you she made a mistake and she wanted you to forgive her, didn't she?"

He nodded. "Yes, you're right," he admitted. "She did say all that."

Sal felt the pain slice like a knife.

Trent continued, "I couldn't turn her away because she needed help. Yes, I let her stay the night, but she slept on the couch. Anton can vouch for me. The next day Sonia left for Tauranga to stay with her parents. I told her, although I would always care for her and a part of me will always love her, I was no longer in love with her because I was in love with someone else."

Sal felt like her head was under water.

He gave her a little shake. "I love you, Sally Gelee."

Sal sniffed and fished desperately in her handbag looking for a tissue. Trent grabbed a serviette from the nearest café and handed it to her to wipe her eyes and blow her nose. She couldn't speak.

"I know, right. For some in explicable reason I love you just as you are. In fact, I'm crazy about you, Sally Gelee, and I hope you are crazy about me too."

Kat was wiping away her tears and cursing her hormones for making her such a sook. Diane was watching discreetly and nodding her approval. The shoppers nearby were waiting to see what Sally's response would be.

`Sal buried her head in his chest. Diane and Kat high-fived each other, and the crowd clapped and cheered.

One old man said to his wife. "Don't expect security to kiss them, do you."

Flushed with embarrassment at being the centre of attention, Sal hiccupped back a nervous little giggle.

Chapter 33: Run, Baby, Run

Trent packed and wrapped two white shoe boxes and tied them with black satin ribbon. After checking with Kat, he had gone to the mall and brought the pair of sports shoes he knew Sal wanted. Kat and the shop assistant confirmed Sal's shoe size. He had carefully wrapped the photo frame in white tissue paper and placed it in the shoebox. Would Sal choose the shoes? Or the frame?

Tucking both boxes under his chin, he knocked on the door of No 4, twisted the handle, and let himself in. Kat was in the kitchen and heard the door open. She wanted to speak to Trent first. Kat ambled towards him, a packet of crisps in her hand.

He gave Kat a nervous smile as he carefully placed the boxes on the dining table.

"Nicely done," Kat approved nodding at the shoe boxes tied with black satin bows. Patting his cheek, she whispered, "Good luck."

"Thanks. Where is she?"

Kat raised her eyes to the ceiling. "Upstairs in her room, I'll get her."

"Hey, Kat?"

She paused. "Yeah?"

"Has Sal ever said anything to you about God being a marble?"

Kat rolled her eyes. "Therapy," she muttered and continued up the stairs.

Trent hid the boxes behind his back and took a deep breath.

Kat yelled, "Sal! Trent's here."

Sal popped her head out the door. "Do you want a coffee?" Sal asked Kat.

Kat excused herself by saying she needed to order more baby clothes. "I'll be in my room if you need me," she said, and abruptly closed her bedroom door, leaving Sal feeling puzzled.

Sal bounded down the stairs. "How are you, hon? Would you like a coffee? I'll put the jug on," she offered. Then, she noticed he was hiding something behind his back.

"What have you got there?"

"Something for you," Trent told her, producing the boxes.

"More presents?" Sal squeaked, clapping her hands like an excited child. "For me?"

He held the boxes out towards her; they were labelled box one and box two. "You can open both but can only choose one."

"What are you playing at?" Sal asked intrigued.

"You'll see. Open box one first." Trent handed her that box.

Sal put it on the table and slowly undid the bow.

Opening the lid, she lit up, shrieking, "Oh cool, I love them. I've been wanting these for ages. They'll be great for DanceFix." Delighted, she hugged the shoes to her chest. "How did you know?"

Trent tapped a finger to the bridge of his nose. "A little bird told me."

"Are they...my size?" Sal was about to try on the new running shoes when Trent stopped her.

"Wait. That's not the only present, and remember you have to choose. Would you like to see what's inside the second box now?"

"I don't think you can top these." She dutifully put the shoes aside and took the second box from his outstretched arms.

Trent studied her as she cautiously opened the lid and gently unwrapped the tissue paper. Sal lifted out the silver photo frame and stared at the photo. It was the one taken of them in Queenstown at Walter Peak station. The photo she had put in the box of exs. Sal looked at him blankly waiting for an explanation. "I've already got this photo," she told him.

"Read the wording on the front," he said. "Look at the fine print."

Sal read, *I'm a keeper.*

"Now turn the frame over and see what's on the other side."

Sal slowly turned the frame over and discovered a diamond engagement ring sellotaped to the back. The words, *Will you marry me?* written in white marker upon the velvet.

She stared at him slack-jawed. The breath knocked out of her, all she could manage was, "Oh!"

His mouth was as dry as cotton candy. "This photo is not for your box of exs, Sally Gelee, because I'm a keeper. But you have to choose. If you want to run then choose the shoes. If you want to be with me then choose the ring."

She stared at him, then at the ring in wonder. It was the solitaire she had said to Kat if she ever got married, she wanted a ring just like that.

Her silence made him nervous. Panicking, he began to babble. "Kat introduced me to Diane, and they told me you loved this ring." He unpeeled the tape and took the ring off the back of the velvet. Holding the gem in the palm of his hand, he sucked in a breath and blew out his cheeks. "Say something, you've got me worried."

Sal found her voice. "Kneel. Please."

"Fair enough, you are an old-fashioned girl after all." He felt vulnerable as he got down on one knee. Trent held up the ring and said, "Sally Gelee, will you marry me?"

Pondering the question, she hesitated, "I...I...love the shoes..." Then she leaned down and checked his thigh by giving it a firm squeeze. Yes, it was a good thigh. A strong, stable, reliable, loving thigh. It felt right.

"You are hanging me out to dry."

"If I say yes, can I still keep the shoes?"

He sighed, resigned. They both knew she was going to get her way. "You drive a hard bargain, Sally Gelee. If that's what it takes to secure the deal then, yes, I suppose so."

"Then I accept," Sal replied, eyes shining. He slid the ring onto Sal's finger. Slightly too big, it went on easily. Admiring the beautiful sparkling diamond, she held her hand up to the light.

"Can I get up now?" Trent asked. "I'm beginning to get cramp."

Sal drew him up, threw her arms around him and kissed him passionately. "Thank you for the shoes, darling," she joked.

"Careful or I'll wear my superman costume as my wedding outfit."

Hoping he was joking, she laughed.

Unable to stand the suspense, Kat came downstairs. "What's up?" she asked trying to look like she wasn't in on it.

Trent replied with an air punch. "She said yes!"

Chapter 34: Celebrate, Come On

The night before the wedding Sal opened her box of exs for the very last time. She had been contemplating what to do. She couldn't leave the box in Kat's garage. Ethan was renting his house out and moving in with Kat so she could afford the rent. There was no romance between them, they were just good friends. Anton had decided to move in with Yulia, and because she was moving next door Sal couldn't leave the box behind, nor did she want to take it with her. She'd helped decorate Trent's house, she had made it a place she'd like to be, and that made moving in so much easier, but she couldn't take the box of exs with her.

Reasoning it was best not to take the past into the future she took out the photos and ceremoniously tore them up one by one. Except the one of Trent and her taken at Walter Peak. On that one she crossed out the broken heart and drew a heart with an arrow through it and wrote 'Trent and Sal for eva,' then placed it on her bedside cabinet. Closing the lid on the past, she went outside and dumped the silver box in the rubbish bin. There was no pretty jogger going by this time. No one to know the momentous shift that had just taken place. Only she knew she was moving on and getting on with her life. It was between her, her counsellor, and God.

Worried Sal might get the jitters and change her mind, Trent wanted to be married before the end of the month. If Trent had his way, they would be married on a tropical island with the sun setting, not in the Serenity Shores rest home chapel. But Sal wanted everyone to share in her joy and that included the residents and the staff. After all, they were her extended family and she loved them to bits. She sold it to Trent by saying, there's a lovely garden for the photos, and think of the money we will save. Besides, we can go to Rarotonga for our honeymoon.

Everyone was invited; the residents, the staff, friends and family. Sal's mother and her partner, her brother and his family had flown up for the occasion. Sal had promised so many people that if she ever got married, they could be her bridesmaid that she couldn't remember who they were. So, she told everyone it was a dress up. They were to come to the wedding dressed either as a groomsman or as a bridesmaid. Trent went along with it, saying whatever makes you happy, little one.

Trent organised a fire truck to deliver him to the wedding. Pearl offered to be chauffeur and picked Kat and Sal up from the apartment. A hibiscus tucked behind one ear, Pearl was wearing a chauffeur cap and outfit. She drove the rest home van which was kitted out Island style complete with tassels and flowers.

Daisy was in charge of catering and had even made a spectacular three tier wedding cake as a present for Sal. Ruth had arranged the flowers for the chapel and bouquets were peace lilies tied with white ribbon. Although Cherry offered to do Sal's hair, Sal decided it was better to go to her usual stylist. Gino congratulated her on marrying the man she loved. Then turned his attention on Kat, saying her pregnant body was as *beautiful as she was*.

When Kat told him she was going to be a single mum he asked if he could marry her, and be the baby's father. Kat rolled her eyes and told him she wasn't going to be someone's ticket to residency, but she would appreciate it if he could make her hair look good for her besties wedding.

Sal had her hair styled in a bun with kiss curls, and Kat did her makeup for her; the effect was subtle. Kat helped Sal get dressed. Sal hoped that Trent wasn't serious about wearing a superman outfit. He had teased her every day since his proposal that he would. Although she kind of liked the way he filled out his budgie smugglers, she didn't want anyone else to perve, and if she was honest, she preferred more formal attire. She liked her man in his uniform.

Looking resplendent in her full-length, emerald-green satin dress, Kat wore her hair down. She looked elegant even with the bump, even though she didn't think so. Now almost full term instead of gliding into a room, she waddled.

Sal's Mum was dressed in a sparkly little blue sequin number. Joyce swept into the room and told Sal how proud she was to be able to walk her baby girl up the aisle. They both shed a tear that Norman wasn't there but told each other that he was watching over them, and he'd be proud of his little butterfly.

"Thanks, Mum," Sal kissed her mother's cheek leaving a smudge of pink lipstick behind.

Kat kept checking the time.

Pearl knocked on the door. She was ecstatic when she saw how lovely the girls looked and wouldn't stop complimenting them. She said Sal looked like an angel in her long white lace gown. Pearl patiently waited for the girls and Sal's Mum to get in the van. Then they were off careering down Beach Road past Waiake and up again, then down the road that led to the rest home. Sal wasn't sure if it was her old fears rising that she felt like vomiting or if it was because of Pearl's erratic driving. Kat had gone very pale. She leaned over and whispered that she thought she might go into labour early because of Pearl's driving. Sally said a quick prayer and crossed herself for good luck.

To announce their arrival, Pearl honked the horn as they drove into the rest home carpark. A fire truck was parked outside the main entrance. Sal was surprised as her DanceFix group, dressed as bridesmaids, danced out of the lobby into the carpark and performed a flash mob dance to Bruno Mar's *I think I want to marry you.*

Sal cheered as they finished their routine, then the dancers ran inside to form a guard of honour.

Inside the chapel everyone was either dressed as a bridesmaid in their best evening dresses or as groomsmen with suits and buttonholes. Since most of Trent's friends were in the services, they wore their dress uniform. It was like one big costume party where there was a Chaplin, a bride, a groom, and a huge wedding party made up of bridesmaids and groomsmen. Cherry had done a hair and makeup wedding special so the residents looked like Marilyn Monroe or Errol Flynn replicas. RuPaul would have been proud. Andie looked spectacular in his aqua blue satin frock with bouffant hairstyle.

Natalie's fingers were poised hovering above the piano keys, ready for Kat's signal. Sal took a huge breath and held her stomach as she tried to calm her nerves. Kat was watching her carefully, waiting for any signs that Sal might turn tail and run. Kat gave Natalie the nod and she began to play. The crowd stood; heads turned to await the bride's entrance.

A look of pure panic on her face, Sal turned to Kat for reassurance. Kat wasn't feeling great either.

Kat spoke calmly. "You checked his thigh and it felt right, remember?"

"Yes," nodded Sal. "Yes, it felt right."

Kat reminded Sal to breathe, and put one foot in front of the other, everything was going to be alright. "You know how to breathe; we have been practising at antenatal classes," she told Sal.

Sal let out a nervous giggle. "If I start to pant, they will think I'm hyperventilating and may chuck me on oxygen."

"Ready?" Kat asked as she opened one of the double doors.

Sal picked up her bouquet and nodded. "Ready."

Trent was standing at the altar and to her relief, he was wearing his full-dress uniform. There were no sudden heart palpitations, or shallow breathing, no fear of suffocation. Her heart flooded with pride. He looked so handsome. Every woman in the room would be jealous, every woman – and Andie.

Sal gripped her mother's arm for support, she took another breath and started the slow walk to the altar.

"She looks bloody marvellous," yelled Marvin from the back of the room.

A smile tugged at the corner of Sally's lips and if she hadn't been so nervous, she would have laughed out loud.

"Thanks, Marvellous," Sal whispered as she passed.

Keeping her eyes fixed on Trent, trying to ignore her increasing heart rate and the butterflies in her stomach, Sal walked haltingly towards him. Kat walked behind; her large bump impossible to miss. Sal reached Trent and the music stopped abruptly. Joyce backed away and sat in the front row beside her beau, Bernard. Sal's sister and brother and their partners beamed up at Sal, nodding their approval.

"Wasn't sure you would come," Trent whispered, his voice husky.

"Was touch and go," Sal admitted. "Don't blow it now." Sal raised her gown so he could see she was wearing her running shoes.

He laughed, and reached for her hand. "I'll have you know, even though they aren't regulation, I'm wearing my superman socks."

"I'm just relieved you aren't wearing the cape or worse, the whole outfit."

Iris, the rest home Chaplin, took the ceremony. When Iris asked if there was anyone who knew why these two should not be joined in holy matrimony to speak now or forever hold their peace there was silence. Sal breathed a sigh of relief. Don was finally gone.

Kat tugged Sal's arm, and in a hushed whisper said, "I don't know how to tell you this but..."

Sal noticed a few beads of sweat on Kat's forehead.

"Are you alright?"

"I think – I might be in labour."

"No, not now," Sal replied.

"I think I need to sit down for a wee bit."

"One moment please," Sal said to Iris. "Kat, go swap places with Andie. Tell him I need him to be my best man. Give him your bouquet, I'm sure he'll be delighted. Promise me you'll keep your legs closed and that baby in until after the ceremony."

Kat nodded gravely, and went and swapped places with Andie. Andie stood as proud as a peacock by Sal's side.

Trent asked Iris to continue but to hurry the formalities a little.

Somehow Sal managed to choke out the words,' I will', and

'I do' in the right places. When Trent asked Anton for the ring, Anton looked like he was doing the mac-arena, patting all his pockets with a panicked look on his face.

Trent glared at him.

"Just kidding," Anton grinned. producing the ring he ceremoniously handed it to Trent.

Sal almost expected the ring to burn her skin as Trent slid it over her knuckle and into place. Her hands were clammy and she was trembling but Trent anchored her, holding her hands firmly in his.

Smiling generously, Iris instructed Trent that he may now kiss his bride. He did so, planting a long lingering kiss on Sal's lips to the delight and amusement of the witnesses.

"Bloody marvellous," bellowed Marvin from the back of the chapel.

Everyone cheered when they were introduced as Mr and Mrs Powell. Sally blushed.

Kat cried, "Nooo!"

Sal rushed over. "You ok, chick?"

Kat's eyes were like twin saucers. "I think my waters just broke, either that, or I just peed myself."

Vikki arrived, her heels click-clicking with efficiency she asked everyone to move out of way. She hauled Kat to her feet and started asking questions whist shepherding Kat towards the clinical room.

Sal apologised and asked everyone to entertain themselves for a minute promising that she'd be back as quick as.

Trent followed, "You're not getting away from me so easily, Mrs Powell."

Sal phoned Kat's midwife but she was sick with the flu and said someone called Rita was covering for her. She mouthed an apology to Trent as she closed the door to the clinical room leaving him out in the corridor. While Vikki examined Kat, Trent and Ethan paced the hall.

"Timing," Trent shook his head. "Kat, you have lousy timing."

Vikki phoned the resident doctor asking him to come quickly.

Sal came out to give them the news that judging by the rapidness of the contractions, Vikki feared they wouldn't get Kat to hospital in time as Kat was already well dilated.

"Don't babies take days to come?" Trent asked. "My cousin was in labour for days."

"Not this one," Sal replied slipping back inside to see Kat.

Kat didn't want to ruin Sal's day. "Hon, go back to your guests. Ethan will call you when I need you, ok."

She went back out into the hallway and asked Ethan if he'd cover. Ethan agreed, promising to stay away from the business end, and saying that he'd call Sal when Kat was about to burst.

Trent put his arm around Sal, "Come on, babe, they'll call us when it's time."

When they arrived back in the main lounge the DanceFix group had just finished a routine and the Serenity Shore Hip Op group were showing off their dance moves. Distracted, Sal kept popping back to check on Kat only to be told go away, not yet. Trent and Sal cut the cake, then Sal popped back to see how Kat was getting on. She was pleased to see the doctor had arrived.

Vikki shook her head, "Not yet."

"Go," insisted Kat waving her away.

Sal hurried back to the main lounge. The band took their places and started playing the waltz so Sal and Trent could have their first dance. Sal was finding it difficult to concentrate. "Ethan hasn't been to training, I have." She told Trent "I'll just pop back and check on her."

Suzie interrupted them. She was hanging off the arm of a handsome muscle-bound man. "Hey Sal, congratulations. I'd like you to meet Lance."

Lance? Sal's eyes widened. This was the famous Lance Suzie had been trying to set her up with.

Suzie's eyes lit up. "You know I spent so much time banging on about how great he was, I thought, man, why am I trying to palm him off on anyone else, he's a great catch. We have been going out about a month now. Funny how life turns out, isn't it?"

"It sure is," agreed Sal.

Ethan tapped Sal lightly on the shoulder. "Now."

Pleased she had her running shoes on, Sal picked up her skirts and ran.

Sal flew through the door and grasped Kat's hand. "Breathe!"

"Arrgh!" Kat cried, bearing down.

"Now push!" the doctor commanded.

Kat did as she was told and wee Brodie shot into the world. It was the first time they had had a birth at Serenity Shores Rest Home. After giving Brodie a thorough checking over, the doctor congratulated Sal and Kat on the birth of their daughter. Trent had been pacing the hallway with Ethan. Upon hearing the baby cry, Trent tapped on the closed door and asked if he could come in.

The guys were allowed in and introduced to Kat's daughter. Wee Brodie lay content in her mother's arms wrapped in a warm blanket pinched from the rest home stores.

Tears streaked Kat's face. "Wish my mum and dad were here to meet her."

Sal tried to comfort her by saying, "They would adore her. They'll be smiling down on her."

Besotted by her daughter, Kat kissed the top of Brodie's fuzzy brown crown.

Sal introduced Trent to the doctor as her husband. The doctor looked confused and muttered something about modern families these days.

Ethan looked chuffed as he held little Brodie in his arms. "This little one is now my favourite lady."

Trent grinned. "You tell all the ladies they are your favourite, mate."

Ethan offered to go and collect the car seat from the flat then take Kat up to the birthing centre so she could stay there, rest and recover while she got to know her baby girl.

Kat gave Sal a sideways hug. "Go on, join your guests, and have fun. We are fine."

When they were told of the arrival of little Brodie, and that mother and child were both doing well everyone cheered. As they were about to sit down for the wedding breakfast Andie reminded Sal it was time for her to throw the bouquet.

All the bridesmaids lined up, ready. Sal turned her back and threw the bouquet high behind her sending the flowers cartwheeling through the air. Fighting off several staff members and two seniors, Andie elbowed his way in and made a brilliant catch that any international cricketer would be proud of.

"It's mine, baby!" he shouted triumphantly holding the bouquet high. His eyes lighted on Harold, all dressed up in his tails, and he blew Harold a kiss. Harold winked back!

Trent endured ribbing from the guests and his groomsmen during the wedding breakfast toasts. Suzette and Josie told him they would have turned for him.

Sal noticed she didn't have the jitters. She didn't feel the need to run. She could breathe. To double check she reached under the table and gave Trent's thigh a small squeeze.

He raised his eyebrows.

Sal grinned. "Just right."

"All in all, it has been a very good day wouldn't you agree, Mrs Powell?"

"It has been," she agreed. Sal picked up her glass of bubbly. "A very good day indeed, Mr Powell. Here's to a wedding, a birth, and to the death of my commitment phobia."

He smiled and tapped his glass against hers. "And here's to happily ever after."

"Love you, Superman."

Trent kissed the top of her head. "Love you, Smurfette."

ABOUT THE AUTHOR

Michelle Kelly

Michelle Kelly lives in Auckland, New
Zealand in a cottage she affectionately calls
The Writery. Her sons, Paul and Mike were
the inspiration for her first novel, Payback.
Payback became a finalist in the Junior
Fiction catergory in the NZ Post Book
Awards in 2009.

Her Historical Fiction Riverstones series came to her in a dream
and was a gift that was meant to be shared.

She says, A Box Of Exs In My Garage was loosely based on her
dating disasters over the years, and quipped that she wasn't
sure if the genre should be called Romantic Comedy or Personal
Tragedy. However, like all good love stories hers has a happy
ending.

BOOKS BY THIS AUTHOR

Payback

Junior Fiction

Lasting Legacy

Biography of Victor Albert Hartley OBE

Riverstones

Historical Fiction book 1 in a series

Scattered Stones

Historical Fiction book 2 in the series

Sticks And Stones

Historical Fiction book 3 in the series